These old mountains are smart, Lucy. They're alive. They can be gentle like mamas; oh, sure, they'll croon and they'll kiss you and they'll whisper while you sleep, and you'll learn what all the old rocks are saying, all these ancient ghosts, all their starshine wisdom. But these old mountains, sometimes they know you can't hear them any other way but to get smacked up along the head. You watch out, Lucy P, for you got the Charm, like us Netties do. You're a guardian of these mountains, and they're a guardian of you. They will warn you any how they have to.

They will slap the near life out of a Charmer.

They're doing it to make you and Gus listen. To make you ready.

—Delta

Praise for Deborah Smith's *The Crossroads Café*

Wall Street Journal Bestseller
Number One Bestseller, Amazon Kindle
The first novel in _The Crossroads Café_ Series

"Unforgettably poignant."
—*Booklist*

"A top five romance of 2006."
—*Library Journal*, starred review

"A perfect 10."
—*Romance Reviews Today*

"The best romance of 2006."
—*The Romance Reader*

"A true treasure."
—*Romantic Times BookClub*

"A book that readers will open again and again."
—*Romance Designs*

Winner of a HOLT Medallion and a Reviewer's International Award (RIO)

The Novels of Deborah Smith

From Bell Bridge Books

The Crossroads Café

The Crossroads Café Novels:

The Biscuit Witch, Book One of The MacBrides

The Pickle Queen, Book Two of The MacBrides

The Kitchen Charmer, Book Three of The MacBrides

The Moonshine King, Book Four of The MacBrides

The Crossroads Café Novellas:

The Yarnspinner

The Apple Pie Knights

*

A Gentle Rain

Sweet Hush

On Bear Mountain

Charming Grace

The Stone Flower Garden

A Place To Call Home (Audio)

Silk and Stone

When Venus Fell

Blue Willow (Audio)

Miracle The Mossy Creek Hometown Series (Contributor)

Sweet Tea Series (Contributor)

Alice At Heart

Diary of a Radical Mermaid

Hot Touch

The Silver Fox

The Kitchen Charmer

by

Deborah Smith

Bell Bridge Books

This is a work of fiction. Names, characters, places and incidents are either the products of the author's imagination or are used fictitiously. Any resemblance to actual persons (living or dead), events or locations is entirely coincidental.

Bell Bridge Books
PO BOX 300921
Memphis, TN 38130
Print ISBN: XXXXXXXXXXXXX

Bell Bridge Books is an Imprint of BelleBooks, Inc.

Published in the United States of America.

We at BelleBooks enjoy hearing from readers.
Visit our websites
BelleBooks.com
BellBridgeBooks.com
ImaJinnBooks.com

10 9 8 7 6 5 4 3 2 1

Cover design: Debra Dixon and Deborah Smith
Interior design: Hank Smith
Photo/Art credits:
Sunburst/compass textures © Sofka_QWE – Fotolia.com

Textures: © Yobro10 – Dreamstime.com, Title lettering: © Jaguarwoman Designs, Closeup portrait of an elegant blond woman © Konradbak | Dreamstime.com, Conceptual portrait of the sand man © Konradbak | Dreamstime.com

:Lckl:01:

The Kitchen Charmer

Afghanistan, February

"HE TOOK THE explosion on the left side. Left leg looks bad. Internal injuries, too. And his left ear's hemorrhaging."

"Captain, can you hear me? What did you say, Captain?"

"I think he said, 'Lucid,' Sir."

"Yes, you're lucid. We can understand you."

Not lucid. Luce.

I searched for my voices. The essences. Mama, Dad. My sisters. Luce.

Find the hunger, and you find the pain.

Feed the body, and you feed the spirit.

Share the table, and you share the love.

Love. Luce.

I tried to ease into the psychic hammock where Luce always joined me. The essence of her could cross thousands of miles between Afghanistan and North Carolina. A taste of honey and crushed fruit, blueberries too sweet to make a dark beer . . . Luce came from tender starters, that's how her brew always tasted in my mind, but there was something fragile, too . . . something easy to break.

I felt needles in my arms. Oxygen hissed into my nose. Darkness rose and then opened like a curtain.

I faced a stranger with an unknown face. Covered in blood and war, like me.

"She's mine," he said. "I earned her. Women are always the collateral damage in a man's world. You know that."

Behind a curtain of see-through lace, Luce stood with her naked back to me and him, her head turned just enough to let us know she was listening.

He stepped closer to the curtain. In the darkness I saw just his hand reach through a streak of overhead light. He anchored it in the delicate knitting. "I'm taking her, and you can't stop me."

"I'll kill you." But when I tried to move, my torn leg had rooted to the floor.

He laughed. "A real man will kill to get what he wants." He lunged at her. Lucy turned, but all I saw was her face, filled with terror, a hazy blur that came into focus as a terrible feeling surged in my chest.

I am him, now.

1

Two months earlier
December
Rainbow Goddess Farm
North Carolina

A LOT OF PEOPLE believed our highlands were a fortress against some future apocalypse. A breakdown of law and order? Invasion of a foreign army? Pandemic? The Rapture?

We could survive as long as we stayed put.

I wasn't like them. I could take my fears with me everywhere. I was the kid who got excited when the teacher said to read silently. I liked going to the library. Museums and concerts took me to fantasy worlds I could sense—I reached out to the veils that separated ordinary life from miracles.

I believed in joy and the Holy Spirit and the purity of chaste minds and untouched bodies and now I realize it was all some sort of defense, some kind of bargain with God, like promising to clock in on time every day at a job. Of course I knew God didn't hand out credits for good behavior, and yet . . . shouldn't He?

No. He didn't care.

It had been three years since the attack, but I relived the memory every day.

What's that thumping noise?

It must be Mr. Nguyen binge-watching CSI episodes with the TV turned up too loud again. Or Anita Suarez's kids turning over furniture while they played Wii tennis. I loved the mix of people and cultures in my in-town neighborhood. My little hatchback had an easy commute to grad school classes at UNC Charlotte, and on nice days like today I walked the few blocks to a small private prep school where I tripled as the art, civics, and Spanish teacher.

I had grown up in the city; my sixty-ish father was pastor of one of Charlotte's oldest Methodist churches. His aging congregation adored him and pish-toshed rumors that he was gay—while discreetly accepting that the rumors were true.

I had a number of beloved uncles, who were kind and fatherly and fun. Most were pastors.

My mother had been older than Dad by a decade. They married, birthed me, and a year later she died of uterine cancer. "You were born with demons on your heels," one of the church ladies told me. "God put a rocket engine on your angels."

I had never felt that angels were hovering over me until after the . . . attack. It wasn't that I felt tainted as a child, or a convenient beard for a gay man. Dad doted on me, and me on him. I was good at being a minister's daughter. A believer but not a fanatic. Neither was he. We all live with our curtains around us, our charades.

Now 24 years old, with a happy job and close friends, I lived in a world of safety and goodwill.

That noise again. Somebody's moving furniture around.

Under the light of a lamp above the apartment stairwell, with the scent of spring flowers rising from below, I brushed away moths and unlocked my door, fumbling with my iPad. I stepped inside, reading an article titled, 'A Cracked Door Lets In the Light. An alternative Christian perspective on the misfits, outcasts, free thinkers, soothsayers, and oddballs who may be chatting with His authentic messengers.'

Dad had emailed it to me with his excited note in all caps.

> INSPIRATION FOR MY EASTER SERMON. DO YOU DARE ME TO FOLLOW THROUGH?

Smiling, I was about to drop my shoulder bag and a tote full of my students' paperwork on my contemporary Scandinavian something-wood Ikea table by the entrance. I looked forward to exchanging my sweaty yoga pants and long tee for a shower and a UNC nightshirt.

My workout shoes toed a large, shaky object in the floor.

Still reading, I glanced down and halted. The Ikea lay there. In pieces.

"Get her," a voice said.

"Let's party, bitch."

A hand, stinking of sweat and dirt, slammed into my face.

And the nice, pretty life of Lucy Parmenter ended.

BEEP. ON THE plank wall above my head, a yellow metal box with a guard dog logo uttered the beep again. The farm's new security system was Alberta's idea; not only connected to the internet, the sheriff's office, the county's 411 emergency response system, but it also included a loud intercom function. Tensions were high in Jefferson County, just like elsewhere in the country. Divisions. Radicals. Threats of violence against the gov'ment. Any gov'ment.

I'd tried to detox the alarm system's Orwellian effect by surrounding it with my photos of mountain wildflowers and the mystical beauty of the old buildings at Free Wheeler.

"Heads up, Parmenter." Alberta's twangy voice. "Just giving you a follow-through on the situation. Monzell's chicken kickers are spamming us again."

"Oh?" My voice was reed-thin and high.

"I'm taking our website down so they can't hack it. And let's postpone that test-run on the crisis hotline. Unless you want your volunteers to get their ears burned in the flame war."

"I'll double-check all of our virus protection."

"We're on alert."

After she clicked off, I opened a drawer and fetched the adorable little handgun she'd purchased for me. I shucked my skirt and fitted the gun's holster around my waist, over my leggings. The belt part was elastic with Velcro fasteners. The holster part was made to look like denim—cozy—but also waterproof. No sweat and no female juices would seduce my pretty little weapon. I had named her Louise, after my long-dead great aunt in Charlotte. Great Aunt Louise had shot a burglar with her vintage forty-five caliber pistol. He lost a thumb.

Soft and snuggly, Louise fit in the fake denim along my lower belly, with her muzzle imprinting atop my mound.

Now, I had a penis, and I could hurt people with it.

IN THE DISTANCE, the main farm house glowed with light, fragrant smoke rose from chimneys, and the small communal lodge hummed with music. Alberta and Macy organized events, speakers and classes for the women and kids. Tonight their Log Splitters' band was playing. Heavy on the steel guitar (Alberta) and electric fiddle (Macy).

They were crushing a Bonnie Raitt song like dragons stepping on petunias. It didn't matter. They changed lives here, simply and sincerely, and against the odds. The average stay for women was two months, and during that time, Alberta and Macy hoped to impart more than give them a temporary refuge from a stalking husband or boyfriend.

Thanks to Cathy's patronage, the success rate at the farm had increased even more in recent years. There was money for referrals to specialists, for follow-ups after the women graduated, and a foundation Cathy and Tom had set up funded scholarships for their kids.

Some said I was one of the farm's success stories. Technically, I was no longer a patient. But I'd never been a domestic abuse case to begin with. I was a survivor of a violent sexual assault by semi-strangers. I was now an employee—management, actually, "Head of Fiber Arts and Wool Production," which was a fancy way of saying I taught spinning, knitting, crocheting, shepherded the woolies, and oversaw how their wool was sold as fleeces or turned into commercially spun yarn. I was proud that my three years at Rainbow Goddess Farm coincided with the herd paying for itself and making a small profit.

But I was fooling everyone but myself if they thought I could hold down a job in the outside world, leave this sanctuary, and live as anything other than a recluse in a sheep barn.

The farm's dairy cows watched me from the low light of the milk barn's doorway, chewing their cuds like baseball players nursing gum and tobacco.

More trouble's coming, Miss Lucy. Watch and listen. You're one of the voices people need to hear.

Skeins of black and blood-red stitched dark patterns in the winter sky above the Ten Sisters Mountains. I had begun seeing visions and hearing Opal's voice in my head not long after my doctors sent me to Rainbow Goddess. Opal had a country drawl. Her voice was young, and she enjoyed sassing me. She'd never told me her name—I just knew it, the way I knew certain things now. Predictions. Prophecies. Warnings. Like Cathy Deen Mitternich being pregnant with twins she wouldn't miscarry this time.

I predicted that. A movie star's successful motherhood.

The ability had terrified me at first. Hearing voices, seeing bright splashes of light and color and patterns. My Sunday school teachers hadn't covered psychic powers.

Tasting and smelling. *Clairgustance— psychic* tasting and *clairessence— psychic* smelling. Sub-sets of general clairvoyance. For a minister's daughter like me, all of that *clair-this and that* had always been secular nonsense. Carnival fortune-telling talk.

But then the . . . incident . . . that sent me here to the farm had wiped out any certainty that God cared about me or that the universe revolved around us in spiritual ways I truly understood. When the broken part of me reached out for a way to pray again, God answered in the only way my heart could receive—through an angel who spoke via the soft, safe wool. So now I was . . . *clair-wooly*?

Focus.

But *Now* wasn't going so well for the world. I was just a fleck of shrinking soul hood in the midst of a storm.

Some of the shop owners in Turtleville had stopped doing business with the farm. Said they couldn't sanction our lifestyle. They were afraid of blowback.

Some of the churches had become emboldened to preach that Macy and Alberta and I were demons. Lesbian demons, converting disobedient women to witchcraft and sexual perversion. They didn't want to risk losing the donations they got from Howard Monzell, owner and president of Monzell Poultry. The processed-chicken-selling king of the Appalachians had made it clear he was on the side of Alt-Right Makes Might.

And that he would wipe our infamy from his pure American community.

That he would get rid of me, in particular.

"Lucy, they arrested Mr. Khangura last week. Came right here into the library and hauled him away from his gardening books. He's lived in these mountains for fifty years. He let my kids try on that funny turban of his. Our sons grew up in his barber shop. But the new Native Born American Act says he doesn't have the right papers. That he's been put on a terrorist watch list. That's just butt-damn stupid. Can you help? Please? Use your witch spells. Something. Please."

"Miss Parmenter, I tracked them with my own two eyes. They had North Carolina gov'ment license plates. They went up yonder outside Turtleville to that property that was the German prisoner camp back in World War I. They did some surveying. They had big design papers spread out on a table. You know what they're gonna do. They're gonna build a new camp. But this time it'll be for Americans. For the Muslims and the gays. And for the rest of us, too, if we spit in the wrong face. Please talk to your yarn angel and ask her what to do."

"Lucy, can the farm take in even one more woman? I know y'all got too many in your shelters already, but Evelyeen's hiding in the storage room at my shop. Her husband caught her using birth control pills and beat the shit out of her. Said God and the Klan needs more white babies.

Please work some magic on him. A hex or something. Please."

I felt helpless. I'd been elevated from patient to counselor at Rainbow Goddess, helping to provide food, shelter and counseling for nearly two hundred women and children. Every cabin and communal bunk house overflowed.

Macy and Alberta, the farm's owners and head of Rainbow Goddess Refuge, couldn't hire trustworthy outside help fast enough to take up the slack. Even with the financial support from the MacBrides, Cathy Deen Mitternich and Jay Wakefield, we were under siege. The cuts in social services. The rise of extremist groups that wanted women at home, barefoot and pregnant. Bruised.

And the wars.

War came first. War always comes first, when people are schooled to hate and fear one another. We had troops in parts of the world that would have been unthinkable even a year ago. Not just stationed there, but fighting new battles in wars that no one understood.

The shortages at home helped pay for them. Cutbacks in social services. Medicine, food, public education, the arts. Riots occurred almost every month in the biggest cities. Crime had skyrocketed.

Here in the Cove, people did what they had done for centuries in these Appalachians. They pulled in close, like cattle in a storm, heads together, backs to the enemy.

Only looking into each other's worried eyes, and kicking, hard, blindly, whenever anyone new or strange or unsettling came near.

They believed the leaders who held the golden keys. The jobs, the power, the promises.

In Jefferson County, North Carolina, home of the county seat, Turtleville, the Cove and the Crossroads Café, just over four thousand tough, hardworking people were scattered across ridges and hollows where memories went to be forgotten.

Most of them earned their living growing fryer chickens.

All of them worked—either under grower contracts or in the processing plants, for Monzell Poultry.

Howard Monzell owned them.

His son-in-law, Chief Deputy Sheriff Kern Burkett, wanted to own *me*.

Kandahar province, Afghanistan

BLOOD-RED BEER gushed over the rubble. The burned oatmeal

stink of over-cooked hops and bitter ale mixed with the mushroom scent of the dust and the acrid flavor of broken concrete. I tasted the mortar hit. Burning plastic and ammonia, like pissing on a fire full of milk jugs.

Now the bloody beer flooded around my boots and began to fill what was left of the tiny house. It rose fast; rising above my knees as I squatted beside the grieving mother and the bodies of her children. She and they disappeared in the crimson brew. So did I, taking one last breath as the raw swallow of death and guilt filled my lungs.

"Captain? We've confirmed that Sarbanri was here when you ordered the attack. Someone tipped him off."

I looked up at my translator, Sergeant Inez Sanchez. Riley's replacement. Texas twang, like Riley's. Tequila and pulled pork barbecue and hand-tooled cowboy boots. Bright pink lipstick behind her face shield. All heart and duty.

Tipped him off. I shoved my helmet backed and cursed silently.

"You had no way of knowing, Captain. He used this family as a shield."

I have a way of knowing. Why did it fail me, this time?

Suddenly the woman made a high-pitched keening sound—not the ululation of lips and tongue but a sheer, piercing, singsong shriek that gutted me. Her eyes, dark and glazed, shifted and jerked, focusing on me, cradling her dead daughters, their blood soaking her burka.

Words stuck in my throat.

I have sisters, I wanted to say. *I don't hurt women and children. I protect them. My whole life is about being a man who takes care of others. I failed once. I can't fuck up again.*

Sanchez nudged my shoulder with her knee. Riley had filled her in on my little secret. "Cap," she said gruffly. "A *bruja* is still just a poor sinner waiting for God's Word. My *abuelita* could tell you who would have babies the next year and when to plant tomatoes for the best harvest. One hundred percent accuracy. But she couldn't predict the addiction that killed four of my uncles."

"I've called it right so many times. But this time . . . "

"That's why we trust you, Captain. You're not perfect, but you're sure as hell talking to angels."

The woman's voice became a sob, then freed itself to fire angry words at me. Sanchez stepped closer, listening, her face as still as dark granite. She looked only at the woman, and I could see the strain in her eyes, how rigidly she kept them trained away from the bodies.

My mouth filled with blood. "Translate," I ordered. I knew enough Pashto to catch some of the words.

Sanchez blew out a breath. "She says she's put a curse on your soul. She will take your spirit away."

The woman's song rose to an unearthly *aieeeee* that echoed off the crumbled block walls. I took off my helmet and dropped it in the sand and blood between my boots. How must I have looked to her, a red-haired, ruddy-skinned killer from the other side of the world? I wanted to tell her I came from dirt-poor Scots-Irish immigrants who built cabins in wild southern mountains covered in blue-green forests, a place of tough but compassionate people who did not send their men to kill the innocent.

I stood. "Let the medics know she has something wrong here." I made a rubbing motion below my navel. "She needs antibiotics."

Sanchez nodded. "Probably a UTI. I'll make it sound like she told me herself."

"CAPTAIN, YOU'RE TO stand down where Sarbanri is concerned. He's above your pay grade."

"He's murdering villagers."

"Not your problem, Captain. Don't rock the boat. You've got seventeen years in; you've got a file full of pretty commendations to offset your crazy shit. You got a month's leave coming in a few months. Enjoy your career."

"If we're not here to fix things, why are we here at all?"

"Hell if I know. Just follow orders. Let others worry about the big picture."

I couldn't do that. I saw the big picture, I smelled it. I woke sometimes with its blood all over me and the pitiful bawls of calves begging not to die.

The slaughterhouse smell of psychic death. Liver. It came to me as well as Tal and Gabs. The one kitchen charm that spoke to all of us.

He's always goin' to be with you, Gus.

Big hands on my shoulders. My cop uncles took over for Dad, that day. Sergeant Charlie Osgood led the way. A dozen others standing nearby. Their wives tried to comfort Gabby, who stood rigidly, guarding Tal, who sat under a hospital gurney with her back turned to us all. Gabby was ten. Tal was only five years old. I was twelve.

"Gus, he wouldn't want you to do this. Your mama don't expect it, either."

"I promised him, Uncle Charlie. I'd be the man of the family, if anything ever happened. It's my job."

I walked through the doors they opened, and through other doors, and into bright lights that made it hard to think about what was behind the white screen in a room with tile on the floor you could wash down with a hose.

And then Mama stepped in front of me. She looked a thousand years old, not thirty-two. Apple pie and the essence of dad's brew-man soul swirled around us. She took my hand and pressed a silver crochet hook into my palm. All the filigree had worn down where MacBrides had gripped the metal since time began, leaving tendrils etched in the shadows where their fingers once lay. The hook was bent at a terrible angle. I started shaking inside. Dad always carried it in a pocket of his uniform. He crocheted and knitted, no matter who laughed at him. He taught me how.

"It's yours, now," Mama whispered. "We'll get it repaired."

Nothing can fix it. Nothing can fix what's on the other side of that screen. Or inside me.

"I want to see him," I said.

"He's not here," Mama whispered. "You know that."

"I smell his cigar. I smell beer, and barbecued pork."

She took my face between her hands. "Of course he's with us that way. He's everywhere we'll ever be, forever. I've been talking to him, and he's not in pain, and he's not afraid, and he's not worried about us. He knows we'll be okay. That's the blessing of the other realms. That's the wisdom and the wonder of passing over."

I nodded, tears rolling off my face and down into her palms.

Mama and I held hands and walked over to view his body. Charlie and my other cop-uncles had tried to warn me. Dad had been hit by a tractor-trailer while working an accident site on an icy road north of Asheville. It was bad.

He was broken in a lot of ways.

So was I, from then on.

2

I WAS UNDERGROUND the first time I saw Gus. Showing his sister the concrete root cellar at Rainbow Goddess. Telling Tal, who'd come to the farm in search of Dr. Firth, her handsome Scottish veterinarian, how much I'd like to live in the cellar, alone.

"The root cellar is built like a big war bunker. It has air vents and a toilet and a secret escape tunnel hidden among the shelves full of jellies and canned veggies. It's very cozy, actually."

Tal handed me her phone. "Let's talk about something positive. Here's my favorite picture of my big brother."

Good bread with a hard crust and soft center.

A pickle grown in tough red clay but so sweet that even a salt brine can't sour it.

That's how Tal and Gabby MacBride had described their brother Gus to me. I didn't want to know how Tal and Gabby saw me, what flavor, what scent. I had always wanted sisters. Giant, red-headed sisters who towered over little five-six blonde me.

"Let us tell Gus about your background, Lucy. He's trained to deal with soldiers who've been hurt in battle. He'll understand. You're a wounded warrior. It's no different."

"It's very different."

Gus MacBride sat cross-legged on some barren, beautiful Afghani ridge, in front of a grill and a hot pile of embers. On the grill sat a large iron skillet full of *qabli palaw,* a traditional Afghan dish made with rice, raisins, carrots and lamb. He was dressed in his desert camo but wore an Afghan hat and fringed scarf. One hand posed to slide a spatula into the pan.

He gazed straight into the camera with a somber smile, his face handsome, square-jawed, and ruddy from the sun and wind. The hat perched jauntily on his bleached crew cut and shadowed his green eyes. He looked big and confident and . . .

Swarms of honey bees surrounded me. Millions. A cloud of soundless yellow and brown, their small wings feathering my face and hands. I smelled the aroma of the honey they made. They merged into a soft weave, a cushioned blanket, around me. Swaddled in warmth, I felt safe and hidden. A flavor blossomed on my tongue. Wheat, corn, more honey. Caramel and berries and chocolate.

Cool and hot. It traveled down my throat, filled my stomach with heat, and bloomed in every direction.

Every. Direction.

"Lucy. Lucy?"

I blinked. Tal was bent over me. I had settled gently onto the floor, dazed. I cradled her phone—the image of her brother—to my chest. I sucked down deep breaths. "Does he . . . does he know he had this effect on me?"

"Well, we get psychic hugs from him, if that's what you felt." She studied me, her eyes crinkling. "But . . . I'm betting you got a whole lot more than a brotherly hug."

"Does he know?" My voice rose. "Can he see me? 'Who's that odd woman having a mental orgasm in the cellar?'"

She hunkered down beside me. "No! That's now it works, with us. He may be out in the Afghan hills somewhere wondering who tapped his keg, but he can't find you if you don't want him to."

"I don't. It's embarrassing."

"You pulled those sensations off his vibes. You slipped a straw into his milkshake and . . ."

"Please, no more metaphors."

She sat down and put an arm around me. "Look, every charmer is different. You, for example, get your sensations as fiber textures. That's your main circuit, so to speak. I use pickles—sweet and sour, brine, spice. Gabby uses bread, flour, sugar."

"What does your brother use?"

"Not to pry, but . . . tell me what you tasted."

"Cold, hot, sweet, fruit, chocolate, roasted, thick, smooth, hard . . ." I halted. *Him. I tasted him.* "He's your brother. He seems . . . likable."

Tal bit her lower lip to keep from smiling. "Look, there's the ordinary ways to taste flavors and aromas. Sniff with your nose. Your brain gets the signal. Taste with your mouth and tongue. Your brain merges the feel and the scent. It sorts out what's bitter and what's sweet. Salty, sour. It even has a special talent for meat and broth. Researchers call that one *umami*. A Japanese word. It means *savory*."

Gus is all of the above. Especially savory. I kept that to myself. "There's more to it than taste buds and brain chemistry when charmers are involved."

She nodded, gesturing at the ether somewhere above us. We connect to other . . . realms. Just like you do, only without petting a sheep or a shawl."

"Gus connected with me."

"*You* connected with Gus. Charmer versus Charmer produces some unpredictable effects."

"As long as he doesn't know he reduced me to a puddle of . . . beer. That's what it was. Beer!"

A huge smile lit Tal's face. "You found him, all right. He's a brewer. A beer man. Just like our dad was."

I touched the photo. Suddenly I began babbling like a girl with a new crush. "The hat is a *pakol*. It's made of wool. It's very baggy until you put it on and roll up the sides. Then it looks a little like a beret with a fat rim. The scarf is a *dismaal*. Thin, probably made of cotton. Woven on looms. The Afghans are exquisite weavers. Especially the women. Afghan rugs are classics."

"So, what kind of wool is Gus?"

"A good one. Strong and special."

"What kind of wool are you, by the way?"

I kept looking at Gus's picture. The giddy moment faded. Reality crept back, cold and tasteless. "Angora rabbit."

"Hey, that's nice! Luxurious, fluffy . . ."

"Helpless and an easy catch for predators."

I gave her phone back.

"I'll see you tomorrow at the Crossroads," she ordered. "I've got a plan."

I COULD WALK the two miles from the farm to the Crossroads Café, going through the deep forest of the abandoned bike village of Free Wheeler and past Gear House, where Tal and Doug had moved in together, with Tal's daughter, Eve. The café was scented with pine and cinnamon, and there were lights and trees in every dining room. Out by the pasture fence, under one of the big oak trees, Santa Joe Whittlespoon's famous chainsawed log Nativity scene gleamed with silver garland.

The elder brother of our county sheriff, Santa Joe was the biggest weed grower in western North Carolina.

His Baby Jesus looked like a piece of knotty pine.

The Crossroads Quilting Society met at the café every Wednesday afternoon to sew and gossip and do good for the community. I came to sew and listen and practice not having panic attacks in public—at least not noticeable ones.

Today we were finishing lap quilts for the local churches to hand out as part of their Christmas Share program for needy families. In years past, their numbers hovered around fifty. Now there were three hundred. Food stamps were gone. The free clinic wasn't free, anymore. Most of the kids who had gotten subsidized school lunches now depended on donations.

"Lucy? Can I get you a tissue?" Cleo McKellan ordered. "If you were a little girl, I'd smear your fingertips with cayenne pepper. Stop chewing your nails." A large photo pendant clanked against the heart and cherub charms on the back strap of her hat. Trey looked out at us—not the shaggy woodsman with bitter eyes and a prosthetic leg, but a handsome marine in full dress uniform, ready to serve God, country, and family . . . before an IED took his left leg above the knee.

I flinched at the embarrassment: a drop of blood drying on my right forefinger, where I'd ripped the nail tip off while listening to the group discuss the dark new world of deported immigrants, KKK rallies, foreclosures, and brutal contract terms for the many chicken farmers who depended on Monzell Poultry for their incomes.

Tal handed me a tissue while glaring at Delta's right-hand woman. Cleo, Delta's sister-in-law, and Cleo's husband, Bubba, had just come home from a hospital in Asheville. Blood pressure problems. Both he and Pike had been struggling with it.

"Did you hear who had to file for bankruptcy? Lost her chicken house and both tractors. Monzell saw something she said about him on Facebook. Cancelled her fryer contract."

"They say he's got secret Mexicans working for him."

"Not at the Daw Ridge plant. There's not a brown face in that place. Too many Goggers on the factory lines. Monzell sends the Mexicans to his plants in Arkansas and Tennessee. He wants his Goggers right under his wing, where he can keep brainwashing them."

"Beth, what in the world is a Gogger?"

"Guardians."

"Oh. When did those knuckledraggers start calling themselves Goggers?"

"G.O.G. Guardians. Of. God. We made up the name from that."

"Oh."

"Big ol' mouthy idiots with Nazi tattoos. They hate Jews, Muslims, Democrats, and colored people."

Mabel, whose family had immigrated to North Carolina from Cuba when she was a child, peered over her glasses at the rest. "Y'all, please. Don't say colored people. Say people of color."

Cleo slammed a package on the table. "As long as they're Christians, I don't care if they're brown, white, pink or purple. God-fearing Americans. We need more discipline. We need more patriotism. My son is right when he tells y'all we have a lot to be afraid of. He saw it in Iraq. He's seen what those people want to do to us."

Cleo was a tough wool. Silence gathered. She was devoted to Delta and the café. She was the grieving mother of Trey, a wounded veteran of Iraq who had vanished after returning home.

Or so she thought.

I pressed hard on my bleeding fingertip, trying to squeeze the guilty truth back into my veins.

She was the adoptive mother of Chief Deputy Sheriff Kern Burkett. A handsome sociopath.

No one in the quilting society wanted to pry open the lid of Cleo's Pandora Box. At least, not during Christmas.

She is burning with confusion and sorrow; I smell the stink of wet and destroyed fleece.

Tal carefully set a wrapped quilt in front of her. "Dr. Firth is Scottish and an atheist. Everybody knows that. Does that mean he can't live in this country anymore?"

Since Tal was newly engaged to Doug Firth, our veterinarian, everyone took an extra sip of mulled blueberry wine and waited for the fireworks to start.

Cleo drew herself up to small tank mode. "If I confronted him and said 'You are a Godless man,' he'd try to convince me he's a deacon in the Jefferson County First Baptist. He only tells the truth when he's prescribing medicines for kittens and hogs."

"Oh, *mierda*," Mabel said.

Tal's face slowly turned the color of her hair. Her freckled skin had merged into dangerous freckle storm clouds. "He rescued me and my daughter from a dangerous situation, last month."

Yes, with the help of Fluffy McFainty, there." Cleo nodded toward me. Then she cut her eyes toward Tal. "I'll say this much for Dr. Firth. He does his job well, and he loves animals. And . . . at least you're not consorting with a Wakefield, like your sister."

Fingers stopped tying bows. More sips of wine were taken from sturdy pottery mugs.

Tal swiveled toward Cleo. "You want to say that to Gabby's face? I can arrange a meeting."

"I'll say it to her face, you bet. Taking up with a Wakefield. After what his people did to your family and this county. After what his uncle tried to do to you and her and that dangerous brother of yours."

Gus MacBride. My skin tingled. Dangerous?

"Tissue," Cleo shouted at me. "You're dripping again."

"Sorry." I dug into my knitted tote. I was a traveling drug store—psych meds, tissues, affirmation pamphlets, dream journals, worry stones, yarn, crochet hooks, knitting needles, pepper spray . . . tissues. I wrapped my finger then hid it beneath the table.

"Bring some bandages next time," Cleo snapped. "I was about to say a prayer that the Lord not think we were holding an Old Testament sacrifice here. Tal, quit being so thin-skinned. You're engaged to an atheist and your sister is tangled with a Wakefield. Your brother hasn't been home in almost twenty years. And your little pet—" she stared at me, "—is causing nothing but trouble. Ever since she wrecked Howard Monzell's marriage. She brought down his wrath on everyone who stood up for her."

"She offered his third wife a refuge from abuse."

"No. She meddled in their marriage and used her peculiar influence. No wonder you took her under wing. She's a practitioner of the dark side. Just like you and your sister and brother. You put weeds in your biscuits—"

"Herbs."

"—and chili peppers in your cornbread. Your apple pies are . . . "

"You leave my pies out of this. That's my mother's recipe." Tal stood, towering over Cleo. "Something in your heart is in pain. I smell the scent of burned grains; I feel the dried-up flour with no leavening to bring it up. What's tormenting you?"

Cleo leapt to her feet. "Don't try that voodoo on me." She held up a hand. "But I forgive you. 'Bless those who persecute me; bless and do not curse them.' Romans 12:14."

As a minister's daughter, I knew Bible verses. I was practically the iPhone Siri of Bible trivia. "'The Lord will fight for you,'" I said quietly. "'And you have only to be silent.' Exodus 14:14." I stared at Cleo. "I think you should be silent, now."

She put her hands on her hips. "Well, hallelujah. The little bleeding lamb has grown a backbone."

Tal put a hand on my shoulder to hold me down. Her bodacious, denimed butt cheeks blocked my view of Cleo. "I don't like how you speak to my friend."

Cleo snorted. "I have my sympathy for Lucy's peculiarities, but *I* deserve some sympathy, too. I've got a son I haven't seen in two years since he came home crippled from the wars." She glared at me. "And people around here are talking trash about my other son."

"That's not Lucy's fault."

"She's luring him."

Mabel snorted. "No, she isn't. Kern's a hound dog. Everybody knows it. He's trying to push Pike out of office and take over. God help us all if that happens. He does what his daddy-in-law tells him. Monzell wants to own us all. My husband's cousin was fired at the Daw Ridge plant for passing out union pamphlets."

Cleo's short, dark hair, going lighter with every hair salon visit to hide the silver, glowed with a halo of fury. I saw colors and yarns around people, sometimes. "All I ask is that Kern gets fair treatment. He's a war hero, and he's doing a great job cleaning up this county. I won't have him accused of flirting with women who aren't his wife." She pointed at me. "You're not right in the head. Your imagination gets the best of you."

Lucy Parmenter encouraged my clients, Your Honor.

My skin crawled. Tal's broad hand still clamped me into my chair. I craned my head around her hip. "That's a lie." Small voice. Then, gathering the storm inside my chest, I said it again, louder. "A lie."

Cleo lit up. Radiant static floated the finest small hairs under the brim of a Crossroads Café baseball cap. On the front of her Proud Military Mom sweatshirt, her gold cross and two American flag pendants shimmered on their necklaces. Two sons. One, mysterious and adopted. One, born of her body. Both veterans.

She shouted, "I don't fiddle-faddle around when there's work to be done, I don't mince words, I don't suffer fools lightly, and—" her voice rose and her finger pointed at Tal—"I don't cast my pearls before swine. You MacBrides were nothing but moonshiners and thieves. Now what's left of you has come back here to cause nothing but trouble. But you're weak. Your brother's a coward who won't come home."

Big swirls of coarse red wool shot out of Tal's hair. I stared as the Medusa of tangled yarn reached the ceiling and began to form a cloud of deadly intent over Cleo's head.

I struggled to my feet, having to wedge myself between Tal's butt and the table. "'For she that will love life, and see good days, let her refrain her tongue from evil, and her lips that they speak no guile.' 1 Peter 3:10."

Cleo shot back, "Proverbs 15:28: 'The heart of the righteous studieth to answer: but the mouth of the wicked poureth out evil things.'"

"Exodus 20," I shouted. "'Honor thy father and mother.' What did you do to drive Trey away from home?"

Cleo stepped back as if shoved. Her mouth gaped. Three shocked blinks and tears poured from her eyes, even as she screwed up her face in a tourniquet of rage. She pivoted on squeaky jogging shoes and hurried out the front doors, slamming one so hard the Christmas wreath fell off.

I winced. "I shouldn't have . . . how could I . . . "

"A toast to Lucy," Mabel said. The others grabbed their mugs.

I stood with head down as they gleefully clinked the crockery.

Tal put an arm around me. Wool twined around us. The heat of baking ovens surrounded us. Handwoven towels cushioned crockery pie plates. Bread cooled on neatly knitted cotton runners. "Good job, Yarn Witch. You're ready for your close-up." She pulled me down a hallway to the kitchen.

Since she was putting together a Christmas shipment of her home baked cookies, Gabby's gourmet pickles, and other gifts for Gus, I had contributed one of my scarves. Hand-spun and hand-dyed.

"Hold it up," Tal ordered, as she positioned her phone and peered through the camera app. "No. Not in front of your face."

"I don't want to send a picture."

"Show your face. Eyes, mouth, nose, chin. The whole thing."

I used to be pretty. Very pretty. But that pretty young school teacher and minister's daughter didn't want to be noticed, anymore.

Tal shook the phone at me. "Either cooperate or I'll follow you around until I get the picture I want."

I slowly lowered the scarf.

Tal took the picture. "Terrific."

I looked at it and winced. A rat's nest of long, white-blonde hair, multiple shawls over a large sweater, no makeup on solemn eyes, and a flat, unsmiling mouth. If she'd sneaked a full-length portrait, Gus would see an ankle-length work skirt over thick tights and muddy boots.

Not interested, stay away.

THAT NIGHT, AS usual, I sat outside in the cold. The security sirens began to shriek. Half past two a.m. forty degrees with icy winds coming down off the Ten Sisters. The dogs were already barking. I sat in the broad pastures behind the sheep barn. They dipped and curved into the forest next door, leading to the haunted forest of Free Wheeler, where Claptraddle bicycles made with fine woods, studded with Appalachian gemstones had whirled along the trails between the factory village and the workers' cottages.

A huge barn owl soared across the dark sky.

Miss Lucy, Opal said. *You are either the hunter or the prey. Decide.*

Gunshots exploded from the front field. The goddess statue was under attack, again. Angry men always dishonored her on their way to the main buildings. She was now missing fingers, nipples, toes, and tendrils of her concrete hair. They spray-painted her with swastikas, penis drawings, and KKK symbols. We glued her parts back on, and repainted her.

Spotlights sprang on, bathing the barns, the cabins and communal dorms in stark light. At the main house, a rambling old farmsteader with multiple chimneys and porches, the Christmas lights went dark.

I tried not to lose my shawls or my knitting tote as I ran. I heard voices. They floated through the sky, settled on the ice frost on the fields, boomed like bass drums from under the forest floor below Rainbow Goddess. Ancient voices. Spirits. My yarn angel was among them.

You gonna handle more than usual tonight, Miss Lucy. You gonna learn how.

Opal, I can't. I can't.

Yes, Lucy, you can. You were meant to lead this fight. You're meant to find me. Avenge me.

Behind me, heavy hooves crunched on the frosted grass.

"I'm okay, Brim." I stopped to stroke her nose. She was a big, gray-brown mule, with a sneer on her yellow teeth for anyone but me.

My phone beeped. Alberta barked, "Four armed men in the front pasture. Lockdown Level One. You take the storage cellar."

Ten minutes later I shut and locked the cellar's heavy door then clambered down its concrete steps. More than forty women and children huddled in the chill under fluorescent lights, crouching around tables and chairs scattered among bins full of last autumn's harvest. Potatoes, winter squash, pumpkins, radishes, giving off their good earthy scents. Tall shelves glistened with thousands of canning jars. The farm had a commercial kitchen where we produced jellies, pickles, and soups to sell.

"What do we do now?" a woman called out. "You're some kind of witch, they say. Cast a spell. Wave a wand or something."

My hands shook. A panic attack crawled up my spine and seeped into my lungs.

It doesn't work that way. I hear voices. I get intuitions.

I fumbled in my skirt, patting the plastic container that held my medications. I'd already swallowed too many pills. A fog began to settle over the terror. Not in a good way.

"Who wants to learn to knit?" I called out. I dragged my tote bag off one shoulder; dug out a pair of needles and a skein of yarn. This is a special blend I make, here at the farm. Merino wool spun with the longer fibers of bluefaced leicester . . . "

Someone pounded on the cellar door.

I jumped. I was now shaking uncontrollably. I felt disconnected from reality; trapped in an invisible coffin.

The door lock rattled, and the bolt slid aside. Women screamed. I, however, was frozen in place, feeling two pairs of male hands all over me, inside me, hitting me, tearing me apart again and again.

I reached inside the waistband of my skirt. My fingers edged into the holster that nestled between my thighs. Alberta had been giving me lessons, despite Macy's disapproval.

Click off the safety, pull the pistol out of the holster, curl a finger around the trigger . . .

Keys rattled. The lock turned. Sheriff Pike Whittlespoon shoved the door open. Picture a graying John Wayne in the khaki and leather jacket and baseball cap of a Southern sheriff. A good one.

"All clear, ladies," he boomed.

The women flooded past me. "Quit diddling yourself," one snapped.

I pulled my hand out of my nethers. Other than that show of dignity, I couldn't move. It was like having seizures in public. Helpless and humiliating.

I'm a loser. I'll always be this way. I'm weak.

"Lucy, are you all right?" Pike's deep, fatherly drawl was muffled by the roar in my ears.

He looks tired and pale. What's happening in our community—our mountains, our nation—is tearing him apart. He's been their Andy Griffith for thirty years. But he can't handle the tidal wave of darkness coming at us, now.

He tried again. "Can you hear me? You want me to call Delta?"

Delta, the maternal force that fought this evil. The kitchen charmer at the center of the legendary Crossroads Café. My surrogate sister-mother. I would not have survived except for her and her magical biscuits.

I shook my head. "I'm fine. Just leave me here to catch my breath. Thank you."

"You know, I get these calls, but by the time I make it to the scene, the trouble's been scared off. It's almost like you've got folks in the woods around here, watching out for the place." He cleared his throat and said nothing else.

He knew about the Knights. Delta knew, also. As long as he was in charge they wouldn't be harassed, even though most of them were wanted for petty crimes.

He held out a hand. "Let me help you up the stairs."

I drew back.

No man touched me. Ever.

That night, I texted Tal not to send Gus my scarf or my photo.

"Too late," she texted back. With a *Grin* symbol beside it.

3

I SAT ON MY cot in the glorified shipping container that served as my home on the base.

A pistol was always beside me, then. Always daring me.

My phone chimed. A text from Tal.

She's a charmer, like us. Wool is her thing. I'm sending you a scarf she made.

I'd heard that before. My sisters were a kitchen charms dating service. Always trying to lure me home.

I clicked.

A photo filled my phone. Gorgeous white-blonde fairytale. Wrapped to the chin in scarves, burrowed inside shawls, blue eyes above blue shadows, not wanting to know me, afraid of me, haunting me.

This is Lucy Parmenter.

The scent of blueberries and honey surrounded me. I drank an old, rich wine, peppered with the broken hulls of sugared muscadines. Only the ashes saved it from curling my tongue. Charcoal. Fire and burnt dregs. Pain and fear and the sour dust of memories. *We're alike.*

Deep inside me, she found what was broken.

And I found her.

I set the pistol aside, but not too far.

CHRISTMAS EVE WAS the most depressing day of the year at the farm—women who felt hopeless, with no place else to go, some of them as young as eighteen, some with small children. Several hid bruises still healing under makeup; one or two wore splints or slings. The recent attack had frightened them even more.

The large den at the community house was full of light and music, with a giant, decorated fir tree. The logs of the wall were chestnut, a foot thick and two hundred years old, salvaged from an old grist mill up on Walking Dog Creek. Even an assault rifle couldn't penetrate them.

Presents were piled in mountains of colorful wrapping and large bows. Cathy, Delta, and wealthy patrons like Gabby and Jay Wakefield made sure there were gifts for all.

Macy, dressed in shimmering robes with pointy ears, her long gold hair plaited with gold Christmas garland, handed out stockings stuffed with gift cards from local shops. Alberta played Santa Claus. Most of the youngest children had not caught on that Santa was Miss Al, the female Marine veteran with the longish butch haircut who dressed like a lumberjack and taught them kickboxing.

I was in charge of face painting, given my arts background as a teacher. Armed with a kit of small brushes, non-toxic body paints, glitter and hair decorations, I'd transformed every child in the room into something resembling a deranged Whoville kid in *The Grinch.*

My last project was Tim, a quiet three-year-old with soft brown eyes, caramel skin, and curly black hair.

This so-called farm is taking in the runts and the mutts. Giving welfare to lazy baby mamas. Teaching them to hate men and God.

Howard Monzell's words.

Tim wore red pants and a Rudoph t-shirt. He sat in a chair facing me, gazing solemnly at the mirror beside me as I followed his instructions to give him Christmas soldier paint—red-and-green camo splotches with patriotic glitter stars.

As I painted big stars on his cheeks, I pulled a small, red-and-white scarf from a bag by my feet. Each child got one. The soft wool shimmied against my fingertips as I tied it around his neck.

Suddenly Opal spoke to me.

You gotta talk to him on that phone of yours. You gotta.

My phone played *Jingle Bells.* Tim pointed toward the sound in my skirt. "Santa."

I shook my head. Only a few people had my number. "Santa's over there showing everyone how to kickbox the tree."

"No, that's Miss Alberta. Mama says she's a man inside."

Tal and Gabby's brother is calling you. Gus MacBride is calling you.

My hand jumped. I smeared white glitter paint across Tim's cheek.

He's alone in Afghanistan, where it's dawn of Christmas morning. You have to answer.

I pulled the phone from my skirt pocket as I cleaned up Tim's star with a cotton swab. I tapped the speaker function. I needed not to be alone with Gus MacBride and his orgasmic psychic effect.

"Lucille Parmenter here. I'm on the speaker. At a children's party."

"Luce? This is Captain MacBride. Tal and Gabby's brother. Gus. I could turn on my speaker but I'm alone in my rat can with the scarf you sent me. I think the scarf can be trusted."

Luce. His voice was deep, a good musical drawl, and he created a new version of me with it; he sang me a nickname no one else had ever used, before. The effect caught me between breaths; it pulled me like the warm stroke of cashmere wool.

"Luce?" he said again. "Or is it Lucille? Or is it Lucy? No, it's Luce. I get 'Luce.'"

"Luce is fine," I said. And then quickly, "I'm the face-painting elf at a Christmas party, and I'm just finishing up the snowflakes on a small friend's cheek. His name is Tim, and he's three years old, and he's convinced that you're Santa calling."

Now, Tal's brother will say an awkward thank you for the scarf and then goodbye.

Instead he replied gruffly, "Hello, Tim. I'm not Santa, but if I see him I'll tell him you're bein' *real* good."

Straight for Tim's heart. He's dropping his correct adverb forms and his g's.

Tim's eyes lit up for the first time. "You will?"

I said, "Tim, Captain MacBride is a soldier. And he's—"

Tim leaned over the phone urgently. "Do you know my daddy? He's a soldier, too."

Oh, no. I searched my mind. Something came to me about Tim and his mother's records. A missing biological father in the military.

Gus plowed forward. "What's his name?" His voice was careful.

No. No. There's no way out of these sad questions.

"His name's 'Daddy.'"

"Daddy. Hmmm. Let's see."

"Captain MacBride, let's change the subject."

"I may have met him."

"Please don't . . . "

"He loves ice cream—"

I drew up in a knot. *Don't try to fool this child with a guessing game.*

"Strawberry. With Reese's Pieces crumbled on it. Tim, he said you call them 'Pinky Pieces.'"

Tim gasped. "Yes! Mama says he left for the war 'cause he couldn't get a job. Where is he?"

"I don't know. I saw him a long time ago. But I know this much: He loves you and your mama, he'll never stop loving you."

"Okay!" He leaned over and whispered into the phone, "You really are Santa, aren't you?"

Gus whispered back, "No, but I'm one of his bigger elves. You stay strong. Take care of your mama. She needs you to tell her you love her.

Tell her every day."

"I'm goin' to go do that right now!"

Tim hopped down and galloped toward an outside door. His mother could be seen through the windows, huddled on a patio alongside several other women, smoking a cigarette under a security lamp made only slightly friendlier by a Christmas wreath. Macy waylaid Tim and looked my way. I nodded. Macy wrapped him in a coat then carried him outside.

He dived into his mother's arms. He whispered against her hair. She flicked the smoke into the yard and hugged him tightly, her face burrowed against his.

Stunned, I finally found my voice. "You were right," I whispered into the phone. "She needed that. But his father's . . . missing. She just hasn't told Tim, yet."

"He's dead." Gus said the words flat, like slamming a brick onto the fresh mortar in a wall.

I shivered. "Yes. I felt it when I gave Tim a scarf. The wool shrank under my fingers. That's a death sign."

"Talk wool to me. Tell me the other signs you get."

"There are too many. And it's situational. I rely on a voice."

"Do you have a name for it?"

"Opal."

"Why?"

"I just know that's her name. I heard her not long after I came here. She told me Cathy Deen Mitternich wouldn't miscarry, this time. She was right. That's when your sisters and Delta Whittlespoon told me I had the gift. I was a Charmer. Like them. And you. But you all were born with it. I just . . . "

"You always had it. You just weren't ready to hear the voice and the visions until the right time."

"Do you hear a voice?"

"No, but if I did I'd call him Wolverine."

"Why?"

"He could grill kabobs with his knuckles."

I did the impossible. I burst out laughing.

He chuckled. There was whisky in it, and drugs. "That's a good sound. Let's play guessing games. "You like the harvest, not the planting, not the waiting. Too much can go wrong in the prep stage. Cook it, store it, pour it, drink it."

"Is everyone some kind of beer, to you?"

"Says the woman who thinks everybody's a sheep."

"You're not a sheep. You're . . . "

I halted. *Take it easy. Don't go all fan-girl on him. Keep it smooth.*

"Don't go soft on me *now*. Finish it. What am I?"

"A wolverine. That's what you like. Wolverines."

"Nooo. Wolverines look like a cross between a bear and a skunk. Just say it. What am I? A yak? A camel?"

"I need to think about it. Tal says you're a yarner. Knit, crochet, even a little needlepoint."

"My dad taught me. Said men who knit get more dates."

"And he taught you to make beer."

"Another way to get the girls."

"You miss him."

"You miss your dad, too. I can feel it. He hasn't been gone long."

Silence. Dad collapsed while I was in the hospital. Died of a heart attack. I still feel responsible.

"Whatever happened," Gus said quietly, "it wasn't your fault."

How much can he learn about me without me telling him?

"I can't look where you don't want me to look, Luce."

He knows what I'm thinking.

"Not really, it's just a deep intuition."

Stop thinking.

"I promise you, I can't read your mind. You can't read my mind, either. Just bits and pieces and guesses."

I finally got my voice back. "What you can do—what we can do—is far more than hunches and guesses."

"Aw right, yes. But I'm not going to plow into your private spaces and violate your trust. You have my word. And I ask the same promise from you."

"I promise."

"Read me. Go ahead. See what you find."

I took a deep breath. I saw long scenes of their childhood in foster care after their parents died. Their father killed directing traffic on an icy winter road. Their mother dying in an Asheville hospital a few months later, from a blood clot brought on by grief and stress. A custody fight and the time in foster care. Frustration and helplessness. The subjugation of boyhood pride to the reality of a system that put Gabby at the mercy of older boys while Tal huddled in corners.

Kiss him, Opal ordered. Kiss him right where it counts. Save his life.

I pressed my mouth to his. How coarse and interesting his skin would be, stubbled, quickly razored after a long patrol, freshly showered but still scented with the vast cold terrain of the Afghan mountains. Not like our mountains, capped in ancient forests of evergreens and hardwoods; no. Scraped raw by bony celestial fingers. A beloved land to its people in ways our mountains spoke to us. Secret whispers.

Like the kiss I brushed across Gus MacBride's open lips.

It's Christmas Eve, Gus. I haven't kissed a man in years. I desperately want to. There.

"Merry Christmas to me," he said hoarsely.

She asked for it, your Honor.

I drew back. Physically as well as mentally. Leaned away from the phone.

"It's okay," he said quickly. "Please. Whatever happened to you, I feel it. I respect it."

"I'm uncomfortable with this conversation."

"Let's back up and change the subject. You still haven't told me what kind of wool I am."

"I have to go. Thank you for calling . . . "

"Buffalo? Gorilla? You're not goin' leave me thinking I'm gorilla wool, are you?"

I struggled to breathe. "Wensleydale, Captain."

"Is that good?"

"Old Irish breed of sheep." I was hyperventilating now. "Tough. Long strands. Almost completely waterproof when spun and knitted. Not always comfortable when it's next to the skin. Best used as a shawl. Coat. Scarf."

"Alright. Not easy to touch, but protective. That sums me up."

His misery flooded me. I heard lambs in Gus MacBride's rust-red river. Lambs crying. He'd seen death. A lot of it. Close up. Even just a few days ago.

"Do you really like the scarf I sent?"

"You bet. I'm having a good night. I've got your voice in my ear and a big box from *home* between my feet. There're cookies and pickles from my sisters. And the scarf you made, yeah. I'm warm for the first time in days."

Deep breath. "It's merino and alpaca. We don't have merino sheep here in Jefferson County, so I barter for that wool. But the alpaca is from our animals. You're wearing Shirley."

"Tell Shirley she feels like a warm hug. So . . . exactly where are you doing this face-painting tonight, playing Christmas Elf? The shelter at

Rainbow Goddess?"

"Yes."

"Sounds homey."

He knows it isn't homey at all. Might as well be honest.

"Not exactly. We have security cameras everywhere, a dozen big dogs who bark at everything that moves, llamas that spit at strangers, goats that attack with no warning, and miles of wild mountains in every direction. We don't publish our address. It's too risky, these days. And we make the farm's main entrance hard to find. It looks like an old hunter's trail from the road, with a steel gate and a rusty *Do Not Enter* sign. Feels like we're guarding an outpost on the frontier, sometimes, except for the goddess statue near the gate. But it's beautiful, here. It's a sanctuary. At least for now."

I stopped.

"Are you safe?"

I'll never feel safe again.

"Yes, of course. I'm a counselor here. It's my home. Are *you* safe? No. You're not."

I *felt* him back off. "I'm safe enough. I'm sipping bourbon out of a metal cup in my metal tin can of a home. Keep talking. Please."

A vapor curled around me. Hops steaming in a deep of water. Aromatic herbs and grains, fermenting.

"Just keep talking to me," he repeated.

"I live in a one-room efficiency in the sheep barn. If I walk outside in the pastures and follow the slope of the hills into the hollows and the forest, in twenty minutes I'll be on your family property at Free Wheeler. The old bicycle village your grandparents built is sad and beautiful and impossible to describe to someone who hasn't seen it in person. All the empty buildings. It's magical. It really is. My outpost isn't nearly as stark as yours, but I can understand how you must feel on a holiday night, alone."

"You've got no family left."

"Afraid not."

"You're not alone. Not when you're talking to me."

Heat traveled through me; his voice carried it, but a current of sensations traveled in sync. Down my body, into my arm, through my hand, which gently smoothed my work in progress, the scarf, atop my thighs. *Change the subject.* "What are you knitting, right now? Current work-in-progress."

"All right, wool charmer. Here's a test. I'm picking up my current knitting project. In my hands. Right now." His voice shifted to a lower timbre, daring me. "Can you tell me—"

"Camel, because it's soft and handspun, with imperfections, and the color is natural; it's the color of the landscape there. I think it was a gift from a villager. You like all those things about it."

He gave a low whistle. "All *right.* Next, Miss Smarty Yarny, tell me what . . . "

"Fingerless gloves."

"You're good at this."

"Not better than you, Tal and Gabby. Do you think there are others like us?"

"I hope so, but until you came along, I'd never met one."

"Me . . . neither. I didn't have this ability until I came to the farm as a . . . until I came here. I had never knitted or crocheted or spun wool before. I . . . touched a handful of wool and suddenly found a connection. Magic. Homespun intuition. Your sisters are my buddies. And Delta Whittlespoon. And Cathy Mitternich."

"I'd like to be considered a friend of yours. If I cross a line, just tell me. Deal?"

My mind pulsed with the urgency that flowed from him, but also the discipline. Controlled desire. *He saw my ugly snapshot and still called.* Desire for me. *I want to be wanted.*

"Deal, Captain."

My breathing shallowed. I wasn't in a pit looking up at a sky I'd never see again. I felt desire for a man. A real one, not a faceless impulse attached to my own hand at night.

"Those fingerless gloves," I said. "You're having trouble with the pattern?"

"The holes are too small for my fingers. When I add stitches, I get gaps. So I frogged that version, re-knitted per the original chart, then did a wash and block to see if I get some stretch."

"Did you try soaking the finished piece in hair conditioner? That softens wool the same as it does human hair."

"Tried that. Didn't work. The holes haven't relaxed at all."

"Try a few simple increases around the rims."

"I get puckers."

"Try tucks. A tuck by the knuckle of your forefinger. A second tuck by the knuckle of your little finger. Then add two small tucks underneath, palm-side, below the middle fingers. The pattern just needs to be . . . tucked."

Silence. I heard my own breathing, and his. He cleared his throat. "I could use help with my patterns. You up for that?"

I could barely form words by then. "Send yarn. I can do that much. Send you yarn. I know your sisters send you boxes full. It's hard to get, there." *Pull yourself together*. Deep breath. "Captain, yes, I'd love to talk to you again. Knitting, crochet, spinning. Wool is my passion. What else can I send?"

"Luce," he said in a deep drawl that caressed my sweet spot, "I'll be happy with whatever you give me, and I'm yours to command."

I was plunging down confession lane with this big, macho stranger. I blinked and saw him vividly. Sitting on his ugly little bed, bare-chested, my scarf around his neck.

And a loaded pistol beside him.

My entire body went cold. I *saw* the pistol lying next to his hip, on the cot.

"Captain. Gus. I don't like that gun. Put it away. Your mother is with you. She's all around you. I can feel the love. And your father is there, too. He's saying something about the crochet hook. You carry a crochet hook of his?"

Long silence. I know the sound of a man trying hard not to cry when he speaks.

"Yeah," Gus answered.

"You need to come home," she says. "You're needed here. She means North Carolina."

"I never . . . planned to come back. Too many memories."

My face was wet. I was crying. "Put the gun away. Put it away. They're saying put it away. And come home."

"I'll make you a deal, Wool Witch." His voice was a deep, fractured mess. "You stay alive, and I will too. I've got a leave coming, in March. I want to meet you."

"I'll be here. And between now and then, we'll talk by phone and work on patterns."

"Deal," he said.

THAT NIGHT I had the worst panic attack in months. Ended up feverishly working at my wheel on the little stoop outside my room in the barn, while sheep, llamas, alpacas and Brim dozed around me. My spinning wheel, an antique Delta had given me, sat on the walkway outside my room at the barn. Bags of unspun wool roving were piled around it. The long stranded varieties, from the Bluefaced Leiceisters, were easy to spin. The short, ultra-soft merinos were harder. The Angora rabbit fur was like fitting fluffs of cotton into a strand.

The long, coarse wools, like the shaggy Wenslydales, could rub my fingers raw.

Hadn't you been leading them on, Ms. Parmenter? Flirting with these two maintenance workers at your apartment complex? Bringing them cookies in the evenings after you came home from your teaching job? Engaging them in conversation?

Sir, that's . . . that's how I how I was raised to treat my fellow human beings. That's called outreach. Ministering. They had drug problems.

Move to strike that comment, your honor. Prejudicial against my clients.

Ms. Parmenter, just tell us your own motives.

Yes, Ms. Parmenter, tell us if you were trying to get sex and drugs from my clients—two hardworking men who were charmed by a pretty blonde school teacher looking for thrills.

I should tell him the truth. I was drugged, raped, and beaten by two meth addicts. They held me hostage, in my apartment, for hours. No part of me wasn't damaged.

If he came home in March, I would talk. Look him in the eyes and read the book inside his soul and find out if he was a dream come true or just another nightmare.

4

January

AFGHANISTAN TIME was eight-and-a-half hours ahead. Nine p.m. on a Sunday night at the farm was five-thirty a.m. Monday at Gus's base. When Gus wasn't on patrol, he called me before dawn, his time; meaning early evening at the farm. I sat on the knoll outside my barn, looking up at the cold night sky, wrapped in shawls and blankets, with the farm dogs snuggling me.

Whenever we could arrange the schedule, Gus phoned me during the afternoons, my time. I introduced him to Brim on a blue-sky Tuesday when the temps hit a balmy fifty degrees.

Brimmy. Brim. Short for Brimstone. Daughter of a quarter horse mother and a donkey father. A *molly mule*. Like all but a few exceptions in the mule world, her mixed parentage made her a sterile hybrid. She was smarter and stronger than a horse, able to survive on less food and in worse conditions, a hard worker, a loyal friend, and hell on anyone or anything who threatened her territory—or me. Her owners, a young married couple planning to live off the grid up here in the mountains with a mule to pull their garden plough, had boarded her at Rainbow Goddess the fall before.

They went home to visit family and never came back. Brim's lack of quaint country charm may have been a determining factor in their return to city life.

I'd fallen in love with Brim from the first day, when I walked up to her in the pasture before I heard the warnings. She bared her teeth at me then tried to eat my hair. Her eyes shifted my way with bored disdain. They were such a dark, walnut brown; I had to look closely to find the pupil in the eye nearest me. Suddenly I was in my psychic zone. Her energies pummeled my face with intense sensations, alive with meaning. I saw every tiny hair on the dark skin around the smooth round jewel of her beautiful oculus. The dark well of the pupil had a fire deep inside it; not a hellish one that deserved her name but a heart of bleak, dull sorrows.

I had pulled my shawl over her head and swept it around us both in a hugging motion. We stood there, tented inside the wool-scented warmth, our heads bent together. For a moment she drew her head up. I waited. Slowly, she relaxed. I leaned my face against the hard, bony plane of her temple.

Sorry. Hurt. Sad. Friend.

She snuffled my shoulder. And then she answered.

Sorry. Hurt. Sad. Friend.

I'd offered the owners one thousand dollars for her plus two queen-sized crocheted bedspreads.

Since Brim's transfer into my keeping, she and I had spent a lot of time in couples' therapy. She had abuse issues.

Gus officiated via the speaker on my cell phone. Two empaths communicating with a mule empath.

Me: *Friend. Safe.*

Brimstone: *Friend. Food.*

"I smell carrots," Gus had said. "How does that make you feel, Luce—bein' regarded as nothing but a root vegetable?"

His deep voice massaged me. "It's not like that. I bring her carrots as a treat."

"I'm sensing some co-dependency issues here. Brim, is that true? Mmmm. I see. Go on. Really? Luce, she says y'all are as alike as two peas in a pod."

"Well, I do like carrots."

"That's not what she means. Have you ever had an urge to bite me?"

The first time Brim heard his voice she lunged at the phone and almost snapped it out of my hand. I had to hold her by the halter while Gus communed with her from a distance. After that introduction she tolerated his voice, although she cast unfriendly looks at the phone each time and flicked her ears back. Her owner had said she was trouble around men in general, and he'd had to work with her a long time to earn her trust.

I understood.

Gus went on. "Like Brim, do you have that urge to bite men in general, Ms. Parmenter?" He kept his tone light.

Not if they respect my personal pasture space. I tried to do the same.

Brim accepts carrots from you as a show of trust. What gift would you expect from a man?

His trust, in return. I paused. And socks. I like socks. A crochet and knitting challenge.

Brim jabbed her muzzle toward a small canvas pouch tied around my waist. Several carrots poked out, along with my phone. She snatched a carrot and the phone, slung the phone aside, and kept the carrot. The phone sailed at least twenty feet and landed in clumps of brown winter grass.

I ran to it as if Gus were physically inside. Are you still there? Can you hear me? The connection was gone. As I began pressing commands and preparing to call him back, his text message came through with a large smile emoticon attached. *I'm knitting socks for you. BUT NONE FOR HER.*

I laughed out loud.

I LIVED FOR THOSE calls to Luce. I'd sit, wearing my winter gear and her scarf, on the wooden steps outside my tin can, looking at the night sky or squinting into the cold gold dawns. Average daily high—forty-something. In the twenties at night. Dry cold, coming off the steppes and the grasslands, not like the misty damp of the Appalachians.

She described every phase of the moon over the Ten Sisters. "January is the Cold Moon," she told me. "That's what the Cherokees call it. A time for resting, and repairing tools and clothing. It's ceremonial to put out your hearth fire and start a new one. Renewal."

"My grandmother's family has a lot of Cherokee blood. The Netties. My mother said our talent for insights and predictions came from them."

"You were born with it?"

"I've had it as long as I can remember."

"I wonder what explains *me*. I wasn't born with this ability. I'm not part Cherokee or any other native tribe, that I know of."

"It comes to different people in different ways."

"How many others do you know?"

"None like me and my sisters and our mother. No one like you. But hints of the gift in people. Yes. There's an old villager here at the base; he runs a shop near the PX. Cigarettes, pirated DVDs, cheap sunglasses. The first time we met, I smelled a spice aura around him. He was staring at me, too. He waved me to the back of his shop and introduced me to his grandmother. I sat with her beside a small grill and a stone oven. I don't speak a lot of Farsi and she spoke no English. Regardless, we talked. I've never done that before. I sensed what she wanted to say and she sensed what I said. She taught me to make *mantu*. It looks like ravioli, and it's stuffed with minced meat. I've been back every week since then. She teaches me to cook, and we communicate in separate languages."

Luce said softly, "The first time I touched a section of wool roving and it 'spoke' to me, I thought I'd completely lost touch with reality. Lost my mind, Gus. That was right after I came here to the farm. I told Cathy Mitternich I wasn't raised to believe anything like that was possible. But . . . looking back, I think I *was* raised to believe. The power of our senses goes so far beyond what we use them for ordinarily . . . who knows how much they'd tell us, if we knew open how to open those channels?"

"I and my sisters learned early on not to share our talent with strangers. Especially after I told my third grade teacher her husband liked to grab her married sister."

Luce never quite laughed, but I could feel her smiling.

"As a child," she went on, almost whispering—as if her sheep and dogs and Brim the mule would overhear and gossip—" when I was sick with colds I remember my great aunt smearing mentholated salve up my nose and around my throat, then wrapping and pinning an old scarf of hers around my neck. I felt like a vapored mummy. But that scent of the salve and the musky odor of the scarf is a memory that comes back to me; it makes me feel so safe, now. I wonder if . . . even then . . . was I tuned into the scarf's energy, you know? That the wool was comforting me?"

I'd like to comfort you. I didn't say it out loud. Didn't have to. Her breath broke and we were both silent for a few seconds.

"Those memories are always tied to sleeping with her for extra warmth, if she wasn't in a mood. She told me to call her 'Mr. Auntie,' because she was Dad's aunt. That made sense to her, if not to me. Mr. Auntie kept her side of our duplex super-warm. She had a coal furnace she refused to give up, even though Dad was afraid it would burn down the entire house. He had trouble finding a supplier to deliver coal in suburban Charlotte.

"The old furnace rumbled and gushed heat up through a main grate in the hallway outside her bedroom door. I imagined that furnace burning black diamonds. That's what the coal looked like to me. I dreamed dreams in her side of the house I never dreamed elsewhere. Scenes of beautiful fairytale places I just knew I had visited in a previous life. I asked Dad if I was going to hell for believing in reincarnation, because, being a minister's daughter, it meant God would judge me harder than others. Being the daughter of a Southern Methodist minister carried even more responsibility.

"Dad said, 'Lucy, God gave us the brains to think up all sorts of heavens. If He hadn't wanted us to ponder them, He'd have made us too dumb to care.' Then he hugged me and added, 'If you tell anyone in the congregation I said that, I'll trade you to the Episcopalians for a case of wine.'"

I laughed, the first laugh of a long, brutal week. "When I come home on leave, I want to hear a *whole* lot more about him."

"There's a lovely half-moon tonight over the Ten Sisters. They have moon shadows on their tops. It's beautiful."

"When you change the subject like that it tells me you don't want to talk about your dad." She was quiet for a long time. "I hear you knitting," I said.

"Thinking."

"Talk."

"You're leaving on another patrol, soon. You don't have to say so; I'm just guessing. I'm sitting out here in the pasture with a few of the farm's sheep snuggled around me. I can sense them thinking, 'This odd creature has no wool. So she wraps herself in ours. We must stay close to her shawls. They are part of our flock.' Delta says every month's moon has a different meaning. This month, January, is a Sleeping Moon—it's all about hibernation. February is a Dying Moon—death to the weak and helpless in a severe winter. March, when you come to visit, is a Renewal Moon. The edge of Spring. A time for waking up, preparing to set new roots and grow new life. I love the old Appalachian folklore."

"Well, my mother called March a *simmering* month. She said it was a time to check the liquor in your cook pots. She didn't mean alcohol; she meant the essence of the meals you'd cooked all winter. That boiled-down gravy. Soul gravy. I wonder what your dad would think of my soul gravy? About you pen palling with a godless army captain who claims he and his sisters can taste and smell the food aromas of other people's thoughts?"

"He'd threaten to trade you to the Episcopalians for wine." She paused as I laughed again. "Dad would say, 'Your strange Appalachian food witchery probably rates *two* cases of wine in a barter with the Episcopalians.' But he'd like you. He'd be impressed with your honor, your kindness . . . and your knitting and crocheting. He did needlepoint.

Mostly quotes from Franklin Roosevelt and Bible verses. But once he did a big one that just said, 'Jesus Gives.' He took it to sell at a church fundraiser.

"Everyone was bewildered. 'Jesus gives . . . *what*, Reverend Parmenter?' Dad told them that was up for interpretation. I always wanted him to do a companion needlepoint that listed some possible answers: 'Jesus gives . . . Good advice. Jesus gives . . . More than He gets. Jesus gives . . . Back. At work. A damn. A hoot. Coupons.'"

I laughed until my sides ached. I felt her smiling again. I also felt her shifting her thighs, the love warm and wanting inside them. For me. Whoever had abused her, no matter what her ugly history—a boyfriend or ex-husband or—hell, it made me sick to think about it, a member of her own family—she'd tell me in her own good time. And we'd work it through, one touch at a time.

"Your voice is a warm liquor," she whispered. "Mr. Auntie took me to visit a branch of her family in Tennessee when I was a child. They gave me a little cup of Ginger Ale spiked with moonshine. I wandered the backyard talking to butterflies. Mr. Auntie never suspected. That's how your voice feels, to me. Like a warm day in a garden where everything's safe, and it's safe to run free."

I felt a sudden fear in her, the drawing back that happened whenever either of us got too close.

I changed the subject. Told her some lame news about the yarn club on base. I was one of its leaders. Painting a word-picture of hard-ass, young soldiers with dead shadows in their eyes. The ones who burned the air with threats if anyone dared tell the girlfriend or the boyfriend or the old buddies back home that I Am Sittin' Here Fuckin' Crocheting a Fuckin' Scarf. How a lot of them quietly came back, each week, to slouch in folding chairs under hard fluorescent lights, talking trash and pretending they didn't like it, while the yarn and the crochet hook or the knitting needles moved like prayers in their sunburned hands.

"What you love doing with your hands," Luce whispered, "Is what you love doing with your life."

"How did you end up at the farm? My sisters won't tell me—they say it's your choice. I won't push you to talk about it, if you don't want to."

Her stark silence filled my mind with the cold rot of a dead lamb in the sun.

"You'll tell me when you're ready," I added quickly. "I can't and won't even try to read your mind. Relax."

She never said another word that night. Pain came off her in waves that made me sick to my stomach. There's an old Celtic word. *Hiraeth.* A homesickness for a home you can never go back to because maybe it never existed to begin with. It hurts. It's a grief. You see pieces of it in dreams, and you never want to wake up.

I'd been looking for redemption since Dad died on my watch and Mom not long after.

Luce was it. My home. I desperately hoped that I was hers.

I SPENT FAR TOO many hours gazing at photos Gus emailed me. They scrolled across an electronic photo frame beside my computer. I put my fingertips on his face. The big, broad-shouldered man in desert camo with reddish hair bleached almost as pale as mine. I saw his sisters in him—saw their strong-jawed Scots-Irish father and red-headed part-Cherokee mother, who'd both died when the three of them were children in Asheville, caught in a blood feud between Jay Wakefield's uncle and an old legacy of land rights at Free Wheeler that tangled in most of the old families of the Crossroads Cove.

I saw strength and pride and pull-yourself-up-determination.

I saw his smile, and the lines creasing the corner of his eyes, and the enameled-green gaze that looked straight out at me and sizzled farther down into me than I could ever let any physical touch travel.

I loved Gus MacBride, the most beautiful man I'd never have sex with in my life.

Gus thought I was funny. Nice. I liked it that way. We were penpals. Text buddies. I loved the pictures he texted me of him cooking over campfires while local children and burka-clad women watched him eagerly, as fascinated by him as I was.

Okay, I loved him from a distance. The best way. He would never come home to stay for good—he did not want anything to do with his memories of growing up in North Carolina, said Tal and Gabby, although I'd begun to worry about a change of heart. Both of them had returned to the mountains. Tal was with Doug Firth now, her and her daughter Eve. And Gabby had become the talk of the entire state with her Christmas drama alongside Jay Wakefield, up in the Little Fin Valley. They were a team. A couple. She wasn't going back to her home in California.

What if Gus had a change of heart, too?

A storm's coming, girl.

Opal's presence sang in my head. I adjusted the water flow to the livestock troughs. The water, from one of the farm's three deep wells, was so cold it burned my fingers. I looked up at a clear blue sky.

You don't mean snow and ice. That's not in the forecast. Not yet, anyhow. It's still only January.

There's a lotta kinds of storms, Miss Lucy. This one will be all kinds, put together.

What do I need to know? I shivered. What do I need to do?

Practice your courage. Every chance you get.

I went inside the barn, which was warm and fertile with the scent of the animals. I sat on my stoop atop a wooden stool behind the spinning wheel. Spinning always loosened the vines of fear. I rested a foot on the treadle and pumped. The wheel whirred and turned. Feeding a fluffy streamer of roving into the yarn I'd started previously, I watched it twist into a slender strand, pivot through the orifice and wind neatly onto the bobbin. Below my little porch, the sheep and llamas and Brim snoozed under heaters that hung from the tall ceiling, their eyes half shut and muzzles mumbling in dreams. Some of the farm dogs and cats were curled up in the thick shavings among them.

My four-legged family. I loved them all.

My phone lit up. Ping, ping, ping, inside a knitted pocket attached to my skirt. My ringtone sounded like mice playing a xylophone. Nervous but organized.

The roving gnarled in my fingers then leapt into the air, spreading tendrils and weaving a soft net, gray-blue, sad.

Not too bad. Not something horrible.

I pulled the phone out and read KNIGHTS on the I.D. But when I clicked to answer, the connection failed. I tucked the phone back in its pocket.

They'd asked me to quit calling them the Apple Pie Knights, a name I had given them to make them seem less threatening at first. They still hid in the woods at Free Wheeler, but no longer sent all their messages written on notes delivered by Patton, the four-pawed military veteran who suffered from PTSD just as they did. He still stole small items from all over the neighborhood. Extracted, not stealing, the Knights called it.

The Knights trusted me. Their phone messages ran the gamut from wistful to wild.

"Yarny—I keep dreaming about a bronze Cadillac SUV with a fat copperhead in the driver's seat. It went up the road to Turtleville. The snake has new hair plugs. He drives with your hands. He wants to bite you. Watch your back. I can kill him if you want me to."

"Hiya Yarnspinner—Night Owl says it's okay to just think about blowing shit up to get the anger out of my brain. You agree?"

"Yarny Sista—Gutsy has a problemo. Gutsy is horny. Gutsy doesn't fuck the men-soldiers in her unit. Band of sister-brothers. Get it? Ditto for Miss Dragon. Gutsy and Dragon warn you—keep Larry Pretty Boy Dishwasher out of our woods. We did our recon on him: He's over eighteen so that means LEGAL. Tell him to ix-nay on his stupid-ass 'science' in the woods. We're not 'rockycockers' but you let us get our hands on him and we'll sure rocky his cock."

The phone seemed to squirm along the waistband of my skirt. Interesting, what years of operating in the thin altitudes of sleep deprivation and cat naps did to a person's perceptions. Throw in a little extra stress and I felt more porous than usual; colors became brilliant and tactile; the sensual flow of the messages came and went through my skin.

I'd become too obvious, staring into the eyes of others, especially the women staying at the shelter at Rainbow Goddess, or really anyone I knew to be in emotional danger. I'd see a desperate glow in the darkness behind their pupils; they needed answers to questions they didn't know how to ask.

And I'd be overwhelmed with information.

Later, I'd find a way to say something.

You mentioned that you feel guilty for coming here to the women's shelter, because your husband's never hit you, and he only calls you names when he's been drinking. But I've been wondering . . . you listed two pre-teen sons of his from his previous marriage. One's eight and one's eleven. Boys can play rough. Are they respectful to you?"

"Why, sure. Look, I didn't come here to talk about anybody but me and him. I don't think I should talk to you. People say you're psychic. That's of the Devil."

"My father was a Methodist minister. I was christened in his church." I pulled out the cross he'd worn.

She pursed her lips. Then, "Awright. Buck gave me a roof over my head and I vowed to be a good mother and wife, and he pays the bills. I just . . . I just . . . "

"You have my word that what you tell me about the boys won't get them in any trouble. Have there been problems with his sons that your husband didn't manage the way you would have liked? This is about him, not about the children."

"You swear? You've gotta way about you. My granny called it the mustering. It was an old superstition up in these high places. That some folks could bewitch people into telling their secrets and their sins. Whether they wanted to or not."

"I swear."

Her jaw hardened. She nodded. And nodded again, then fought and lost to angry, shamed emotion.

"Buck's boys shove me and punch me and grab me," she whispered, with a quick shift of her eyes. "Down there and—she indicated her chest—here. They call me names worse than any he ever does. Say I'm not their mama, I'm their daddy's whore, and that makes me their whore, too."

"Did you tell him about their behavior?"

"I told him the first few times. He whupped them and hollered at them to keep their hands off his property. That's how he put it—his property. After that they quit touching me. But they hated me for tellin' on them. So every chance they got—and I was there alone with them, a lot—they'd say awful things to me, and bring over friends who'd do the same. Tear up my flower beds and tape dirty pictures inside my purse. Text me photos of their 'parts', you know, on my phone."

"Your husband wouldn't tell them to stop?"

"He said that was just boys being boys. That I wasn't much of a woman if I couldn't handle them." Her control shattered. Tears spilled. "If y'all could teach me how to do it right, I can go back. I came here to get some lessons. I heard she's ol' bull dyke who used to be a marine, that one that owns this place, Alberta? She can teach me how to tame those boys, can't she? I got no other place to go, and no good way to support myself. I have to go back. So just help me get some lessons in being a good mother to tough sons. I'll work hard at it."

"Certainly. But in the meantime, I saw on your records that you worked for Dixon's Heritage Seed business for five years. You handled all their mailing lists and their mail orders."

"I don't remember telling anybody that, or putting it on paper."

"You know how to set up spreadsheets and databases. You can design websites."

"Yeah. Got a knack for that stuff."

"Do you know that Rainbow Goddess is mostly self-supporting? The work done by the women who stay here pays for their program and helps pay for the future. The berry harvest, the goat and cow cheese, and now the yarn and fleece business—it's important. I've been hoping to find someone who could organize all the yarns and the roving, the fleece, everything, and set up an online store for us."

"You're saying I can stay here and pay my way by doing that work?"

"Yes."

"I don't care what it pays. I'll find a place to live . . . I'll sleep in the woods . . . "

"No, you'll have room and board here. That's part of the deal. We can't pay much, but you get a place to live, and safety, and friendship, and help."

She smothered tears behind her hands. "I don't want to believe what Mr. Monzell and his people say about you. You're not trying to lure me into witchcraft or being a lesbian, are you? Like you did with his third wife?"

"No, I promise." I held out a hand.

"I accept. But I'm not touching you. No offense, alright?"

"No offense."

This was my life. To be needed, pitied, and feared, except by a few people who knew about me and understood who and what I was.

The mice played the xylophone again.

This time, a text message came through.

Nighthawk's dad died. Bring some Jesus, quick.

"WE'LL SET UP IN the old bakery," Tal said when we met in Free Wheeler. "The Knights feel comfortable there. Lots of good spiritual energy. The ghosts of pies and cakes and bread. The people who lived in Free Wheeler loved the bakery shop. It was a gathering place. You can feel that serenity."

Puffing along beside her with a heavy backpack riding my shoulders, I caught enough breath to ask, "Why did you hide your truck inside the Lube and Fuel?"

The Lube and Fuel was our nickname for the village's tiny gas station, designed like an English cottage with a peaked roof and window boxes for flowers. Currently it sat at the end of Main Street, with tree stumps protruding between the cracked paving stones, its windows and garage bay shuttered and barred.

It was hard to imagine hand-built bicycles skimming along the paths in the 1930s and 40s. Mountain Flyers and Star Riders and Spinning Roses had been built and assembled at The Hub, a grand two-story brick building that occupied one entire side of the village's paver-stoned main street. Over its tall double doors, a granite arch was engraved:

Enter the Hub of Imagination
The World of Clapper Motion Machines

Inside those doors was a large marble foyer inlaid with a huge mural of colorful marble chips. The shops of Free Wheeler, the Ten Sister Mountains, blue skies and white clouds; happy adults and children rode bicycles as onlookers waved. A tall, smiling man and red-haired woman waved from the Hub's doorway. Sam and Rose.

To own a Claptraddle bicycle was to claim a part of Appalachian artisan history; to own a piece of the ancient mountains themselves, and their peoples' pride, and their tragic memories: the inlaid chestnut wood from ghost trees long extinct from the blight; the ornamental chips of mountain sapphire, ruby garnet, and even specks of gold . . . the metals refined from mines dug by immigrant settlers, mines with bloody and dark histories of greed and politics and power, not the least of which had been the MacBrides versus the Wakefields.

Now it was all ghosts and memories.

So quiet.

But not quiet at all.

Tal paused to steady the stack of boxes and plastic tubs on her hand cart. My skin prickled at the tension in her face. "Sour, rotting, moldy. That's what I smelled during Carl's funeral. Everybody called him Bubba, because that was the nickname Delta gave him when they were kids. Her older brother. Her bubba. But the funeral program called him Carl. He was a sweet man. He and Cleo were married thirty years, but she didn't shed a tear during the service. She's not a crier. I got 'flattened soufflé' from her. She's a lost soul. Except for holding onto Kern. He was there for her."

She unfastened a padlock on the bakery's back door. The heavy wood creaked as she opened it. Tal pulled a propane lamp from her cart, lit it, and hung the glow from a low rafter over a long marble counter. I stacked a dozen thickly crocheted lap throws on the counter—the Knights needed all the coverings they could get, since—so far as we could guess—they lived in a primitive camp in a hollow or under a rock overhang. I gazed at gracious old walls tiled in pale colors. A tile floor in a checkerboard pattern. Empty shelves made of beautiful, hand-carved wood. The forlorn spots where ovens and sinks had stood. With the windows all boarded, it felt like a dark chamber lost in time. I closed my eyes.

I loved the tea cakes, Opal whispered. *They had molasses on top.*

This was the first indication that Opal had a local history, a past I could trace. She disappeared in the ether before I could ask.

I finally caught my breath enough to say, "The bad smell. What does that mean? At the service. Why did you hide the truck? Just tell me. I'm getting better. I can handle it."

Tal turned from setting a tub on the counter. "The bad essence came from Kern. I felt him watching me. I think he suspects that his brother is hiding in these woods. I'm worried he'll find an excuse to search. We can't let him discover the Knights. Most of them have open arrest warrants. Drug charges in some cases. In others, what you could call 'unfortunate meltdowns' due to PTSD."

"I can't tell if Kern wants to hurt his brother or just bring him home to Cleo, like a gift."

"I take it that Gus hasn't told you the story about him and Kern fighting, when they were kids."

My ears pricked. Invisible antenna lifted from the top of my head. "Not yet."

"Ask him some time." She paused. "Kern definitely wants to hurt Trey."

I told myself maybe she was just on edge. A lot was going on in the world and in the MacBride family. Gabs and Jay had finally reunited over the holidays, but in the process, he'd gotten shot in the chest by his own aunt. "Wakefields put the func in dysfunction. They're a wee bit malevolent," as Doug Firth put it. "It's a wonder Jay grew up without horns and a forked tail."

I began unzipping my backpack. "I know Kern and Trey had issues as kids. I can feel it every time I'm near Trey. Shame and anger. And fear."

Tal put a finger to her lips. "Night Hawk, not Trey. Let's stick with the code names. You never know who's listening."

Standing in a 1930's village that had been deserted for nearly eighty years, in the middle of a wild Appalachian forest full of steep hollows and granite ridges, I would have said she was being paranoid. Except she was a kitchen witch, and I was a yarn witch, and when she said that with all the intuition she possessed, every fiber in every woolen article of clothing on my body stood on end.

"You smell like ripe bananas," Tal said. "And raw cocoa. Stay calm."

"I feel like a yarn porcupine."

"We can handle Kern. I don't really think he'll track me here. This is private property." She put a fist of power to her sweatered chest. MacBride land."

We set up food along the counter, along with paper plates and plastic utensils. It was a cold feast of fried chicken, ham, potato salad, cole slaw, mounds of biscuits and rolls. The iconic Southern funeral repast. Tal unpacked a small army of bottled beers. She sighed. "Even if they're warm beers, they're still beers. Besides, the Knights are not picky."

I picked up one bottle and studied it. "This is fine. This kind of ale is meant to be served at room temperature. The hops really pop at room temp." I glanced up into Tal's puckish expression.

"You and my bro have had a lot of discussions about beer?"

"And needlecraft," I said primly.

Tal checked her phone. "It's time. Are you ready?"

I took a shaky breath. "I'm not a minister."

"To them, you are."

TREY MCKELLAN limped out of the forest with a haggard expression on his face. I didn't need my gift to deduce that grief and guilt tormented him. He looked much older than 28. When he pulled a heavy sock cap off his head, his roughly clipped hair showed a feather of silver among the dark strands. He nodded to us. "Thank you for doing this. It's not for me. It's for him."

"Sit," Tal ordered gently. She pointed to an old wooden stool from the bakery. He lowered his lanky body atop it awkwardly, extending the bad leg to one side. His baggy camo pants couldn't hide the clumsy prosthesis that formed his leg from the mid-thigh down. He always rejected our offers to supply him with a better model.

I felt the watchful eyes of the Knights, somewhere in the fringe of forest and evergreen rhododendron. They were experts at vanishing in plain sight. They stood guard.

I stepped into place a few feet from Trey, while pulling a soft gray scarf from beneath my shawls. I held it out. "This was one of the first things I made, after I learned to knit and crochet. Just a few months after I came to the farm to live. I gave it to your dad. He gave it back to me right after Christmas. Told me to save it for you. Put it away, and take care of it. His blood pressure was causing problems. He was worried about it. He never wanted to be disabled by a stroke. I learned that he'd made the same agreement with other people around the Cove. 'When Trey comes home, this is for him.' Photos, your old baseball mitt, things like that."

Trey's face contorted. He looked away, his throat working.

I laid the scarf on his knees then stepped back. "He understood your pain. Don't ever doubt that. I touch this scarf and I feel a father's love and understanding. He felt that he failed you."

Trey turned stark eyes back to me, shocked.

"Failed you," I repeated. "Failed to protect you from Kern. He always knew that Kern bullied you. He kept quiet because your mother doted on Kern."

The winter forest hovered over those words. Bare limbs of old trees bent closer, listening. Wild creatures woke from their sleep to taste the air of sorrow.

"He didn't realize how much he misunderstood until after you were gone. How badly Kern had treated you. How much it had hurt to be lesser in Cleo's eyes. Those are not words he said to me. These are beliefs I feel from the connection I made with him." I gestured to the scarf. "He was kind, and brave, and he loved your mother dearly. He wanted to love Kern because Kern meant so much to her. I can't explain her devotion for Kern to you; there are some things I can't see. People store their regrets in deep places. But I know he loved you, and he would be proud that you've become a leader to a group of people who've been hurt and cast off." I took a deep breath. "He wants you to forgive him."

Trey scrubbed a hand over his wet eyes. "I want to believe what you're saying."

"I do understand how you feel. My father died of a heart attack in my hospital room, after the rapes. He felt he'd failed to protect me. That his God had lied to him and . . . and had dishonored my father's service to Him. And yet . . . I watched him die, and decided it was all my fault. I will never stop feeling guilty for being a victim. For causing my father's deadly grief and his loss of faith. But you didn't kill your dad. You didn't choose the life that isolated you from your mom and drove you away. He knew that."

Trey struggled to control his tears.

Fucking crybaby.

The words sprang in my mind like paint dripping off a brush. One of the many taunts Kern had thrown at him when they were kids.

Tal made a book opening gesture at me.

The Bible. Make a detour from Trey's deeply personal pain.

I cleared my throat. "'Peace I leave with you; my peace I give you.'"

Tal twirled a finger. *Speed it up.* I stood there in bald-faced sacrilegious intent. I edited God's word for a short take. "'. . . Do not let your hearts be troubled and do not be afraid.' John 14—"

Tal made a Cut motion.

I began cherry-picking from the Bible. Dad could have preached an entire memorial service from each bit I chose. "'God will strengthen you and help you . . .'" Isaiah. Next up, the Psalms. "'Nations are in uproar, kingdoms fall; He lifts his voice, the earth melts . . . He says BE STILL, AND KNOW THAT I AM GOD . . .'"

Tal pressed down with her hands. *Don't shout like that.* Trey glanced at her, frowning, then back at me.

I was beginning to sweat despite the forty degree air. "'The peace of God, which transcends all understanding, will guard your heart and your mind . . .'" *Philippians,* I added silently. "'For I am convinced that neither death nor life, neither angels nor demons, neither the present nor the future, nor any powers . . . will separate us from the love of God.' Romans, 8: . . . shit." I halted, mortified. "I am so sorry for that language."

Trey was now rubbing his chin and hiding his mouth a little.

Guffaws came from the forest.

"Romans ate shit," someone whispered loudly.

More guffaws.

Trey bent his head into his palm, laughing.

Tal blinked for a moment, then broke out a big smile and gave me a thumbs up.

Suddenly Trey grabbed a phone from inside his jacket. His face deadly serious, he read a message then pivoted on the stool to look into the forest, giving a curt hand signal.

All laughter stopped.

He lurched to his feet and turned toward us. "Kern's here."

Tal ran to him and jammed her arm beneath his. She was as tall as him and very strong. "You'll never limp fast enough to get back in the woods in time. Come with us."

With her supporting him and me running to open the bakery door, we covered the brown winter earth quickly. Once inside Tal locked the door's iron bolt. "How did you know?" Tal asked him.

"We have cameras along the road."

Tal and I traded a startled look. The Knights seemed to be low-tech, all the way. Primitive camping, no running water, no electricity. We'd been surprised to find out they had cell phones.

And where did they go to charge those phones?

And now . . . security cameras in the woods?

Trey put a finger to his lips. He held up his phone.

We watched a live feed showing the clearing outside.

Kern drove up, a Lexus slinging cold dirt and winter grass. When he got out he slung a pistol from inside his leather jacket over a dark suit. He fired into the air until the chamber clicked empty.

"He died because of you," Kern yelled at the woods. "He looked for you for the past two years. You broke his heart, you fucking loser. You couldn't make it through Ranger training. Couldn't even earn your sergeant stripes. Ended up just a PFC mechanic patching up Humvees and going for joy rides on a colonel's motorcycle. You got your leg blown off racing a stolen Harley through a mine field. That's some retarded shit, baby brother.

"You always acted like you were the real son and I was just a stray puppy Mom took in. Everybody treated me that way. But I proved I'm the one she and Dad could count on. The one to be proud of. She knows it. I was there today, burying him. Standing beside her.

"You're too ashamed and afraid to show your face and admit you're a fuck-up. Too afraid to be compared to me. I got the scholarships. I got the officer's commission. Top of my Ranger class. Ten years and I came back here a badass hero. I take care of business, now.

"I know you're in these fucking woods somewhere. Come out of hiding. Be a man. If you don't, I'll find you. Don't make me have to come looking. I'm in charge, now."

Kern looked from the wooden stool to the bakery. We held our breath.

He grabbed the stool and slung it so hard it splintered when it hit the shop's brick wall.

He headed towards the bakery, focused on the door with laser intensity.

Trey pulled a pistol from his camo jacket.

Tal grabbed me by one arm. "Climb those stairs in the corner. Hide in the attic. It's better if I do the talking. He'll freak out if he sees you here."

"No. He'll torment you. He'll find a reason to arrest you. He's cruel."

"Not while Pike's still sheriff."

"He's working behind Pike's back. Even Delta says so. He'll hurt you. He'll find the Knights."

Trey whirled towards us. "If I don't open that door and talk to him, the Knights are going to start shooting."

I staggered back, jerking my arm from her grip, pivoting to head for the stairs.

A hand closed around me.

Invisible, ethereal, gentle.

I looked at Tal and she was transfixed, not looking at me but staring into space.

"You feel it too," I whispered.

"Yes."

Kern slammed a fist on the door. "Open up. Goddammit, Tal, if you're in there hiding him . . . "

The explosion rattled the bakery's windows behind their plywood shutters. The concussive force washed over us.

And yet it made no sound.

A sonic boom with no boom.

Silent thunder.

We heard Kern's footsteps retreating on the bakery's stone stoop. Lights danced in my vision. The encompassing hand faded away. The shawl I wore rose like wings and twirled in the glitter of the air.

"I don't know what the hell just happened," Trey said, "But the only other time I've seen him scared like this was when . . . " His voice trailed off. "Anyhow, thank God he's gone."

Tal's voice, full of wonder, was telling me how the pies and cakes smelled and looked in the handsome shelves; how the breads scented the air as the big ovens browned them. "And over there, in a tall glass case with filigreed metal racks, I see trays of taffy and butterscotch drops. Marzipan fluffs with candied dates in the middles. And . . . "

"Teacakes soaked in molasses syrup," I finished. "Opal liked them."

We stared at each other.

The Knights pounded on the door.

Tal put her finger to her lips. I nodded. She went to the door, pulled the bolt back, then opened it wide.

"Something must have spooked that fucker," one of the Knights said.

They hadn't heard or felt a thing.

The Knight we called Doc pushed forward. An older man with sad eyes and the red blotches of a heavy drinker. Doc looked at us both as if diagnosing a secret. "Whatever happened just now, it stopped one brother from killing another."

"That's what's important," Tal said.

Heads were craning. Noses sniffed.

"Let's eat," someone yelled.

"Beer!"

And they poured inside, leaving Tal and me standing in the shadows, sorting out mysteries.

Trey leaned against a wall, looking away from what his brother had said.

5

We have to talk. I don't like it when you keep secrets from me.

Kern's text message cut me in half. I spent most of a day trying to breathe.

"This goes into his file," Alberta said. She tapped a key on her laptop, sending the screen-saved image to a folder named BURKETT HARASSMENT.

Macy hugged me. "Say the word, and we'll let Pike know that Kern's stalking you, again."

"No. I'm going to handle this. I've got to get stronger."

"You're trying to impress Gus. We get that. But Gus is thousands of miles away."

"No. He's close by." I whirled a finger at the air.

They studied me the way they looked at over-heated hens wobbling around the chicken yard in August. Alberta arched a brow. "Can he use a *Star Trek* transporter? Have you let him know about Kern? Or about Monzell always looming over us?"

"No."

"I thought he could do hokey pokey psychic voodoo, like you."

"There's nothing he can do about Kern, not from the other side of the world. And why should he? We're just friends."

Macy rolled her eyes.

"I saw that," I said. "Look, I have to learn to take care of myself. That's why I came here originally. To heal. To toughen up."

Alberta sighed. She thumbed a hand toward my hidden crotch holster. "Then let's at least teach you to shoot something bigger than that tiny metal dildo."

Gus

I knew where Kern Burkett came from. At least, as much as anyone knew. He was raised hard, and abandoned at the age of ten by his mother, one month after his father, a shift foreman at one of Monzell's processing plants, died of cancer.

Kern got off the school bus at their trailer in the woods of the Big Walk community. Late November. The start of a week-long Thanksgiving holiday.

His mother had piled boxes of his favorite Captain Crunch cereal, loaves of raisin bread and jars of peanut butter on the kitchen table, stuffed about a hundred dollars into the knock-off Air Jordans his dad bought for him from a roadside flea market, and taped a note to a framed picture of his dad holding him as a baby.

Sorry. I know this is hard.

But it is harder on me.

I am not your mother. You might as well know it now and get used to the idea.

Here is a list of phone numbers. Don't be stupid. Call and somebody or other will take you.

I did right by you. I forgave your daddy for bringing you home to raise.

But raising you by myself wasn't part of the deal.

Have a good life. Happy Turkey Day!

Mom

Kern tied all the food and camping gear he could handle onto the battered four-wheeler he and his dad had used on the hunting trails. He stopped at the Big Walk Drive Up, a tiny gas-grocery store on a dirt road, and bought bullets, matches, cigarettes and batteries. None of which rang any alarm bells thirty years ago, even if the customer was a third grader wearing an imitation samurai sword his dad had bought for him at a gun show.

School had been back in session for a week before T. K. Jefferson Elementary teacher Olivia Clayton called her sister Vivian, a loan specialist at the bank in Turtleville, to ask if Marcia Burkett's phone number at the trailer was out of order. Olivia was hunting for Kern.

From that moment on, the grim news spread swiftly: Kern Burkett had last been seen driving the four-wheeler along a forestry trail on the lower ridges of the Ten Sisters before Thanksgiving.

There had been five frigid nights below twenty degrees since then, with most days not getting much above freezing. One of the coldest seasons on record.

Pike hadn't been sheriff for long. He was still recovering from a knock-down-drag-out fight with the Clayton brothers, Olivia's cousins. He'd broken up their dog-fighting ring in the county, once and for all. They were headed to prison—not for animal abuse, but for assaulting a sheriff—and Pike was propped up in a Lazy Boy recliner at the office in Turtleville, with three broken fingers, a concussion, broken ribs, a ruptured spleen and two broken toes on his left foot, where Cirius Clayton had slammed him with a sledge hammer.

The Clayton brothers were worse off than Pike, by far.

Delta dove into her cooking to help make ends meet, baking biscuits non-stop. Her grandmother's empty farmhouse, sitting no more than fifty feet from the Trace, was the perfect place to open a tiny diner in the front rooms.

Cleo McKellan, Delta's new sister-in-law, took charge of the search for Kern. Short, strong, like a vintage Kewpie Doll and fond of leg warmers that matched the scrunchies she wore in her curly black hair, she was never shy. She declared herself head of the Jefferson County Volunteer Rescue Team.

"I can out-shoot and out-track any man in these mountains," she said. "Because Jesus is my guide."

"Does she say stuff like that in bed?" the menfolk joked to her husband, Bubba. He always had an affectionate comeback about her well-armed Jesus talk.

Cleo was nursing their son, Trey. She strapped him to her chest and went to look for the missing boy. Five brave men followed her, including Bubba. The rest laughed and went in the other direction.

She found Kern on a high ridge. He'd made a camp using a rocky overhang as a windbreak. He knew better than to build a fire that would draw attention, so his only warmth had come from thawing his hands over a camp stove—until the fuel ran out. He wore heavy camo coveralls, which helped. He'd wrapped himself in blankets, stuffed leaves inside to add insulation, and survived as well as any experienced outdoorsman might.

No one could understand Cleo's uncanny sense of direction. She tracked him the way a cat tracks its kitten, the men said later. Bubba kept asking, *How do you know where you going?* But she just kept plowing forward, with Trey along for the ride as if he were still inside her, hidden under layers of sweaters and coat.

Kern was tucked in narrow gulley where the fallen shell of a massive tree formed a burrow. She crawled into that dark hiding spot to the spine-freezing sound of Kern saying, "I'll shoot everybody and myself before I'll get thrown away somewhere."

No one could hear what Cleo said to him in response, because Bubba was diving into the gulley at the time. She stuck her arm out of the burrow with a pistol cupped in the palm of her hand. Bubba took the loaded .35 caliber weapon and watched incredulously as she crawled out with the half-frozen Kern in tow.

The sweat in his black hair had almost frozen to his scalp. Patches of frostbite dappled his face. He was stiff with the cold. The skin beneath his pale blue eyes was nearly purple. The coldness in his eyes would never depart. He managed to stand up and glare at her and Bubba.

There was no childhood left in him.

"I found him," Cleo announced. She looked up at Bubba. "Jesus sent me straight to him. He's mine."

Bubba was flabbergasted at the way she said all that. But, having been raised with Delta as his sister, and accustomed to nodding rather than admitting his heart had just died, he only said, "Well. Okay."

Trey shifted on her chest and made an unhappy sound.

Some said it was fear.

Lucy

I SAT AT A cluttered desk in the darkened back room at Bah Spa, amidst the fragrances of storage shelves filled with goat milk and herb soaps, lotions and bath balms. I smiled at one of Gus's text messages on my phone.

His name's Bazir. He looks like a kid in a Disney movie. Big bright eyes, big smile, shaggy black hair. I've got him and Eve trading pictures with their pet goats. My niece and Bazir, two kids grinning at each other beside their goats. Maybe world peace starts with that.

Outside, sleet stung the rooftops of Turtleville, seat of Jefferson County, where a tall statue of a pioneer cradling a goat stood atop a fountain in the park near the courthouse. Farlo Jefferson, the legendary goat man, had founded the town back in the 1840s.

Delta, a Jefferson descendant, said there was more than a little goat in all the old families.

Bah Spa was one of my safe places away from the farm. The Crossroads Café was the other. The little shop—Delta and Cathy's idea, with proceeds going to Rainbow Goddess—sat along a narrow road beside the river, where mists feathered passing cars and enormous oaks pronged their roots from the craggy banks like the claws of large birds.

Living with the river running through town was a challenge at times, especially during heavy rains. At the Turtleville Kiwanis' Forked Tongue Spring Storytelling festival every year, there was an entire category of River Tales. Delta had won a grand masters' blue ribbon for hers.

"A jury let my mother's great aunt Molene walk free even though she shot her business partner dead in broad daylight in front of a dozen witnesses. It was 1932, hot and muggy, August, and the courthouse back then had no electricity and no way to move air except to open the big windows and fan yourself with a cardboard fan from the Jefferson Funeral Home."

Don't tarry, we bury.

Jesus is ready for you, and so are we.

"Nobody wanted to serve on the jury in August.

"Especially not when the river was up. And loud. The bugs got worse. Chiggers and mosquitoes and blue-bottle flies came in slow and buzzed loud next to your ear, *brrrr.* There was more sweating and slappin' in the courtroom than in a tent revival full of married people confessing who they'd hugged too tight at the last carnival dance.

"Town had just been hit by two weeks of frog-drowning, goose-wallowing, mud-sloshing, Baptist-baptizing rainstorms that turned it into such a monster that old Grandpa Joe Walking Cloud, the last Cherokee Indian who had escaped the Removal, then a hundred years old, Grandpa Joe called that monster river of 1932, Weehatcheedonnawallachokacola.

"'The river with a name that goes on for miles' . . . "

"Lucy?"

I clicked the phone off. "Yes?"

"Give me that phone. You can't help Gus until you get better at looking after yourself. Take it from the original 'Me' Girl."

I'd never been good at resisting authority. I turned it over. Cathy barricaded the phone behind photos of her husband Tom, their teenage girls and the twins.

Cathy Deen Mitternich, the woman who'd been the highest paid female movie star in the world, the actress named *The World's Most Beautiful Woman* by more than one major magazine not that many years ago, had survived a near-fatal car accident in California that left her with burn scars on the right side of her face and body. She'd hidden in her

Nettie grandmother's isolated home here in these mountains, just wanting to fade away and die. Thanks to Delta, she'd met Tom, a hard-drinking widower, and they'd fallen in love.

Bah Spa was only one of her enterprises. She was a major board member at the farm, and children knew her now as the beloved voice of *Dazzle the Dragon Rider* in a series of movies and videos. Bah Spa sold soaps and lotions and candles, all made locally. The Bah Spa online store was slowly building a customer base across the South. Women I'd taught to knit and crochet sold soft cotton face scrubbers there, also felted wool slippers, hand-knitted cosmetic bags, and rice-filled heating pouches. I'd written a brief note for the bi-fold card attached to every item:

The women of these mountains, both Cherokee and immigrant pioneers, were experts at making rugs, clothing, and housewares from plant and animal fibers. Near here, a large spinning and weaving mill run by the women of the MacBride families in the Little Finn Valley made the finest wool cloth in the Appalachians. The craft and business of textile work instilled progressive ideals of education, confidence and leadership in mountain women.

"Lucy?"

"Sorry. Daydreaming."

Cathy pointed to the computer screen. She tapped a key. The screen filled with digital sketches of cartoon sheep smiling in bubble baths.

"And here's my sweet girl," she said, flicking to the next sketch and pointing to a brown-and-white cow wearing a Carmen Miranda headdress of fruits and vegetables while reclining in a spa tub. The cartoon cow was inspired by Cathy's namesake cow, Cathy, who lived at Rainbow Goddess. Tom had named her after giving emergency assistance at her birth.

I focused on Cathy the cow's headdress. "I don't consider myself a real artist, but . . . "

"I don't consider myself a real actress, and if I read all the things people say online about my burn scars, I wouldn't think I deserved to live, much less show my face to a camera. Your point is?"

"I could hit you right now, and there wouldn't be any witnesses."

She laughed. "And?"

"Why does Cathy the Cow have vegetables and fruit in her hat? You're selling milk-based products."

"The ad agency says those say 'health.'"

"To me they say 'Go on a diet.'"

"That's not good."

"I love cows and sheep, but many women might see them as negative symbols. Follow like a sheep, be cowed, fat as a cow, et cetera."

Cathy sighed. "I never had to work at staying thin when I was in the spotlight. I had to lie about it all the time in interviews; say how much I starved myself, so women wouldn't hate me." She gestured toward her scarred face. "I admit I don't understand what it's like to be called fat. *But* I understand how it feels to hear some successful comedian joke about me looking like 'a grilled hamburger with tits.'"

I reached over my shoulder to touch her burn-scarred right hand. "When you moved to the Cove, did you feel hidden and safe?"

"Yes. Tom felt the same way when he came here from New York. And Doug said it when Delta lured him here. He called the Crossroads Cove 'Little Scotland.'" She donned a hooded coat and wrapped one of my scarves around her neck. "Speaking of sanctuaries, I have to get home to Wild Woman Ridge. The girls are here from school, and Tom is making a big dinner. The twins expect me to make my semi-famous sugar biscuits for dessert."

"Learning to make biscuits was a turning point for you, wasn't it?"

She nodded. "Partly because I overcame my fear of anything hot, including ovens, but also because I finally understood the magic Delta was trying to teach me. The letting go and letting God in. Or as she puts it, the 'Lard.'" Cathy smiled. "You'll find your own way to make biscuits. Just give it time. Macy will be here in a few minutes to pick you up. Okay?"

My stomach clenched, but I nodded. "I'm expanding my safe zones. Maybe next time I'll walk up the street and buy an ice cream cone."

Cathy cut her eyes at my phone. "Gus is a good influence." She winked as she left.

I wandered to the front, smoothing my damp palms on my skirt. The shop was pretty and pastel; it smelled wonderful; the shelves and displays gave it the appeal of a maze or rabbit warren.

If threatened, I could flee down the narrow aisle between the face soaps and the lip balms. Hide behind the rack of scented neck pillows.

When Kern swung a big Jefferson County Sheriff's Department SUV into a parking space outside the windows, my hands knotted in my skirt. The small pistol rested snuggly against my lower belly, the soft cloth holster rubbing me in ways that were sometimes disturbingly erotic.

Not around Kern, however.

You'll come to my wife's party at the lake.

No. I don't do parties. But thank you.

You'll come. I insist. Don't be shy. I'll protect you.

Under his shirt were the pale ghosts of tattoos covering his arms and shoulders. He'd had them lasered after Howard began grooming him for big things. Eagles and skulls and guns. A snarling bear behind a Christian cross surrounded by lightning bolts—the emblem of the Guardians of Liberty militia.

I had seen those fading tats the summer before—months before Gus and I met—when he came to the farm on one of his usual pretexts of official business. Alberta and Macy agreed he was stalking me. No, it was not a flirtation, not charming, not wanted. He was married to Amber. He had been constructing excuses to see me for a year or more, by then.

And the problem was, he played the game so well that we couldn't risk going to Pike for help. Or even to Delta. He was Cleo's adopted son. Cleo was Delta's sister-in-law and second in command at the café. What could we accuse him of?

Well, he comes by a lot and hangs around. He's charming and friendly and kind, and all the women adore him. Even though his father-in-law hates Rainbow Goddess Farms, Kern comes here to show his support. So . . . that's a problem.

It's a delicate business, humoring the people in power who can do you harm.

So he visited and lingered to hoe weeds and pinch suckers off tomato plants in the farm's five-acre vegetable garden. Or he'd fix a tractor. Repair a window. Talk straight talk to the kids who needed a male authority figure straight out of the comic books to tell them not to do drugs and to stay in school.

Amid the organic compost mounds and the rainwater cisterns, he always stripped off his deputy's shirt, while pretending not to notice my reaction. A dozen women and teenage girls were working the garden around me. They all stared at his muscles and his faded tattoos. Then they stared at me. I was their weather vane.

I failed them. I didn't say, "We don't get to strip down to our nipples, so please don't show us yours." I said nothing.

Shame.

No. Anger. Anger was weaving its way up through the Dorian Gray picture in my closet. Me, the minister's daughter and good girl victim.

No. Me. The woman endowed with second sight and a small pistol between her thighs.

He hunched his big shoulders inside a heavy tan JCSD jacket as he strode to the doors and swung one open. A tall, handsome man, with a hard jaw and deep grey eyes. But the set of his face could go from charming to ice cold in a flash. And when he spoke, his voice was clipped, pruned of southern melodies, or any song, at all.

He stopped several feet away and held up both hands, palms facing me. "Relax," he ordered. "I just want to talk to you for a minute."

"The shop closes in ten. Macy's on her way to pick me up."

"I'll make it quick. Please, just listen." He lowered his hands. "I know about your new friend. He's trouble."

"That's none of your business. This isn't appropriate. Go home to Amber."

"I wish you wouldn't keep secrets from me. I'll do whatever you ask. Just understand that I'm always here for you, and always will be. From the day we met in the field at Rainbow Goddess I knew you deserved better than that life. I've got the money. I've got the power. I'll make sure no one hurts you. Especially *him*."

"I'm not going to discuss my personal life with you."

"Let me tell you about Captain Gus MacBride. Regular army. Seventeen years in. Four combat tours. Record of being written up repeatedly for disobeying orders. Demoted three times. Wild card. Way too friendly with the natives. In Special Forces, we call his kind names I won't repeat.

"And now he's got millions of dollars waiting for him when he comes home. Wakefield money. His sisters tell you it's a debt the Wakefields owe them for stealing MacBride land and framing their grandpa to get mining rights at Free Wheeler. No. It's Jay Wakefield paying a big dowry to get into their family and *keep* those mining rights. It's greed, Lucy. It's Gus trading his sister Gabby for money."

I backed away. "That's a lie."

"Gus MacBride is a troublemaker and a traitor. You've got to cut him off. I knew him when we were kids. No one wanted the responsibility of handling him and his sisters. They were head cases. Jay Wakefield's uncle was their only hope. He tried to take care of them. He put them in a private J-Fac—facility for troubled juveniles.

"Gus was about to be sent to lock-up for almost killing a boy. He broke out and dragged his sisters with him. Delta and Pike took them in and coddled them. Family relationships. I wouldn't know . . . I never had much family willing to lie for me. They were shipped off to friends in California before anyone could find them. That's why they waited twenty years to show up here again. Gabby is marrying Jay Wakefield. Money. Money is all they came back for."

"You're wasting your breath."

"Gus is using you. He wants to get back in tight with Delta and Pike. He knows they care about you. You're special. You're a prize. And he wants that prize." Kern's lip curled. "I don't doubt he knows I want you, too, and that's all what matters to him."

I moved behind a counter, trying not to expose my fear, not to tremble. "All right, I've listened to you. Now leave."

He held out his hands. "You have such amazing powers but even you can't—or won't—see what's coming. America can't afford to be soft anymore. No more free rides for the lazy and the weak-minded. No more tolerance for complainers and troublemakers. Conformity. Obedience. Those are the new rules. But you . . . you'll always be an outsider, a threat to the dimwitted and easily fooled. You can't fit in—you're special. There will come a time when you'll suffer for it. You need me, Lucy. You need to have friends in strong positions. It isn't just about money; it's about command."

His expression became deadly. "I know how it feels to be used and abused. I will *not* let Gus MacBride hurt you. For God's sake, Lucy, has he told you he's got a woman? He's been hooking up with a British war correspondent for *years*."

"I know. It doesn't matter."

Bleak streamers of gray and rust surrounded him. I saw the red orb of his heart glowing in his chest. Waves of shock and anger rolled off his skin.

"I *will* save you," he said.

He walked out, slamming the glass door so hard the *Closed* sign fell from its suction cup hook. I sat down on a plastic crate behind the cash register.

The woman's name was Dana. Or Lana. Shanna. Vanna. Anna. I couldn't quite focus on her; her presence in his universe jarred my control. *Do not invade his privacy. You promised. He doesn't invade yours at that level. If he did, he'd deduce what happened to you.*

What Gus and I shared was a friendship beyond description. Yes, it brimmed with affection and desire, but there were no vows. If he did come home on leave in a couple of months, the reality of my condition would cool us down.

I couldn't begrudge him a girlfriend. A lover. I wouldn't demand that he tell me about her. Oh, sure, I'd just casually pop her into one of our many long conversations. Maybe when he called at odd hours, and I snuggled on my cot describing the taste of my hot mint tea as the sky lightened in the small window above me.

So, tell me about this woman you sleep with. Vanna, Shanna, Lana.

No.

We all view the world through tunnels we trust.

Kern's was no wider than the bore of a gun.

Mine was as narrow as a strand of yarn.

I HATED THE nightmares. In my experience, they always held a clue to the future.

Luce was here. I heard her voice, felt the aura of her reaching toward me. We wanted each other without touching, without taking it into the obvious sex talk, without any need for explaining. I wanted to fuck her into heaven. And she wanted to fuck me the same way. A Given. But all those scary parts were hidden in the space between a knit and a purl.

All I had to do was get to her before the psychic warden noticed I'd escaped. Before the hellhound tracked me down with its blood and its voice that mimicked her, screaming.

Get up, soldier. Move your ass.

I'm up. I'm walking. No cast on the left leg. Interesting. It was mechanical from the knee down, but nothing fancy; made of simple steel shafts, nuts and bolts, a few big rivets, and wires that connected the joints. Parts began falling off—one at a time, while I walked as fast I could toward Luce. I couldn't see her, but I knew she was my destination.

My toes went first; bolts popping like metal champagne corks. *No problem. I don't need toes.* Then the foot rattled, the screws loosening, washers jiggling, making a loud coins-in-a-glass-jar noise. The components made cartoon *pings* and *plunks* as they fell out.

My balance was failing. *Just walk faster.* I stumbled.

A wire snapped. Then a second one. I nearly fell down. The foot was useless, now. I stopped and shook it. What was left finally popped off the rotating metal collar of a shiny ball bearing.

My ankle.

I set that stump down carefully. *I can walk on this. Get going.*

The ground, or grass, or whatever I'd been walking on before, suddenly turned steel-gray and as smooth as still water. The steel ball shot forward with a high-pitched whine. Skating on concrete.

I went down hard on my back. My leg hit the pavement and shattered into metallic confetti, twinkling above me in absolute darkness. I didn't have to look to know that all I had left was a human leg that ended in a gory steel nub at the knee.

Blood. The smell and taste washed over me. The screaming began.

You hurt women. You're being punished. She'll be punished, too.

KERN STALKED ME through some kind of cave or tunnel. I woke up, clammy and gasping. I always slept with my desk light turned on. I blinked painfully in the glow. A pinging sound jumped through my senses.

Gus calling.

I scrambled to my laptop, hugging a blanket around me.

His handsome face filled the screen. Not the best streaming video quality, but there he was.

He had deep shadows under his eyes.

"Bad dreams," Gus said, looking directly at me from my laptop screen. "You, too?"

"Yes."

"Want to talk about it?"

I shook my head. "Do you? About yours?"

"No." He leaned in, searching my brow. "Is that a turban or a 'do rag?"

"It's a crocheted headband. It's cold in here. My little electric heater doesn't help much in the winter. My ears are chilly."

"Show me an ear. I need to check for frostbite." The slight crook in his lips dared me to demure. I lifted a gloved hand, pulled a scarf down my neck just a little, and nudged the head band up.

He squinted. "Would you push your hair back? I think I see some frost. Need a better look."

I curled the pale blond shank behind my ear.

"Hmmm. Can't tell for sure. I need to compare it to the other ear."

I pulled my headband back into place. Discomfort slithered around me.

He quickly sat back. "Tell me about that desk. I'm getting 'Dirty Pony.' It's a seven ounce short beer, hoppy, forty percent alcohol per volume. Like a shot of whisky. Small but heady."

I smothered a smile behind one hand.

"I see that," he teased, his voice graveled with gentleness but also fatigue.

Still smiling, I lowered my fingers to my phone, bent sideways, and snapped a photo of the desk's stubby legs. I held up the phone so Gus could see. "It's an antique buffet table. Delta gave it to me. She said, 'Cousin Elam Partaine from Nashville cut the legs down to suit her no-good four-foot-tall boyfriend. My mama said our family forgave Mr. Sexy Little for seducing Elam, but not for ruining the buffet table.'"

He laughed. "Show me more."

I bent to the other side, aiming the camera at the desk again.

He laughed harder. "Not the desk. Other pictures on your phone."

Pictures of me. My chest tightened. *Breathe in slowly. Breath out slowly. Relax your diaphragm.* I fumbled with the phone. "Here's . . . this is Shirley. Your scarf's wool donor. And this is the interior of the barn. There's Brim lurking in one corner, trying to bite the king of the llamas. And here's King Llama trying to bite her back. And here's the newest resident in the barn loft. She's a refugee in my No Fry Zone. I call her Fran. She escaped from a poultry truck headed for the processing plant at Monzell . . . "

"Stop," he said gently. "I'm not trying to upset you."

I laid the phone down and took a moment to inhale and exhale several times. Other women sent their soldiers triple-X selfies. I'd progressed to showing Gus that I sometimes wore only a sweater and long skirt. Very sexy—no shawls. "I'm not comfortable with photos of myself. It's one of my quirks. I'm so sorry. I hate being this way."

"Hold up. I wasn't asking for pictures of *you.* I want more sheep photos. I *like* to look at sheep. Nothing creepy. Just as friends."

I tried to laugh but it came out with an unhappy sound gurgle. *I bet Vanna, Shanna, Dana sends him pictures of herself. Naked.*

I fumbled with my neatly organized desk files, knocking over notes and invoices related to the woolies and their management, also notes for the Knights and their work on Free Wheeler's old bike paths. I slumped in the office chair and gazed at an electronic photo frame beside my computer.

I pictured him lying on his narrow bed. He'd sent so many photos that I had put together a panoramic view for my laptop's screensaver. A desk and computer, photos of his sisters and their parents, rest in peace, pictures of Gabby with Jay, and Tal with Doug, and with Eve, and photos of the Asheville police officers who had served with his dad, now balding men with paunches.

And photos of me, shawled and long-skirted, peeking from beside Brim, from among sheep and llamas and alpacas with wintry mountain skies behind me. Oh, and the one very intimate selfie of my feet in the gorgeous socks he'd knitted for me. He'd put that photo in a frame on the file cabinet that served as his nightstand.

Think that thought. Look at that picture of the photo on the nightstand. Feel the slow pull of deep muscles and the thick tingle around them. Shift your legs. Head back. Eyes half shut. Gus inside you. Safe sex.

He was so handsome; the big, broad-shouldered man in desert camo with reddish hair bleached almost as pale as mine. I loved his smile and the lines creasing the corners of his eyes; I loved the enameled-green gaze that looked straight out at me and sizzled farther down inside me than I could ever let any physical touch travel.

"Luce. Look at me. Please."

I forced my eyes back to the laptop's screen. He was writing something on an unseen notepad. Slowly he tore the page out. Then he held it up for me to read.

HANA

I sagged. "That's the only name I *didn't* rhyme with Anna, Lana, Shanna, et cetera. Look, I wasn't prying. I respect your privacy, and you don't need to explain . . . "

"There's not much to explain. I've seen her off and on for years. The last time was six months ago in London, when I had a week of R and R. It's never been exclusive, on her part or mine."

The sex is really good, even great. She's wild and fun and dangerous. She's a broken bird, like me. Her dark side has a hold on him. I have a dark side, too, but it's not fun.

"Speaking of dark sides," he said with an arched brow, a half-smile and serious eyes, "Who's Vern?"

I propped my chin on one hand. *I see you, and you see me. And it's okay.* "Kern," I corrected.

His eyes went black.

DADDY AND MAMA were dead. I was thirteen years old. Gabs and Tal and I were in hiding from Jay's uncle, who wanted everything that lay beneath the surface of Free Wheeler, everything his father and grandfather had tried to rip from the MacBrides for generations. Jay was his nephew—but not much better than a hostage.

Warm spring day. Blue wisteria blooming up in a poplar tree. The aroma of chicken frying beyond the big screen doors at the back of the café. Wood smoke curling from a barbecue smoker in the yard. The Ten Sisters rising over the wide valleys of the Cove. And me, out back between the barns, throwing rocks at a barn wall as hard as I could.

Santa Joe, Pike's hippie brother, red-eyed, pot-scented, and armed with three handguns on his belt, pressed a thick wad of cash into my hand. "Hide it, keep it, use it for you and your sisters in an emergency," he said. "And don't ever forget we're your family." I took the folded bills, unfolded them, and stuck the flat parcel inside the front of my jeans. Pulled my t-shirt over them.

What happened next? Think. Remember. Throwing more rocks. Feeling the muscles in your right shoulder catch on fire. Shaking it out, walking. Getting the vibes. The fear and pain.

I charged around the barn's corner. Kern was older, bigger, crazier. He held his younger brother off the ground, shaking him by the throat.

I'd seen Dad's broken body in the morgue, watched Mother collapse on the floor of our little house in west Asheville, been shoved into a foster care group home where the older, bigger boys threatened my sisters and beat the shit out of me, and onward and upward or what the fuck ever. And now this.

I charged him. Hit him low and hard. Slung a fist into his kidneys. Grabbed Trey and tossed him aside. Trey scrambled up, coughing and vomiting.

Kern hammered my head with his elbow. He pinned me on my back, grabbed a rock, and knuckled it. I watched in slow motion as that rock and hand came toward my face.

His body levitated. An invisible palm pushed him aside. Flattened him on the ground.

Not hallucinating. Trey saw it, too.

I got to my feet. I gaped at him, scared and filled with a kind of horrified wonder. Kern lay there, gasping. Terror pulled the whites of his eyes. "Trick," he yelled. But the fear boiled out of him.

Roasting grains filled my mind. Oats and rice and more. Fermenting in stone crocks, cooking up their magic. Transforming.

"If you ever hurt your brother again," I told him, "That *thing* will come out of the ground again, and it'll throw you so far, you'll hit a mountaintop."

I was just making stuff up. Not my gift. I hadn't called on the *thing*.

Something much bigger was at work.

"THERE ARE GIANTS here," I told Gus. "And they protected you from Kern."

Not the kind of admission I'd make to anyone else.

He finished his story with a long pull on a beer. When I said that, he stopped in mid-swallow. "They talk to you?" he asked.

"I hear whispers. I think they're trying to tell me something, but I don't know what, yet. I'm not saying they're flesh and blood; I'm saying there's an . . . energy. Spirits. Forgotten souls."

"Almost every Native American tribe has legends about giants who were here first."

"The Old Testament is very specific about giants existing. Deuteronomy. 'Only Og, the king of Bashan, was left of the remnant of the Rephaim—the tribes of the giants. His bed was nine cubits in length.' A cubit was roughly a foot-and-a-half. And Goliath was a giant, of course. He was said to over nine feet tall. When you were a boy, did you ever visit the boulder with the big handprints carved all over it?"

He nodded, frowning. "I remember stories Sam, my grandfather, told. He was a broken soul by the time my sisters and I came along. He talked in riddles. He'd mumble about caves and tunnels under Free Wheeler. Underground rivers and hidden palaces."

"I've heard Delta say that during Prohibition your family made moonshine inside the old mines there. She said the smoke from the stills went up through natural cracks in the rock ceilings. The rock filtered it. Hid it."

"Yeah. Not much of the family survived to pass down the details." His voice had an edge to it. "The feds and the money-men made sure of that."

Wakefields. Jay Wakefield's ancestors had destroyed the MacBrides under the guise of helping the government battle the evils of liquor, when what they wanted was control of mines that produced mica, feldspar, gold, granite, and gemstones. Mica alone, that glittery, paper-thin shale children picked up to admire, had industrial uses by the late 1800s.

Jay's uncle had nearly destroyed the new generation of MacBrides because *he* wanted the purest quartz in the world. It streaked the ancient bedrock in a narrow channel tucked in this one small part of North Carolina. To the east, the mines at Spruce Pine produced ninety percent of the planet's electronics-grade quartz. A billion dollar industry.

His uncle was convinced that the quartz beneath Free Wheeler could be worth even more.

I shuffled my hands, warming fingers going cold from nerves and the winter cold. "Whether there are tunnels and kingdoms under Free Wheeler or not, the word I'm sensing is 'sacred.' Protecting the sacred. Did you ever get vibes about them—the giants?"

"Nothing. That day . . . that weird thing that happened to Kern . . . was a shock."

"Tal and Gabby don't get the vibes, either. So maybe I'm imagining them."

"No. There's got to be a reason why you've tapped into that current. Or it's tapped into you."

Goosebumps went up my spine. "I don't feel threatened by them. The energy seems . . . " I searched for words. "Lonely."

Gus rubbed a big-knuckled hand across the pale beard stubble beginning to show on his jaw. "Howard Monzell thinks there's a fortune under Free Wheeler. Kern does, too." He tapped the empty beer bottle on his makeshift desk, hard enough to ping the metal. Everything about his living space was gray and dingy and made of metal. Shadows surrounded him. I smelled the cold stink of armor and weapons and big, empty reaches of land filled with sorrow and danger. His eyes shifted to mine. Hard. "And he wants you."

"It's not mutual."

"I don't doubt."

"He's married. He's got Monzell's money and backing. He's running against Pike in the next election. His own uncle. He's using the sheriff's office as a wormhole to gain control that goes far beyond being an ordinary county officer. He tells people that sheriffs are the highest law enforcement authorities in the country, because they're the only ones who are elected, not hired or appointed."

"That kind of talk comes straight from the militias. They've got a foothold in the government now. It'll only get worse."

"Pike keeps him close, and keeps him under control. For now."

Gus leaned in, his jaw flexing. "You know my family has money. Let us move you where he can't find you. Wherever you want to go."

"I won't run. I can't leave this fight. We have too many desperate people who need all the help they can get. This . . . the Cove, the farm . . . this is my *home*. And . . . I know you can sense this . . . " I stared at the clutter of my small life atop Elam's desk. Frustration tightened a net around every muscle. "I have a problem with unfamiliar places."

"I know you're afraid."

"Panic attacks. Crippling anxiety. The medical term is agoraphobia.

But I'm not a coward."

"I'm scared all the time, Luce. Not about being killed here. About getting other people killed. Innocent people. Civilians. And the soldiers I'm responsible for. And the state of the world. And what's going to happen to my family. The feeling that everything's out of control at home. Things are not right. I couldn't do much to protect my family when I was a kid, and I sure as hell can't seem to do much, now. Until you came along, I didn't know how much longer I could stand the goddamn despair. And now I'm scared I can't protect you."

I reached out a hand and touched the laptop's screen with my fingertips. "You already have."

He touched his fingertips to mine. The thin veil between us meant nothing.

FROM THEN ON, we were a couple. At times, we went quiet and let the psychic connection build sensations between us—aromas and colors, textures. And desire. Unspoken, shimmering and hot, a steaming bath of full-body reactions.

All so safe. And for me, so depressing.

Ms. Parmenter, isn't it true you sent my clients photos of yourself?

I gave them a church newsletter that included some pictures from a social event.

Pictures that included yourself in a very revealing swimsuit.

I was in the background of a large group of people.

Wearing a bikini.

That looked like it came from a 1950s beach movie.

A bikini, Ms. Parmenter.

Opal finally got disgusted with me. *Get yourself up and get going, Miss Lucy, and take even just one little bitty chance at a time.*

WE MET LIKE spies in a film noir. Fog swirled through the dawn fields.

The low beams of a sleek car pierced its silver cloak; the faintest white caps showed on the snowy tops of the Ten Sisters. I snuck glances at the distant darkness of the barns and communal living spaces of the farm, watching for the lights of early risers, Macy and Alberta responding to a barking dog, or a resident alerting them that there might be man-trouble at the edge of the fields, maybe a boyfriend or ex-husband creeping up, or an errant resident creeping out.

My contact walked toward me—a woman in a low-slung fedora, a long coat, and high boots, silhouetted in the car's lights; Ingrid Bergman in Casablanca, impossibly chic and beautiful. After all, not that many years ago she'd been called the most beautiful woman in Hollywood—and one of the highest paid actresses in the world.

I stood there, hypnotized on the other side of a hog-wire fence, a peasant draped in wool shawls and backed by a posse of sheep plus Brim. That's where the glamorous film analogy ended.

As Cathy reached me, she said, "Don't inhale. One of the twins threw up on my coat."

I opened a gate and she walked through. As we made our way to my home in the barn, Cathy clasped my cold, bare hand in her warm one. In the deep dawn shadows the scarred side of her face was almost hidden. She was stunning. More than that, she was my trusted friend. "I understand your caution," she said. "After the accident, I wouldn't even take a selfie anymore. My phone was hacked three times, all by internet thieves looking for pictures of my scars. Did I ever tell you that someone stole the Trans Am's charred steering wheel and sold it? Last year it showed up on one of those pawn shop reality shows."

I squeezed her scarred hand gently. "I'm so sorry. I'm glad I'm not a celebrity."

"You are. You're the gorgeous white-blonde witch of the Appalachians. The mysterious recluse at the notorious farm where covens of man-hating women dance naked around bonfires and draw symbolic vaginas on their boobs."

"How'd I miss out on all the naked dancing and body painting?"

Cathy wrapped an arm around me. We marched along, her long stride to my two-steps. "I told you once that I couldn't believe Tom really liked my face. We'd go to bed, and I'd turn the bad side away from him when he touched me. It wasn't until that day—the day he risked his life to pull me out of the café after the tornado hit. The way he looked at me as he was lifting me out of the building—the love in his eyes—convinced me. You understand what I'm saying?"

I nodded. "The only uncovered thing Gus has seen of me is my face and my feet. And that was so I could show off the socks he made for me. If the rest of me doesn't interest him, then let's get it over with."

"Oh, girl." She shook me lightly.

"Could we change the subject? I'm really nervous about what we're going to do."

"I heard you asked Alberta to teach you more about guns. That you've been target practicing with an assault rifle."

"Yes, and everyone's appalled. They're more worried about me being armed than about me being helpless. Why does society sanctify women as victims but disapprove of them as warriors?"

"That's a great point." We entered the sheep barn and headed toward my little room under the hay loft. Cathy hitched her camera bag higher on one shoulder. "Arm yourself for a different kind of shooting."

She smelled like perfume and peanut butter.

Gus
Midnight, Afghanistan

The snipers sent by Sarbanri had us pinned down in the bombed-out ruins of an old factory. One of my men screamed as the medic worked on him. Another lay silent and still, blood pooling under his head. Everything was pitch black except for the bursts of gunfire. Bullets ricocheted around us. Chips of old masonry hit my cheekbone. The slickness of blood greased the strap on my helmet.

Clear your mind. Listen. Smell. Feel. Taste.

There are three of them. They're behind the walls at home, they're in the rafters, they're running the government, they're putting people in jails and camps. They want power and money. They'll shit on the laws and destroy democracy. Home will turn into this. This fucking no-man's land of fear and death.

"I can't see a goddamn thing through these goggles, Captain."

Bullets shattered the mortar from a new direction.

"We're taking fire from behind, Captain! We're surrounded."

"Stay down," I yelled.

I crouched and made my way through a maze of rubble.

I see you, MacBride. Bleeding and crawling in the dirt and the dark. You're just another Nothing and Nobody. I've got the balls to take what I want. You don't. I'll take your home. I'll take down your family. And I'll take Lucy.

My head filled with the piercing heat of ghost peppers. Burn a hole through your throat. Cry until your eyes fry and shrivel.

Use the pain to light this fire. Light this fucker up.

I stood. I stepped out into the open. I dragged my night vision goggles off and dropped them.

Raised my rifle and fired into the jagged hole that had been a third-story window.

I pivoted and walked through a shower of bullets toward another gaping hole in the old factory.Ready, aim, fire.

I turned toward the bullets coming from my right. Pinpoints of acid ate holes in my skin. Capsaicin melted my brain.

Follow the pain. Smell the heat.

I took a long swallow on a cold beer, ripe with berries and flowers. Sweet beer. Sissy beer. But then came the meaning. Balm of Gilead. Killing the enemy is righteous. Death tastes good. Healing can begin once the dead get what's coming to them.

Kern Burkett stood on the jagged rim of a rooftop.

I shot the bastard until a body tumbled to the ground.

Stay away from her. This is war.

6

I HADN'T YET SENT the photographs to Gus. Couldn't work up the courage.

Get out in the world and get your mind off this thing, Miss Lucy. A watched chicken never lays.

The Crossroads Café had a back dining room where I taught knitting lessons on Monday afternoon. Free, open to all. I practiced being a teacher again. People who didn't know better assumed the café was just another place to enjoy a meat and three. When, really, it was a mother-hug on the lap of the mountains. Dad said such places were endowed with the Holy Spirit. Delta called it Biscuit Love.

At first the women—most of them no older than me—barely talked, just asked questions and took notes and didn't socialize with me. They had come to get a look at the notorious soothsayer who'd lured Howard Monzell's wife away and might be tempting Deputy Burkett to leave Howard's daughter.

Their group vibe came to my mind in one phrase: Rump In. The alpha ewes form a defensive cluster like that when they feel threatened but can't flee. Rumps to the center, faces turned out, eyes watching for trouble in every direction. They didn't accept Delta's free cookies; they even turned down sugared biscuits with whipped cream.

They looked at a stack of brochures about the women's shelter with stern disapproval, and a few made comments.

You should never encourage families to break up. The world isn't safe anymore.

Imagine how much more good you'd do if you brought families together there to learn how men treat women and how women should respond.

I'm sure you think you're helping women, but these kinds of places just make them depend on the government instead of their husbands. That's what America's all about now. Learning to take care of our own families, without government help.

One day, Delta tapped me on the forehead with a plastic light saber her grandson had left in the kitchen. "Use the force, Lucy, use the force," she drawled.

Within a few weeks, they were lining up to hug me as they arrived and left. I told them about the sacredness of wool.

Did you know the good Lord gave us woolen animals from the earliest times for milk and meat and clothing and shelter? Do you know that wool is hypoallergenic, fire resistant, and repels water? Do you know that when added to bullet-proof vests it will stop a bullet even better? That it can be felted as hats, and shoes, and shelters and blankets? And that the most perfect grace of this gift is that it asks for no magic tools—just what God put on the ground in front of us. A rock tied to a stick will serve as a spindle to whirl raw wool into yarn. Two smooth sticks will knit that yarn into a shawl or blanket or cap or mittens.

Once I had them enthralled, they began to ask about the farm. I told them plainly that it was an honest, simple refuge for abused women and children; that some stayed there a long time; that those who wanted to work there in the cheese and dairy or the berry farming business, or helping with the sheep, could do so and earn good wages. That it was self-supporting and had a small budget, but that in recent years the board had added Cathy Deen Mitternich, which gave it a huge boost.

She brought money and her celebrity status, and a big commitment to giving something back to the community she credited with saving her life and giving her the love of her life, Tom Mitternich. So, plans were in the works to add more services, such as dental and medical help, and housing referrals, legal aid and education.

They warmed to the idea that their world view could accept Rainbow Goddess Farm. They began to gobble the cookies and biscuits, to talk to me about their lives, and to hint that they longed for the good old days of only a few years earlier.

Now that Tal was partnering with Delta to expand the café's menu, a signboard on the veranda carried daily specials unlike anyone in the Cove had seen before. The poetry of Tal's promotional lingo knew no bounds.

This week: The BaconZilla
"So big it might attack Tokyo"
Handcut wild-hog Coca-Cola marinated bacon
Your Pick: Butt Farms Mellow Goat or MoozaFella Cheese
Two Fresh-Laid Miz Ted's Laidback Fat Red Hen Eggs
Topped with your choice of Delta's winners!
(as seen on the "Kitchen Star's Showdown" finals)
Kiss My Mama Cream Gravy
Kiss My Foot Red-Eye Gravy

The Crossroads Café. Where the Lard Cooks in Mysterious Ways.

I followed Delta from her truck parked in the side yard, where it joined a half-dozen other trucks and cars belonging to staff. The front lot was full, plus just past the turn-out, vehicles were pulling off at The PickUp Truck—Tal's idea—a big food van that handled takeout orders.

"What are your Knights up to?" Delta side-mouthed as we went in the Café's delivery entrance.

"They're fascinated with Larry's scientific determination to find rockycockers. They've been planting evidence. Tal bought them a pair of dinosaur feet from a Halloween costume supplier, and they glued extra rubber toes on it."

"What'd they use for the toes?"

"Some items that were in Mrs. Z's delivery of intimate 'personal relaxation' aids. The one Patton stole."

Delta began to laugh. The grief under her eyes disappeared. She and Bubba had been close. I had no laughter in me, but I was glad she did. She even tolerated the fact that Cleo supported Kern in his campaign for sheriff. *Against Pike.*

Everyone knew Monzell was funding Kern's bid to uproot Pike, the most respected sheriff in western North Carolina. Monzell had waited more than thirty years for revenge on Pike, who'd been a tall nobody back in the 1970s when he joined the Jefferson County Sheriff's Department. Just a raw-boned rookie deputy who'd served in Vietnam then come home to marry his sweetheart, Delta McKellan, one of the Nettie kitchen witches.

They said she put fierce angels on his shoulder. He seemed fearless because of her. She whispered secrets and advice in his ears. He became a man who stood up for fairness, honesty, and the rule of law. He won the respect of the voters and unseated Monzell's grandfather, infamous Jefferson County Sheriff Denzer Jacobs Monzell.

The Old Nooser, people had called Denzer. During his twenty year reign of unsupervised judgment, more than two dozen men—and three women—had mysteriously found ways to hang themselves in the cells of the tiny Jefferson County Jail.

Three Whittlespoons, five Netties, and six MacBrides.

Not many months after Denzer lost the election—and not long after he gave a speech at the Turtleville Chamber of Commerce's annual Biscuits and Politics Breakfast at the newly opened Crossroads Café, where Denzer shocked the 1970s business community by offering five thousand dollars for proof that Pike had used his wife's witchcraft to seduce voters . . . Denzer was found dead atop the oldest formation of rocks in the forest at Free Wheeler.

Lying there, glassy eyed, bloated and choked, polyester suit stained with spit and vomit, tie torn open. His short gray hair littered with tiny leaves off a nearby huckleberry, fried to an autumn brown in the middle of July. His polished shoes had no walking dirt on them.

It was as if he'd been transported there, into the realms of the Nettie power.

Under his fetid corpse were ancient carvings of giant hands that archaeologists insisted were symbolic, not drawn to size.

Heart attack, was the official report.

The kitchen witches and their giants brought him to justice, the old people said.

Pike's bitch of a wife murdered him, the Monzells said.

I touched Delta's denimed arm. "Kern is part of your family, I understand. But that's not the only reason you don't confront Cleo for supporting him against Pike." I searched for insights. *Open the door, Opal. This situation is darkening into disaster. Unraveling. Please . . .*

The truth about Kern could unravel everything. He's the eye of a storm that started generations ago.

I blinked and came back. Delta held me by one hand. She was at ease with what she called the Cronehood of Cooking; her graying brunette hair shoved up in a messy bun; five small diamonds glittering from recent piercings in each ear. Her eyes would always be Young Elizabeth Taylor, and she would always brag that Cathy Deen Mitternich's famous eyes came from the same hypnotic Nettie source.

"The past is what I can show you," she said. "The future is a recipe it hasn't tested yet."

We passed a chalkboard listing work schedules. My eyes landed on this handwritten note in neon at the bottom—TREY MCKELLAN: DAYS MISSING SINCE RETURNED HOME FROM IRAQ: 672.

I see Kern behind you. All the time. Kern's shadow. But never Trey's. Why one son and not the other?

I know where he is. He's in the woods with the rest of the Knights.

Cleo rounded a corner, sweaty from the kitchen, carrying a clipboard and a phone, her apron pockets stuffed with invoices and pens. "Stop staring at me," she ordered.

I wrapped my shawls tighter around me. *Be kind. She's in mourning.*

"'A false witness will not go unpunished.' Proverbs 19:5."

"Don't you try to out-Bible *me*. 'Do not turn to mediums or necromancers; do not seek them out, and so make yourselves unclean by them.' Leviticus 19:31."

I raised my chin. "'Judge not, that you be not judged.' Matthew 7:1-5."

Delta stepped between us. "Hush, both of you. Get on home for the afternoon, Cleo. Lucy, come with me. Let's set on the porch. I wanna tell you about how Gus's grandma and grandpa met. Right here in this house."

Cleo glared at me as she pivoted to leave. "'If anyone thinks he is something, when he is nothing, he deceives himself.' Galatians 6:3."

"'Do nothing from rivalry or conceit, but in humility count others more significant than yourselves.'"

"Phillippians 22:1," Cleo supplied smugly.

"22:3," I corrected.

She stomped back to the kitchen.

Delta smiled sadly as she zipped up the quilted jacket that dangled over her apron and overalls. "Gus is having a good influence on you."

"ROSE NETTIE WAS born one of triplets—" Delta began, her socked feet propped on a small electric heater on the front veranda. Her rocking chair creaked and moved. Mine was rooted to the wooden floor. I leaned forward, all ears.

"—twin boys, and her separate, but all from the same pregnancy. It was said that when they were kids, the three of them together could call out recipes from the dead. By which I mean, any spirits who wanted to reach loved ones through the memory of food, which is one of the most powerful memories there is.

"So Rose and her brothers would be at a church picnic, or a family reunion, or a funeral—it happened a lot at funerals—and they'd get this look about them, like they were listening to someone only they could see. And they'd hunt out a person in the crowd and announce whatever it was the spirit told them to say—'Cousin Maisie's Pineapple Nut Bread' and they'd chant out the ingredients and the baking time.

"Of course, that upset a good number of people. Scared 'em half to death. But others were brought to tears of joy. Turned out in most cases the recipes had special sentiments or had been lost and mourned. The spirits just wanted to get them back in the family.

"But the other thing the three could do as they got into their teens, was cook together. As if they were one person, a perfect team. Without talking out loud about what they were going to make or how to make it. Not using any recipes, and even coming up with dishes nobody around here had ever made before, or even knew what to call back in those years—this was the 1920s.

"That was when Rose met Sam. He was older, a lot older. This crazy, handsome rich man from the city, building this magic village on a huge piece of land he'd bought in the wild woods. My grandmother invited him to supper in this very house, back when it was her home and the center of her farm. He was her next-door neighbor, so it was only polite to ask him over."

Delta raised a brow. "Especially since it would cause a lot of gossip, which Grandma loved to stir up. She liked nothing better than to shock people with her progressive ways. Sam was Jewish. There were plenty of people in this county who thought he might be hiding horns and a forked tail. And rumor had it that he'd left a wife from a wealthy family on the coast; that she lived with another man there. Whew. That was some strong pepper sauce for folks around here. You'd have thought we didn't have far more lurid scandals going on, with roadhouses and whorehouses and sister-wives and husband-swapping and moonshiners and a whole lot else, but still . . .

"Anyhow, she asked Rose and the boys to make one of their odd dishes, something Rose had named 'Muscadine beef and flatbed potatoes.' It was a hard one, and could only be made when the season was right. They had to have spring onions and wild mushrooms, a bottle of muscadine wine, fresh tomatoes, and wild herbs from the woods. The rest was easier—some good stew beef, chunk bacon, a fat roasting onion or two, potatoes.

"So Rose and the boys got it all together and put on a show. There was lots more to the supper than just that—it was a feast. Grandma got carried away and invited some friends, then got out all her silver and china, and polished all the lamps and brought out the MacBride whiskey. Premium hooch. This was a good five years before the MacBrides would be murdered by the revenuers and the Wakefields, up in the Little Fin Valley.

"Anyhow . . . so up rides Sam Osserman, on a bicycle. The Trace was a dirt road then. There are mule-drawn wagons and Model-T's outside, and he parks his bicycle right amongst them, pretty as you please. He's all dusty but he still looks like the most elegant man in the Sears catalog. Everybody in the house was peeking at him from behind the curtains, including Rose.

"He's got a big wicker basket on the front of the bike, with a lid on it, and he pulls out a big ol' bouquet of red roses. Like a magician. Now they weren't florist roses like we think of today; they were old-fashioned garden roses, but still, it was early for roses, so where did he get 'em? Afterwards, Grandma spent *weeks* investigating those roses. She wrote letters and even paid to put pictures of the flowers in the papers. But she never found a florist or a garden shop that had roses like that in bloom, that early.

"Anyhow, so Sam walks in, gets welcomed and dusted—his hat was hung on the butler you see in the back dining room today—and he presented the roses to Grandma, who called for Rose, then only sixteen, to bring a crystal vase and hurry.

"So Rose steps out of the back, with a long apron still draped over one arm and a beautiful vase gleaming in her hands, and she's red-haired and tall and pink from the heat of the kitchen, wearing one of those slim dresses with the fine little flower prints on it, all sweaty and clinging. The story goes that she had old floppy boot-shoes on her feet, but I'm sure the effect was charming, because every picture of her was a picture of carefree life itself.

"'This is our cook, and she's a witch, a kitchen witch, as are all the Netties,' Grandma said, much to the embarrassment of other family members, as usual. 'Her brothers are witches, as well. They're out back, making certain that the libations used in the main dish are up to par.'

"Sam looked at Rose as if the only magic he saw was in her eyes. The feeling must have been mutual, since she dropped the vase and cracked it." Delta gestured over one shoulder. "It's the one in the big cabinet by the main fireplace. I fill it up about halfway and put roses in it on her birthday, every year.

"So everybody sat down to this amazing dinner in this big ol' farmhouse, with owls hooting outside and deer wandering by in herds among the milk cows, bears not far away, and even wildcats screaming in the woods back then. They ate by the light of big oil lamps. There were biscuits and rolls, and a broth soup, and then, the muscadine beef and flatbed potatoes came out. Rose and one of the brothers set a platter at each end of the table. It must have been a glorious sight and an even better scent.

"I'm sure Sam had trouble taking his eyes off Rose to look at the food, but finally he did. Now, everything I've told you up to this point, Lucy, is seasoned by people's memories and tellings and re-tellings and romantic ideas. I can't be sure it's all true. But this I know for sure, because every version of this story comes down to this moment. Sam Osserman had traveled the world. He knew food, and wine, and women, and bicycles, and money, and who knows what else. He took a bite of the muscadine beef and flatbed potatoes, which Rose and her brothers had been given from the spirit world, and he looked over at Rose with wonder in his eyes. 'I have found you,' he said. 'I have looked for you through so many lifetimes. And here you are, again.'

"She ran off to meet him in his wild woods that night. All he owned—beside a bank account full of considerable money—was a tent and a bicycle and some drawings for the bicycle town he called Free Wheeler. She was the spark that set it all in motion."

Delta blew out a long breath and sat for a moment, looking out on the graveled parking lot and the paved two lane of the modern Trace. I did too, imagining Sam and Rose riding bicycles on the old dirt path. I wanted to stand up and turn around and walk back through time, inside the café when it had been Grandmother Nettie's home. Seeing it that night, watching Sam and Rose meet.

"I know nothing ended well for them," I said. "Tal's told me about Jay's grandfather trying to get the land at Free Wheeler for the mining rights. Framing Sam. Ruining him. How Sam ended up in prison. And Rose . . . when Sam went to prison, it destroyed her. You knew her, when you were a little girl, didn't you?"

Delta nodded sadly. "Her brothers died in World War II. She never cooked again after that. Never called out a recipe from the spirits, never had the magic again. She gave birth to her and Sam's baby girl. My mother took the baby to raise. Rose just wandered the empty buildings and lanes at Free Wheeler. When I was no more than five, Mama sent me to follow her around. Told me to run for help if Rose got hurt or lost."

Delta cleared her throat. "Rose was already hurt, and already lost." Delta pivoted toward me in her rocking chair, a graying mama bear in winter clothing. She reached into a side pocket of her coat and handed me a small take-out box. "But her kitchen charms survived in her daughter and her grandchildren. So did her spirit recipes."

I opened the plastic lid, inhaling cinnamon, butter, and rich pumpkin aromas.

"Candy roaster pie," Delta said. "You think it's pumpkin, but candy roasters are an old timey winter squash. The Cherokees grew them. Rose and her brothers started speaking in tongues at church one day. It wasn't until later some of the old people said they were speaking Cherokee. That's where this recipe came from."

I lifted the sliver of pie to my lips and bit off a large piece. Chewing with my eyes closed, I realized I was crying and smiling.

Delta laid a hand on my sleeve. "Don't tell me you can't see what I see." I looked toward the bare winter oaks at the edge of the parking lot.

The trees shank from towering giants to saplings. Their empty limbs sprouted thick arbors of green leaves. The Trace was no longer a paved two-lane; it was once again a dirt road. The Ten Sisters rose in deep blue-green splendor; the air was so clear that every tree top was etched against the sky. The only sounds were birds and the singing of insects in the high pastures.

Rose stood there, curvaceous in her drop-waist dress with its hem floating not far below her stockinged knees, and Sam, handsome with his mustache; wearing dusty knickers held up by suspenders and a shirt with the sleeves rolled up on thickly muscled forearms.

He slipped a hand around her waist.

She cupped his face in her hands and pulled his mouth to hers.

In that moment, they couldn't see the future. The darkness lay beyond.

"Even the best love comes with sadness," Delta said, her voice hoarse. "Even the happiest."

I SENT THE PHOTOS to Gus. To be safe, I used the farm's high-tech, secure email system, the one we used to transfer confidential files to social service agencies. I coordinated the timing so that a snail-mail package would arrive at the base then. After I watched our indomitable postwoman rumble off down the farm's frostbitten dirt road with my package in the back of her USPS mail truck, I went to my room and headed straight to the corner between the tall shelves full of bagged wool. I sat down with my safety quilt and pulled it over me; making my usual tent. My safe place.

I had been a naïve high school art teacher and devout minister's daughter—much to Dad's dismay, I took a vow of chastity at the age of sixteen.

I wanted to show Dad I could bring lost souls into the fold, and that was why I set out to save my apartment building's maintenance men from their meth addiction. I sincerely believed in the power of faith, of good hearts doing good deeds to reveal the Light to those in the Dark.

Until I opened my door one autumn night to find the duo waiting for me, thinking that my friendship, my ministry, was an invitation of an entirely different kind. They didn't take Bible verses for an answer. They didn't take No for an answer.

They didn't hesitate to hurt me for the next few hours of my life, and to leave me naked and bloody on the floor.

My attackers went to prison for life.

I told everyone in my church and my counseling center that I forgave the men.

A lie.

I wanted to kill them slowly, with my bare hands.

So here I was, still hiding from life. From that fury that lurked inside me.

Opal whispered, *Either you're gonna stop being afraid of life, or you're gonna stop caring whether you live.*

After a minute or two under the quilt, I sneezed.

I am just sitting under a blanket, sneezing.

I got up, folded the quilt carefully, and stood looking down at it for a long time.

Then I went to the stack of plastic crates that served as my closet, and put it away.

7

I WAS DIRTY, COLD, exhausted, and my boots had blood spatters on them.

Two villagers had been kidnapped by the warlord. I found their bodies. I staggered inside my cold tin can and saw the box peeking out of a mail sack I'd dumped on my bed before I went on patrol.

Luce's handwriting.

Still wearing fifty pounds of *battle rattle*—full combat vests and armor—I sat down and turned Luce's mysterious package in my hands, drawing comfort, letting her presence sink into my muscles.

I smelled . . . pink. Strawberry beer. Yeah, it exists. Prying the box open took careful maneuvers of my knife, since I was in a hurry. The fat envelope inside was folded three times and bound with more tape.

Once I got that open, the delicate shawl slipped out like blue silk water. My cock went hard. I lifted yards of soft worlds in my fists. I pressed the cloud to my face. It was sexy as hell, kisses and fingertips on my skin. The swirls of the pattern drifted over my arms and torso, feathering my thighs and draping between my legs.

I dug inside the envelope and found a note.

Gus—

I thought you might like to see that I have arms, legs, feet, and a neck. Check your email for some photographs.

I shucked my gear and sat down at the desk.

I opened the first picture.

Luce sat on a small bed thick with colorful quilts, pushed up tight in a corner against a plank wall painted egg-shell white. There were no windows, no art on the wall, just the clean, plain beauty of her and the quilts against that textured background.

She wore the blue shawl—and nothing else. The see-through pattern swirled around her from neck to ankles, showing me only hints of the skin underneath. Aside from her bare left shoulder and a sliver of her bare left foot and ankle, she was fully covered.

Her hair, wound up in that way women do so it looks like they just piled it on their heads while watching eggs boil, was anchored by a yarn spindle I'd sent her after Christmas.

I opened the rest of the files as fast as my fingers could move. More tantalizing glimpses. A bare leg from the knee down. Both shoulders. Her neck, yes. Her bare feet. I had never seen anyone sexier, or more breakably beautiful, in my life.

It was going to be a long night.

NINE P.M., NORTH Carolina time, when he called. I was in bed with a heating pad turned up high to keep my feet warm. Spinning yarn on a drop spindle. I held a pile of roving on my lap, and let the spindle twist beside the bed.

"Show me your feet," Gus said.

I dropped the spindle.

Slowly I pulled both feet from their warm haven. My skin prickled in the chill.

"I'm laying here with both feet completely naked from the ankles down."

"What are you wearing?"

"A shawl like the one I wore in the pictures."

"No, just tell me. Reality is good."

"My ancient UNC nightshirt and floppy sweat pants cut off below the knees. And the socks you made for me."

"Pull up the pant legs a little. I'd like to hear more about your knees."

I adjusted the sweat pants and stared at my legs. "I put Bah Spa goat's milk body lotion on them. They have a nice sheen."

"Any freckles, bumps, scars?"

"Why?"

"I like details."

"I have a small scar on top of my right knee. In the shape of a circle. I went ice-skating once, during college. I fell on a metal bottle cap. The ER doctor said it was the strangest little wound she'd seen all month."

Suddenly, a soft pressure touched the scar. No more than a wisp of air. Warm. Like his breath on my skin. I gasped.

"You feel that?" he asked.

"Yes."

"Want me to keep going?"

"You know the answer."

I shut my eyes. I watched his thick, suntanned fingers knitting a sock with needles so small only a delicate and skilled hand should have been able to maneuver them the way his large, dusty fingers did. The top of the sock was stretched between four slender double-points—they look like large toothpicks—holding the edging apart like the aperture of a colorful spider web.

I pictured him touching his fingertips to that taut entrance. He circled a forefinger around the rim. He stroked the ends of the imagined double-points, rubbed them. Then, slowly, he slid one finger down inside the soft chamber.

Withdrew it. Slid it down again.

Imagine the warmth of a summer tide on the northern Florida coast. Atlantic side, facing Europe and Africa; gray-white beaches and fruit stands selling oranges; t-shirt shops and biker bars and miniature golf courses. But on the beach, the throb of the surf lulls the outer world to sleep. You sit there in your modest one-piece suit, watching tiny crabs skitter along the rivulets of water; feeling the salty wash of the great, mysterious depths curl around your feet and ankles; the inlets stroke your thighs as they arrive and retreat.

The ocean is coaxing you off the continental shelf and into the magic of the abyss.

Inside your deepest self, you admit you want to be swept away.

The tide hears you. It rises, thick with sensations, bathing you and covering your entire body, sliding the bathing suit down your shoulders, caressing your naked breasts, kissing your belly, your thighs, and all parts in between. You don't need to breathe; suddenly, you can breathe underwater. You're free of the land-born world; you've become a mermaid.

The tide becomes your mouth, your lungs, your body.

And you dissolve into the beautiful ache of its passion.

The JabberTalk
Welcome to the Online Community Bulletin Board for the Crossroads Cove,
Ten Sisters Mountains, and Wild Woman Ridge Districts of
Jefferson County, North Carolina
Dr. Doug Firth, DVM, moderator

"Beware the JabberTalk, my child! The jaws that flap, the words that quack!
Beware the Hearsay bird, and shun The Farteous BanAllfacts!"
On bended knee, Mr. Lewis Carroll, I hope you're square with this admiring fun. DF
Temperature on Devil's Knob as of 9 a.m., highest elevation in Jefferson County and all of western NC—25 degrees
Temperature at WTUR as of 9 a.m., the voice of Turtleville, county seat of Jefferson County—29 degrees
Sponsored by Delta's
Biscuits@TheCrossroadsCafé.com
This week: The BaconZilla
"So big it might scare Tokyo"
Handcut wild-hog Coca-Cola marinated bacon
Your Pick: Butt Farms Mellow Goat or MoozaFella Cheese
Two Fresh-Laid Miz Ted's Laidback Fat Red Hen Eggs
Topped with your choice of Delta's winners!
(as seen on the "Kitchen Star's Showdown" finals)
Kiss My Mama Cream Gravy
Kiss My Foot Red-Eye Gravy
The Crossroads Café. Where the Lard Cooks in Mysterious Ways.

TODAY'S SCIENCE report courtesy of Lawrence T. Potter, Jr., Assistant Table Manager, The Crossroads Café.

"Still no confirmed sighting of Rockycockers around the old Free Wheeler bicycle town. But Sam Carter is missing a wrench he laid on the tailgate of his truck while changing a tire on Carter Road last week. E. Tarl Swetzer found three shirts missing off his clothes line on Swetzer Road on Tuesday. Mrs. Zip says another UPS package that was "for-sure" on her front porch when she left for Joggercize was gone when she came home.

"Mrs. Zip says it is 'confidential' that her latest UPS package contained items of a personal nature for important female relaxation treatments. I'll keep everybody informed if more female relaxation treatments are targeted by the Rockycockers."

MISS LUCY, I KNOW you told me not to walk too deep in the woods at Free Wheeler, and I have kept my promise to stop looking for rockycockers until springtime. Dr. Firth says the ones in Scotland hibernate like bears, so he bets our kind do, too. I've taken pictures of all the giant rocks that might have caves inside them, especially the ones up on the ridge above Free Wheeler. They look like a backbone and have the giant handprints carved on them.

But I do not want to crawl inside their caves. Not even for the sake of science.

Sometimes I hear strange noises in the woods. The squirrels throw things at me. Pine cones and acorns. I have dusted some of them with my kit, and I SAW PART OF A HUMAN FINGER PRINT. I know there are bad people around here, now, so I'll be careful.

But here is why I am emailing you today. When I was clearing tables after lunch at the Crossroads, Miss Cleo went into the back dining room. Deputy Burkett was in there eating his free food. I don't like Deputy Burkett. He makes fun of me but only when no one is watching.

Miss Cleo talks to him like I don't have ears.

This is what I heard, today.

"Word is going to get out. Leave her alone. You're a married man. You're Howard Monzell's son-in-law. You're somebody important."

Deputy Burkett said, "Don't worry, I have plans. I'll make you proud of me. *Mother*."

But he didn't say it in a nice way. He said it MEAN.

And then Miss Cleo said, "Not if you throw it all away for that sickly white-haired demon."

Miss Lucy! That is what she calls YOU. Except to Miss Delta. She never says it to Miss Delta.

Miss Cleo must have you confused with somebody else. I am your loyal friend. I will find the other sickly white-haired demon around here and let you know who she is.

Yours truly, Larry T. Potter, assistant table manager, The Crossroads Café

PATTON STOOD IN the edge of the woods below the sheep barn in the chilly dawn, almost hidden among the broad leaves of the rhododendrons. I picked my way through the frosty foliage. "Good morning, Corporal Patton."

I reached out, hoping to pet him. He backed away, always suspicious of intimacy. I understood. The big German shepherd was often seen as little more than a stealthy shadow, and should have been frightening. His military "extractions" of unaccompanied items from homes in the Free Wheeler area had convinced amateur sleuth Larry that he was a mythical Rockycocker, the source of any odd sounds and sightings in the woods.

But I now know him to be a gentleman, albeit as reclusive as the human Knights. Like them, he was a damaged veteran who didn't trust civilian society. He snarled if his nose caught any person other than me in the wind below the barns. But he dropped the Knights' tin-foil-wrapped message at my feet then stepped back politely. By the time I picked up the slender silver wrapper, he'd faded back into the silver forest.

> *Urgent. Yarnspinner, meet us 14:00 hours. Big Hand Rock. Regards, NightOwl. P.S. Cpl Patton extracted another UPS delivery from Mrs. Z's porch. Dildos. Can't return this one, sorry. Gutsy & Dragon cite morale needs of female troops.*

"EASY, BRIM, EASY. That's just the smell of marijuana and guns. Lots of guns."

Brim stomped along, disliking the western saddle and hackamore, even though I rarely tugged on its reins.

"You didn't have to ride the demon mule down here." Gutsy waved both arms. "Watch out, Sink! She's going for your head."

I scrambled off Brim and held her around the head. Her bared teeth slowly disappeared behind a twitching upper lip.

Sink grimaced and wiped slobber off his camo hat. An AK47 swung gently from the strap across his back.

"You actually came," Cowboy said around the butt of a smoke. "We heard the farm is on lockdown."

"Most of the time, yes. Where's Night Hawk?"

Sergeant Katherine Carmichael, aka Gutsy, kicked a muddy clod. "His stump is hurting. Doc's got him on painkillers and weed. We're running out of weed."

"I thought Santa Joe . . . "

"The feds are watching him and his farmers. From that new task force the Prez created."

"Clean Sweep America," Sink said, and spit. "Need more inmates for the fucking private prisons."

Gutsy nodded, a grim gleam in her eyes. She struck a match on the thigh of her faded corduroys, lifted the flame to a rolled joint between her teeth, and sucked on the little stogie. Gutsy's effect was always startling—she wasn't much taller than me, but was built like a weightlifter—at least from what I could tell of the body hidden beneath corduroy and camo jackets and scarves. "Night Hawk could use more padding. And Berg's arm is pinching his shoulder."

"I'll bring you a new bag of wool. Just make me a promise."

"Yeah, what?"

"Stop throwing things at Larry. No more pine cones and acorns."

She rolled her eyes. "I'll tell Dragon. It's her little game. She really wants to fuck him."

"I've told you. He's autistic. Promise you'll make her stop stalking him."

"I'll do what I can. Show me the money."

I pulled a bulging canvas tote off the saddle. "Blueberry jelly, apple butter, and muscadine preserves."

Sink lunged forward and grabbed the tote. He had impulse-control issues.

Brim did, too. She snapped at him.

"Now tell me what I need to know that's so urgent."

Gutsy blew a cloud of smoke into the air. "We've got intel, Yarny. And it's not good."

My blood chilled. "Monzell."

"Your angel tell you that?"

"It's always about Monzell, these days. And Burkett."

"Toke up." She held out the smoke.

I shook my head.

She rolled her eyes. "Better for you than all those psych drugs. At least we go half and half."

"We're semi-organic," Skin said. Cowboy laughed.

"Quit hesitating," I told Gutsy. "I can take it."

Gutsy pulled a cell phone from her jacket. Clicked a control. "Here. Take a look."

Me. In the blue shawl. Sitting on my bed with one foot exposed, gazing somberly at the camera.

Members of the jury, she knew my clients were in court-ordered rehab. She wanted to play on the wild side. Minister's daughter, school teacher. She lured them to her apartment. She consumed illegal drugs with them. She was a willing participant in the unfortunate sexual violence that resulted. She's not a victim.

My knees went weak. I made my way on the uneven ground to the Big Hand Rock. It loomed over us, a granite monolith the size of a large truck. Down low on one side, five distinct carvings had baffled researchers for years.

Giant hands.

I sat down with my back against them. Breathing hard. The hands curved around me. I felt the large fingertips cradling my spine, my arms, my hips. Rocking me gently.

"She's going dark on us," Sink said.

Gutsy squatted in front of me. "Come back to the now, Yarny, or I'll stick one of Doc's happy pills down your throat."

Gutsy's voice cut through my brain. I looked at her, dazed. "There's no way those pictures were hacked. I used a special secure email service."

"We should have brought Bandit with us. He'd have fun 'splaining how easy it is for the pros to go around those systems."

"But how would anyone even know about them?"

"Somebody knows people who knows people who collect juicy tidbits about other people. Monzell collects a lot of pictures."

"You should see the blackmail stuff," Sink said. "Monzell's got one of his investors in a hooker sandwich wearing leather."

I swayed. "How did you find out?"

"Because we're listening in on Monzell. As much as we can. His security is pretty good."

Cowboy mimed jacking a rifle and pointing it eastward. "Probably got it from the Russians. Fucking Russians are everywhere now."

I took a deep breath. "Monzell could be spying on everyone we know."

"Yep."

"But what good do my pictures do him? They're not that racy."

"You shoulda shown more skin," Sink said. Cowboy nodded.

Gutsy hit them with a wicked side-eye. "We think he's using them to keep Kern in line. All he has to do is have somebody send them to Amber and tell her they came from her husband. She's already hearing rumors about Kern horndogging you."

"I am sorry . . . I'm so sorry to have caused this trouble . . . Sorry. Really sorry."

"Say you're sorry one more time, and I'll smack ya. Own your shit. Get mad. Get fucking furious. Stop lying to yourself, Yarny. You want revenge. You want to fuck up everyone who fucked you over. Stupid whiny weak bitch."

She shoved me.

Brim lunged, and I spent the next moments being dragged around. I clutched her head.

Finally, we all sagged to a halt, me hanging onto her neck while Gutsy, Sink, and Cowboy grinned. "Damn, that was fun," Sink said. "That mule is sick righteous."

"One of us," Cowboy said.

I dragged myself up on the saddle. Brim dipped her head and sneered at the others. "Is there anything else I need to know?"

Gutsy planted herself in front of us. "We're just getting to the good part. The Jefferson County Guardians of God are expanding. Fucking Goggers. They're playing army."

"I've heard. We're fighting back. Petitions, email campaigns, calling our elected officials . . . "

"Petitions," Sink said dryly. He shrugged his shoulders. The assault rifle swayed.

"And calling pols who ain't gonna do shit," Cowboy added. "Because they're all in the pockets of people like Monzell." He hawked a stream of tobacco on the ground. "Ohhh, Imma call my senator, soon as he gets done kissing ass in Washington."

Gutsy gave them a zip-it gesture. Her eyes grim, she dodged Brim's teeth to crowd in closer and tuck a thumb drive into the top of my hiking boot. "Monzell has set up an enemies' list for the Goggers to harass. You and your pals who run the farm are at the top of it."

I'M NOT TELLING Gus about Monzell hacking my photos. I'm burying this so deep he can't sense it. Right beside the compartment with the rapes.

Alberta paced in front of five deer heads mounted above the big fireplace in the main house, a hundred-year-old farmstead cobbled into a much bigger home via added rooms and porches, a covered walkway to one of the dorm buildings, another walkway to a five-vehicle garage, and graveled paths in every direction, all hooded by large trees. The décor was a mix of her hunter-casual and Macy's goddess-worship-therapist style. A giant goddess statue stood in one corner, trickling water into a small pool.

A dozen dogs and cats were curled up on the rugs around it. The goddess had muddy paw prints on her stone feet.

"Well, we're in damn good company on Monzell's enemies' list," Alberta said. "You, us, Tal and Doug, Gabby and Jay, Delta and Pike, Santa Joe and his weed empire, half the ministers in the county, two ex-mayors, the president of the Jefferson County Farmers' Co-Op, the head librarian in Turtleville, and Barry at the dry cleaners. He's the only one I can't figure out."

Macy, seated on a couch covered in one of my knitted throws, said quietly, "Barry headed the committee that accused Monzell's Daw Ridge plant of sneaking their filthy run-off water into the river—again." She sighed and sipped a mug of dandelion tea. "That's why he wasn't re-elected to the city council." She glanced at me. "Kern campaigned for his opponent. Kern has a lot of followers."

In the fireplace, logs crackled and smoked. Deer heads looked down at me, barely blinking. Ethereal vapor curled from their stiff nostrils. I saw them in the pastures, mingling with our flock of sheep, grazing on the bosoms of the green slopes. Waiting for the inevitable doom.

"Earth to Lucy," Alberta grunted.

I settled deeper into a couch filled with dogs and cats, a pet squirrel and a raccoon. "Sheriff Whittlespoon isn't well. That's why he hasn't fired Kern and run him out of the county. That's why Delta is keeping quiet about Kern. She's worried about Pike. If Pike retires . . . Pike's the only major official standing between us and the new regime. He's trying to give Kern the chance to fill his shoes. To do the right thing."

Blood, the deer heads said.

I blinked. What did 'blood' mean? The dead deer heads didn't blink back, this time. Their ghostly breaths vanished.

Macy's phone beeped. She pulled it from the pocket of her pink overalls.

Her face went pale. "Carolina Furniture has cancelled our order for more bunk beds. They say they can't get them in stock."

Alberta slung a beer into the fireplace. "That's bullshit. We've bought furniture from them for ten years . . . "

Macy's phone beeped again.

Her hand faltered, spilling dandelion tea on the screen. "Cray Payton can't repair the fence in the south pasture. His wife is sick, and he's taking care of her full time."

"He's not married," Alberta said. "Unless he calls his pig herd a harem."

Macy's phone beeped ten times in the next ten minutes.

We were on Monzell's enemies' list.

And we were being shunned.

THERE'S SOMETHING I need to say about Alberta and Macy.

I loved them like sisters, the way I loved Gus's sisters—Tal and Gabby—and Cathy Deen, and Delta.

For a while, not long after moving to the farm, I wanted to become a lesbian because of them. As if I could convert, like changing churches. Get sprinkled instead of dunked. They were such a strong couple, so connected, so solid. Nothing rattled their bond.

That Macy is a sweet little darlin', and some lucky yahoo will take her out of this girl hotel before long.

Said by at least one man on the sheep-shearing crews that passed through every spring.

I'm going to introduce Macy to my cousin next time he's here from Birmingham. He loves outdoorsy little blondes.

To which Alberta had replied, "Eee-yep. I can understand why."

And I thought, *A girlfriend would be safe. No violence. No stabbing me with penises. Just kisses and backrubs and touching and all that. In return, I could count on her devotion, and I could stop hating and fearing the male sex while harboring hopes of loving a man.*

One autumn, a tall woman in manure-spattered overalls finished delivering several new heifers for the farm's dairy herd. She flirted with Alberta then grilled me about Alberta's availability.

"Damn, she's hell on wheels with a side order of take-no-prisoners. She's my kind of woman. You know what I mean? Would she be interested?"

Macy was off to one side, entering figures into the farm's big checkbook.

I cleared my throat. "I'm sure she would, if she were free, but she's spoken for."

"At least tell me this much. She's not straight, is she?"

Simple question, or it should have been. Three women, standing outside a barn in the mountains on a late autumn afternoon. Our only witnesses—a penned group of female animals, bred to serve without complaint.

Macy struggled to keep quiet, looking tormented. She hated secrecy, but in the current social and political climate it wasn't safe to be lesbians running a shelter for straight women scared of straight men.

I stepped up. "Alberta's spoken for."

The heifer woman stared at me. Her mouth flattened. She looked from me to Macy, whose eyes turned into big blue moo-cow rounds of suppressed laughter.

"You?" the woman said, pointing at me. "You? You're a *runt*."

"Excuse me," I said. "I'm not a runt. I'm just small compared to *you*."

8

I SURVIVED EIGHTEEN years in the Army and multiple tours in combat zones thanks to my kitchen charms. My company has the best send-em-home-in-one-piece record in the battalion. All because I have this secret ability to sense what makes people dangerous—hungry.

So there I was, stirring sliced sweet potatoes in a pot of oil over a campfire. Furthering world peace through the diplomacy of fried southern taters.

Sanchez stood beside me, translating everything I said to the women and children. She wears a big fluttery head scarf tied around her helmet. Looks like a pirate. She can make eye contact with the women, but I'm not allowed. So I look at the kids. The armed men—husbands, brothers, uncles, sons—lounged around the perimeter—and oh, yeah, they'll let me know I cross a line.

I forked up a slice of fried potato.

"This is called a sweet potato stick," I told the kids. Explaining the name, "French fry," was too much for my storytelling ability and Sanchez's Pashto vocabulary. "But it's not sweet, and it's not a stick."

Sanchez gave me the Stink Eye. Whatever she told them, they laughed anyway.

"Sweet potato sticks are the most important food in my province of America," I went on, wagging the tater like a long, orange finger. "The home of James Brown and Elvis."

Blank stares.

"Coke a Cola."

That got smiles and nods.

I cooled all the fries on a rock, telling stories the whole time. They giggled like crazy. My people and our strange ways. Eating slimy okra pods and alligators' tails and giant fish with whiskers, and these peanuts we pulled out of the ground. As the fries cooled I started to hand them out to the girls first, but Sanchez shook her head. So I spread my hands and said, "Here's what we say when it's time to eat," I told the kids. "Come and get it, y'all!"

Sanchez translated like a drama queen. Reared back on her boot heels and almost yodeled the words.

They looked startled, then burst out laughing. The women smiled behind their covered mouths, and even some of the men grinned.

A woman nudged one boy forward. Shaggy hair, wide eyes; not more than ten. He stepped out of the group and stopped before the fries. "Bazir," he said, pointing to himself. "Thank you, y'all."

While the children and their mothers ate I sat down on a camp stool and perched a stack of small posters on my knee. I pointed to a map of the United States.

"My friend, Luce, drew these pictures for me to show you," I called out. Sanchez gave me a hard look. "Don't you mean your wife, Captain?"

Bingo. Men don't have female friends who aren't sisters or cousins. Not in the view of these villagers. So, what could I say? "Yes, wife."

I laid the U.S. map aside and pointed to the next poster, a large drawing of western North Carolina. "This is my home. My sisters and I grew up right here. I pointed to a large star. This is called Asheville. People who live in Asheville are a different tribe from other North Carolinians."

Sanchez translated.

"Sweet taters," Bazir said.

I nodded. "Sweet taters."

I held up a large photo of Tal and Gabby. "These are my sisters. They are very tall, like me. They have long red hair, but instead of hands they have cooking pots and spoons. They can't clap their hands. They rattle too much."

Sanchez translated dramatically.

The kids were onto my bullshit now. They laughed. The women leaned closer, squinting at the photo. My sisters, posing in the renovated Victorian kitchen at Tal and Doug's house at Free Wheeler, wore jeans, sweaters and full-length white aprons.

"They work as chefs. Cooks."

One of the women whispered to her husband, who spoke to Sanchez. "She says don't they have husbands and children?"

No way would I attempt to explain that my sisters were living with their intended husbands. So I said, "I keep giving them away, but the men give them back. Because they rattle."

Sanchez translated. For a tense moment I psychically smelled burning olive oil. Then the men burst out laughing, and everyone joined in.

But now my sisters have come back to our home. I pointed to North Carolina.

But all I said was, "They want to cook for people the way our family did, before. Our parents owned a restaurant." I held up another sweet potato fry, without much enthusiasm. But when Riley translated, everyone seemed impressed.

Another woman asked a question. Riley squinted at me. "She says, 'How can your sisters live there without a man from their family to be in charge of it? So you will go home soon to take charge of them?'"

"I have new husbands in mind for them," I said. "Ones who like women who rattle and cook."

I held up a picture of you, Luce.

"This is my wife," I announced. "This is Lucy."

They stared at your hair. It's so pale it's almost white in the photo. They traded a lot of shocked looks, and there was a lot of pointing.

Sanchez said, "They want to know if she's Muslim. Because of all the scarves and the long skirt."

"Tell them she's Christian but it's a very modest sect."

Finally the leader of the women spoke directly to Riley.

"Captain, they'd like to honor her with an Afghan name. *Tabana.* It translates roughly to 'The light of the moon.' Because of her hair."

"Tell them it's a beautiful name, and I'm sure she'll love it. And thank them."

Bazir walked up tapped me on the arm. "Sweet tater," he said happily.

"Sweet tater," I answered. He grinned.

I HALTED JUST outside the security light of the barn and sat down, looking up at the January half-moon in a sky of scudding clouds.

Some said we have energy vortexes in our mountains, that they draw "Sensors" to them—people who are sensitive to those vibrations. That the energy is calming, and healing. The Cove—the heart of Jefferson County—is thought to be the most powerful pulse at their center. My dad said such effects were the work of the Holy Spirit. He made me promise not to reveal his blasphemy to his Methodist congregation.

I curled deeper inside my shawls and quilt, watching my breath puff white through their soft igloo entrance they made around my face. The cold night air wisped at my nose.

My phone rang. I hugged it. "Hello, Captain."

"I married you today." Gus's deep voice filled the small theater of fabric. "It was for community relations."

"I . . . you . . . what?"

He told me the story.

"So, Luce, for the sake of foreign relations and maybe even the future of world peace, do you mind being married to me in the eyes of a small village in Kandahar Province?"

I smiled. "For the sake of world peace, I agree to be your Afghan wife by proxy. 'Light of the Moon' MacBride."

"Considering the MacBride history as bootleggers, how about I call you Moonshine? Ready for our honeymoon, Moonshine?"

I went very quiet.

He said quickly, "Take your time, Luce. When you're ready, you'll tell me what scares you."

I rustled around, holding back tears until my face ached. I tapped keys on my phone. Searched for files. "I'm emailing you something. One of our residents asked me if I'd help her work on a knitting pattern she found. You know, I teach the residents to knit and crochet and spin. It's so meditative and calming . . . well, and so . . . Macy encourages the women to explore their sexuality as part of her counseling program . . . solo . . . to claim their personal space, and power . . . it's important for women who have developed the abused mindset to value their own bodies, and . . . "

"Moonshine," Gus said gruffly, "if you're trying to talk dirty to me, just go ahead. I really want to hear about that pattern. In detail."

"Okay. It's a corset. With a matching garter belt."

His psychic reaction was stark and hard and sweet.

ALBERTA SNORTED. "One of your yarn groupies is here to do her cute little old lady routine on you."

I headed down a hall at the main house. A long, blue-sky rug softened the floor. My work. I liked the feel of my foundation under my nervous feet.

I knocked.

Feet rushed. The door swung open. "I want the hug," a small gray woman in camo coveralls yelled. "Lucy!" She grabbed my hand and pulled me into the room's friendly swarm of old couches and lamps and bookcases. One leg winged out from a deformed knee joint. She paddled on hiking shoes crusted with dried mud. A tangle of brown-gray hair fluffed around a thin face canyoned with shallow jowls. A pack of long, thin, fashion cigarettes protruded from the breast pocket of the coveralls.

My instinctive hug mechanism reacted to the misery in her face. Her cushioned arms grabbed me like crab claws as I enfolded her, cradling head and shoulders, waist and back. Then I topped it off with The Sunday Share. What Dad called his *hand-over-hand blessing*, offered to every member of his flock as each left the sanctuary after his 8:30 and 11 a.m. sermons.

A double-link freight-car-puller for the soul, Lucille. Grasp with the right hand, cover with the left hand.

"I don't care what they say about you," Mirelda said, her leathery hands cozied inside mine. "You don't scare me."

"Good."

"I've come to ask you a big ol' favor. I know I shouldn't come here and beg you, but can you take in my friend's granddaughter? She's only a baby, just eighteen, and her mother's run off and my friend is on those vouchers now, the ones the government gives out instead of Social Security. She can't afford to raise the girl."

My fingers caressed the soft human wool of Meery's gray head, opening channels only I could hear.

Her name is Megan. She's not what she seems.

She has been told to spy on us from our weakest point. Me.

But there's more to her than that.

"We'll find a place for her," I said.

9

MEGAN ROWAN WAS eighteen going on a thousand. I saw dark, tangled images around her, too blurry to decipher, darting away, trying to form barricades. A dour old woman stood next to her, claiming to be her grandmother.

Megan's hard gray eyes scoured me like steel wool. "How many boxes of cheap-ass hair color does it take to get that George Washington white-wig-blonde 'do? Where're your dragons, Daenareys? Whazzup with the Amish clothes? You some kind of hillbilly nun?"

Alberta and Macy watched us from beside the desk in Macy's office. I stepped closer to Megan, who radiated cold air from the freezing winter day she had left outside.

I put a hand to my chest.

Megan's eyes flickered nervously at the gesture. I touched my heart point then extended my hand to her. "I can use your help organizing several hundred books I've been collecting. I'm starting a library. I can tell you're smart and you're an avid reader. Could you help me?"

She drew back. "Bullshit. You don't know anything about me."

"You insulted me using at least five different specific cultural references. You have a better command of language than most creative writing students. You're a book reader. Don't even try to deny it. I really could use your help."

She shifted, frowning.

The grandmother hooted. "Yeah, she's a bookworm. But she thinks everybody's trying to mess with her. Get in her panties. Like she's got much to offer."

I pivoted toward this shriveled creature. I stepped closer to her, looking up and narrowing my eyes in concentration, examining her to see where the disguise might let the alien lizard face peek through.

She scowled. "Hey, I don't give a shit who fucks who. It doesn't bother me that this place is run by bush-lickers; I just want to make sure you're not gonna turn my baby girl into a bush-licker, too."

Are you sexually deviant, Ms. Parmenter? After all, wasn't it true your late father, known in the Charlotte church community as a respected Methodist minister, was a closet homosexual who entertained a number of men you called your uncles? How can this jury trust your version of events? Isn't it likely that a young woman such as yourself, who grew up accepting that her father's sexual acts with a man were normal, would be willing to engage in an orgy of drug-fueled rough sex with two men, that, unfortunately, got out of control?

Megan's grandmother added, "Unless the pay-off is some really nice shit like this." She picked up the end of my wrap.

I lunged at her.

Alberta blocked me just in time. She dragged me into their big, folksy kitchen, scattering cats on braided floor rugs and an old terrier who snapped at my shoes. Alberta clamped an arm around my shoulders while planting a wet washcloth to my face. Actually over my face, including nose and mouth.

"Fist DOWN," she ordered. That's when I realized I had my right hand balled and raised.

What is that hand doing? I let it drop and gasped against the washcloth. Alberta let go of me. I leaned against the sink, where tendrils from a windowsill herb garden reached down past a tile backsplash. I snapped off a sprig of parsley and ate it.

"If you're going to start grazing," Alberta said, "we'll put an ear tag on you with your livestock number."

"Palette cleanser. Bad taste in my mouth."

"Are you practicing Kung Fu to impress the captain? What the hell are you thinking? Punching old ladies is a good way to get us shut down."

"That woman is *not* Megan's grandmother. This is a set up. I can't unravel the details, yet."

Alberta gaped at me. Then her eyes narrowed and her jaw clamped. "Monzell."

"Probably. But it's odd. Nothing about Megan feels authentic. She's acrylic yarn pretending to be wool."

"I'm not taking in a goddamn *spy*."

"We have to. It's important." I searched the air with my hands. "She's part of something bigger. I have to know what that is. She's meant to be here."

"You're making it real hard for me to trust your wool witch hoodoo this time."

"Give her a few weeks. I'll watch her."

Alberta stabbed a finger at me. "If you get *any* danger vibes off her, you tell me. Pronto. Agreed?"

"Agreed."

She pointed to an outside door. "Out. I'll get Macy to smooth things over. Beat it."

AN HOUR LATER, when I was filling a hay rack outside the sheep barn, something sharp bounced off my hair.

I whirled.

Megan stood near a shed. Lanky, smirking, prowling. Pulling another weapon from the pocket of a cheap faux-leather coat. She jiggled it in her palm. A rock.

She'd thrown a rock at my head.

She drew her hand back. "Will this get me kicked out of here?"

"No. But it will get you a trip to the ER clinic in Turtleville."

Brim charged out of an open barn door, her big, yellow teeth bared.

Megan jumped and dropped the rock.

"Brim, HALT."

My guard mule slid to a stop with her teeth inches from Megan's pale face.

"Brim, go back in the barn. I'm okay."

Brim, her long ears flattened, her muzzle curled in a sneer of threat, shook her head at Megan then slunk back indoors.

Megan turned toward me, recovering her own sneer. "So you *are* some kind of comic book freak. Reading minds. Controlling donkeys."

"Brim's a mule, not a donkey. And no one controls her."

"*You* stopped her from biting the shit out of me."

"I don't use violence to make a point."

"Coulda fooled me, fairy godmother."

"My offer about the books still stands. Or come learn to spin yarn and to knit. I also teach art. Or just hang out with the sheep and I'll teach you how to work with the herding dogs. There are plenty of things to learn around here."

"Yeah, I've heard that." She drew back her arm and mimed beaning me with another rock. When I flinched, she grinned and walked off, kicking the cold brown grass with the toes of dirty boots.

I staggered back to my room, made a pot of tea with my electric kettle, and sat down at Elam's desk to wait for Gus's emails and phone calls. I would tell him what I had deduced about the mysterious Megan.

Dominate or submit. Attack or surrender. Hit or be hit. Are those the only two choices in life? No, of course not. Patience is a virtue. Time heals all wounds. Forgive and forget.

The Zen of Zen, got your fresh hot Zen right here; we can rationalize your acceptance of any horror the world throws at you, just give it a Zen-something reference. Jesus saves. No . . . remember what Dad said. Jesus gives.

That's the choice. For those who take the Lard's way, as Delta puts it, Jesus gives us only one choice. To give.

FUCK JESUS.

Fuck giving.

There's only love, death, and revenge.

"He died instantly, Captain. He was trying to be a soldier. To clear the IEDs for you."

I stood among the dirt and blood of an exploded mine.

I knelt beside Bazir's small body.

I lifted him into my arms.

I'm going to kill the bastard who did this to you.

February

Gus had been gone on patrol for days. No communication. Especially not even the psychic kind.

"He can wall himself off," Tal confirmed. "All of us can. I thought you'd learned how, too."

I nodded. "So he doesn't find out those photos were hacked. Or sense what happened to me before I came here."

"Same with him. He doesn't want us to worry. Or . . . he doesn't want our pity."

I understood. But the darkness continued to gather.

Something is coming our way. Something very dark. Gus is in danger. I'm in danger. Everyone is in danger. The sky is falling, and it will cover us with decisions.

I printed out one of his emails, folded the paper carefully, and tucked it inside my crotch holster alongside the pistol. I had asked him how he could handle being in charge of other people's lives.

My dad faced that every day, as a cop, Gus wrote back. He said, "Don't let fear get in front of you. Rise above it. Be bigger than fear. Be better than fear. Be smarter than fear. Be braver than fear. Be kinder than fear. Be a leader who's not afraid to die if that's what it takes to do the job."

STEEL GRAY SNOW clouds clotted the mountain sky outside the kitchen at Rainbow Goddess. A human hamster in expensive hiking boots, a gray pinstripe suit and a quilted overcoat parked a Mercedes sedan by the front walkway then handed Alberta and Macy an envelope. "State says you're running fifty clients over capacity and you employ an uncertified counselor named Lucille Parmenter. You have thirty days to rectify the problems."

Alberta tossed the letter into a wicker basket atop some over-ripe bananas. "Monzell had something to do with this."

Macy dutifully moved the letter to a stack of mail. "Kern was here this morning. He wanted to see you but we said you were out in the far pasture. That put him in a mood. He interrogated the Menedez sisters along with Rita Juarez and her kids. Made them show their papers. Said immigration has given local sheriffs' departments more authority to conduct raids."

Alberta picked up a hammer from a kitchen table filled with pecans waiting to be cracked. "All I need is one good swing at his crotch."

I stood at the big double sinks, scraping potatoes. "He has spies everywhere." I held up a spud that had begun to sprout. "Eyes. Lots of eyes. And each eye makes a new plant and its roots grow even more potatoes with more eyes. We're going to be living in a police state, soon."

Alberta pulled the potato from my grip, planted it on a chopping block, and halved with one swing of a sharp cleaver. "Step away from the potato analogy."

I covered the rest of the potatoes with a dishcloth to protect them. "I'm going to buy a rifle. Or a shotgun."

Macy whacked a canning jar with the handle of a heavy knife. She dumped turnip greens into a ten-gallon pot. "As your therapist, I strongly advise against it."

"You can tell Alberta about our therapy discussions. I give my permission."

Macy shook her head. "I don't support your fascination with weapons."

I looked at her grimly. "I need to defend myself better than I did in the past."

STILL FROWNING, Macy dropped me off at the café on her way to town that afternoon.

I trudged across the gravel parking lot bundled in shawls and scarves and a thick wool reggae cap that bundled my wadded-up hair on the back of my head. Pike's blood pressure was bouncing. He'd come home early. Only a few of us knew. The campaign was taking a toll.

Delta met me on the porch. She was pale with blue circles under her eyes. "Good timing, girlfriend," she said with a strained imitation of her jolly drawl. She slid a bulky, quilted jacket over her jeans, flannel shirt and apron. "I'm gonna go check on my man. Take him some chicken and dumplings. Larry's washing dishes. There won't be any dinner customers until four, at the earliest. You can handle the place for a little while. Cleo's out and about. Holler if you need anything."

"No. Wait! I don't know how to deal with . . . "

The café's double doors were already slamming shut behind her.

I sat down in a rocker.

I rocked.

Slow down. All you have to do is sit on the porch and look neighborly. Wave if anyone drives by.

Stop rocking so fast.

Larry slammed the front doors open and tromped out, lanky and earnest, wearing a long apron stained with food and smelling of heat and soap. "You need anything, Miss Lucy?"

Tires squealed on the Trace's aged asphalt. Its muffler rumbling, an old pickup truck barely held its wheels on the pavement as it skidded around the curve that cut through the forest. The truck plowed into the Café's parking lot, slinging gravel, and slid to a stop by the broad front steps.

The driver leapt out. Short, wiry and spinning a red weave of fear. He wore a Jefferson County High varsity jacket over a heavy sweater and camo pants.

"Sanctuary!" he yelled, raising both arms as if surrendering. "We need sanctuary!"

A teenage girl climbed out the passenger side. "Sanctuary! Please."

The term was meant to be quietly shared, not shouted. *Sanctuary.* Certain churches. Specific homes. Burf Roberd's Old Train Museum, off the Turtleville road behind the old mill. The clubhouse at the golf community. Safe places. Sanctuaries.

Rainbow Goddess was on the list. So was the café.

A siren wailed in the distance.

Larry clutched his hands to his chest. "What do we do?"

I stood. "You go back inside and keep washing dishes. We don't want to w-worry Delta and Pike right now. I'll h-handle this."

"You-you-you're . . . "

"Stuttering can be a sign of thoughtful command. G-go."

"Okay." Larry bolted indoors like a blond llama.

"Sanctuary," the teens yelled again, in unison.

I pointed. "Drive to the old barn shed. Pull the truck in and shut the doors behind you."

They scrambled back into the vehicle and spun gravel down the lane.

Delta, come back. Delta, help. I can't . . .

Kern slung a sheriff's department truck into the yard. Big engine. Four doors. Lights, sirens, emblems.

He climbed the wide veranda steps in two long strides. Then he was in my space, looming over me, something desperate and gentle battling with a deep streak of anger. I saw it around him, woven in coarse wool and harsh colors. Lust and ownership. Ambition. My skin began to retract. Exposed nerve endings shriveled in the chill.

He nodded toward ruts in the gravel. "We shouldn't be at odds. I know they're here. Either tell me, or I'll track them down."

"They're just kids. What did they do?"

"I don't want you to worry. Just tell me where they are. I'll go easier on them, if you do."

I smelled the rising anger in him; the casual brutality masked as order and discipline.

They spoke out, Opal whispered. *They didn't obey. Just like the old days.*

"Is this about the protest some of the students have been organizing? The Freedom of Speech rally?"

"It's been cancelled."

"They had a permit. It was all set."

"Not anymore. New town ordinance. Political rallies can only be held on private property."

Only in dictatorships. The words wanted to spit through my lips, but a panic attack short-circuited them. In another few seconds I'd barely be able to hear Kern's voice; my entire battle would be internal, in the shadows, with the demons. "That's unconstitutional."

"It's the way the Constitution is meant to be used. Structure, obedience, respect for the law."

"Howard Monzell wants control over these mountains. He wants to be a dictator. He's bought the town council and the county commission, and he's put you in position to become his enforcer. Can't you see how he's using you?"

"They defaced the courthouse's main doors. Stenciled a resistance symbol on them. That trinity bar. They may be the ones who stenciled the Monzell Poultry trucks at the Daw Ridge plant."

"No. It wasn't them."

"Oh? Your angels tell you that?" He stepped closer. "You can use your psychic ability to make society better. Safer. Stronger. To protect what we have, here. In this county. This state. This country. Work *with* me."

I stepped back and hit the front wall of the house. A *Welcome, Y'all* plaque fell off its nail. When it clattered on the wooden floor, I began to shake.

Kern raised his hands in a plea. I shrank away. "Please don't. I want you to trust me. A strong man needs a wise woman to keep him on track." His hands hovered near my shoulders.

"You have a wife to do that for you. Back away from me."

He didn't. "You and me. My money, my influence, combined with your talent."

Howard Monzell's money.

I frantically side-eyed the shrinking distance between his hands and my body.

Talk. Make words. It's the only hope for those teenagers. And for you.

"Monzell despises me. Because of Sheryl . . . "

"She would have left him, anyway." He rested his hands on my shoulders. "I can run this county. I can run this state. With your help, I could run this *country*." He bent his head close to mine; his breath filled my nose. "You can save me. And I can save you. He swept one long muscled arm around my back and dragged me to him.

Quit fighting, bitch. Come back here. Hold her down. Slap the shit out of her again.

"Let. Me. Go." Sweat broke on my forehead. I fumbled between us, trying to get my shaking hand inside my skirt, fumbling for my handgun.

"Just let me hold you," Kern said hoarsely. "Just relax and trust me. If you'll give me five minutes to hold you like this, I'll let those kids off with a warning."

"And if I don't?"

He pulled me closer.

A shot rang out. A few feet away, the globe on a porch light fixture exploded.

ADJUST TARGET. Hold fire.

I gave orders to an unknown soldier on the other side of the planet. I stood behind a bunker in the dark of a cold Afghan night. He stood in the woods of the high ridge across from the Crossroads Café. I smelled sangria and cheap rum. War and heroin and suicide attempts and pain.

But loyalty.

Someone sent him to guard Luce.

Twenty degrees right. Down ten. Wind from the southeast. *Now.*

"INSIDE. NOW," Kern ordered, shoving me toward the café's doors.

He pulled his gun and crouched, watching the woods across the Trace.

My head light and a dazed smile growing on my face, I walked through the cozy dining rooms, past the server's station with its napkin-wrapped cutlery and canisters for tea and water. I walked down a back hall through the flour-dusted kitchen and the big pantry, then through a side hall that ended at a sturdy door with a screen door inset. I opened both and stepped out onto a side porch crammed with cardboard boxes of vegetables from local farms. I walked down stern concrete steps to the graveled side yard, and I headed straight to a small, drafty barn so old that Delta and Pike parked tractors in it and filled it with hay so their grandkids would bounce if they fell out of its loft.

I flattened myself on the cold gravel and crawled through a ragged hole in the boards.

The teenagers huddled beside their truck.

I stood. "You sprayed the trinity bar symbol on the courthouse doors."

They nodded. "Everybody's doing it," the girl said. She raised a fist. "We're in the Resistance."

I pointed to my right. "Walk down this driveway. Tell Delta I sent you. Me. Lucy. She'll take care of you."

"Burkett will send us to jail. He's beating people up. He gets away with it because he knows how. Everybody says Sheriff Whittlespoon is letting him . . . "

"Sheriff Whittlespoon has people watching him. Did you hear that shot out front? Tell everyone *that* was Sheriff Whittlespoon protecting the people of this county."

"Are you really a witch at the lesbian farm?"

"Yes. Do what I say."

They ducked out the hole in the wall. I slumped beside their car, watching cold sunlight filter through the slats in the barn walls. My knees went south and the rest of me followed.

Breathe. Breathe.

Several minutes later, the big doors creaked open.

"Shit Yarny," Gutsy said, lowering her rifle. "Get the fuck outta here." She spoke into a mic on her headpiece. "All clear." Then, to me. "Dragon will walk you back to the farm. We've got this covered."

"Stop vandalizing the court house."

She looked wounded. "That wasn't us. The Resistance is growing, Yarny. And when they hear what you did today, you're gonna be a inspiration. Five parts inspire." She swiped a hand across my clammy forehead. "Two parts perspiration."

"I didn't do anything."

"You went Voodoo on Berg. You told him to shoot."

"I would never . . . "

She shrugged. "Okay, if you wanta be humble about it, he'll say one of his voices told him to do it."

Gutsy grinned and left.

I sat there in awe.

It was Gus.

THREE WEEKS UNTIL March. Three weeks until I went on leave. Went back to the mountains I said I'd never call home, again.

Back to Luce. She had been there in spirit when I was young. She was there now, in the flesh.

I would never let Kern get near her again.

Groucho Khan, Bazir yelled. Bazir's young voice rode the wind of the high, stark hills of my brain.

I'd broken my rule about never telling my full name. I'd told the kids Dad named me Groucho Marx and my sisters Tallulah Bankhead and Greta Garbo. Mama indulged Dad because he loved old movies so much. The kids had no idea who those stars were, but they understood when I made faces about being called Groucho. So it became our game. *Groucho Khan*! And me making the faces, and them laughing.

Now I felt him tugging my hands when I walked. Pointing. *There, over there, Groucho Khan. That is where he is. At the sunrise.*

I was running out of time to close this part of my life. I couldn't leave for home without making things right.

"Change of plans," I said into my helmet mic." I rolled new coordinates off my tongue.

I felt the curious glances of my men. Beer poured into the light armored vehicles in our small caravan. A tsunami of dark stout, the foam spent, the hops giving off the odor of burnt oak. The essence of fear and excitement. They trusted me. I didn't tell them more than they needed to know, and I took full responsibility for what happened next.

Sanchez, who was seated in the back wearing sunglasses that reflected green, making her look like a fly, said, "New mission?"

"A detour," I answered. "You'll drop me off and wait."

SHADOWS ROSE IN the corners of my vision, but when I looked quickly, they weren't there. I couldn't concentrate on my spinning. Gus had been away from base for days. I shivered. The barn's temp had dropped from a cozy sixty degrees to forty in only an hour, and it wasn't even noon, yet.

My phone beeped.

I stared at the name. Amber Burkett.

I KNOW you tried to seduce Kern the other day. And now I know about the pictures you sent Kern. Why don't you go back where you came from? I'll pay you to leave. Trust me, if you don't leave, my father is going to make you sorry.

As firefly lights began to flit across my vision, the next text message arrived.

K Burkett.

What did I ever do to you except offer patience and understanding? To visit you, to talk to you. To be your friend and encourage you so that you'd see how I could give you a normal, happy life. So why are you trying to destroy my marriage to Amber and my election campaign? I won't let you ruin my life.

Time slowed down. I fanned myself. My hand looked odd. Disconnected. Here it came—the thick, suffocating cloud pressing around me. A waking dream, not a good one. Nothing felt real.

The phone was going blurry.

Block the fear.

Too late. Everything inside me turned rage-red. Stored fantasies sent their tentacles toward the light. I'd executed my rapists countless times, not in vague ways but vividly; I'd even researched the details. I'd picked the exact guns, the knives, the medical instruments; I studied the methods of electrocution and strangling, the forms of torture, the use of painful poisons and crushing devices.

"It's your process, hon, and I support it," Macy told me when I came to the farm. "But let's work on letting go of that anger. Don't be like Sisyphus, pushing his rock up the same hill for the rest of your life. Be Themis, the goddess of justice. The embodiment of wisdom and foresight, of law, order, of balance. Protector of the helpless."

I pointed out that Themis relied on Nemesis, goddess of revenge, when justice failed.

Still, I understood that the rage inside me was toxic and infinite. Every stressful event revived it, fed it. I'd worked hard to stop the gory daydreams. Alberta had offered to teach me to shoot guns, and I took her up on it. Strangely, it helped. I loved them. Guns.

This is giving me flashbacks. About . . . wanting to become Nemesis.

No, hon. You won't become the goddess of revenge. If you try you'll just turn into ol' corrupt Sisyphus, pushing the eternal rock of frustration up the same endless mountain and watching it roll back down, forever. Remember? Use what I've taught you. Practice staying in the moment. You. Are. Themis. Goddess of justice and protector of the helpless. Okay?

All right.

Like an ingrown hair. I'd lanced boils on sheep. Get the infection out. Relieve the suffering.

I TOLD MACY about the text messages.

"Amber has moved out of their house," she said flatly.

I stared at her, mouth open. "It's not public news yet."

She nodded. "A broken marriage won't help Kern beat Pike in the election. And Howard's not going to allow it. Take your meds, go for a walk. Breathe. We'll just wait and see what happens next. Think happy thoughts. Gus will be home in two weeks. Next Wednesday you're going to Asheville to shop for a new outfit. Big trip, on a whirlybird, with Tal and Gabby? You're getting on that fancy Wakefield copter and you're going. I mean it."

Macy's voice, always calm, was filled with an unblocked flow of kind energy, the way a skilled therapist and high level yoga practitioner ought to be. Namaste, you all. Macy Spruill-Groover, PhD in counseling. Wife of Alberta Spruill-Groover, ex-Marine medic and doctor of kicking ass and taking names later.

I would try to breathe.

PIECES OF MY QUIET world ripped slowly down the sides of an old picture frame. I felt the fragile linen fibers of the vintage canvas pulling my skin off my bones. Gus was trapped in the weave. I had to hold warp and weft together for his sake, at least.

Gus's bare shoulder was warm against my cheek. I snuggled next to him on top of his imagined covers, sliding upwards. Soon my head burrowed against his neck, my naked arm was draped over his bare chest and my right leg over his right leg, with my knee sunk deep in the valley between his thighs.

I half-opened my eyes, seeing a stone wall against the other side of the mattress. The black shadows crowded in close around us, just like before. *Inside a mountain, the light never changes.*

Inside a mountain?

His chest and abdomen were a tree trunk of hard muscles. I rode the rhythm of his heart and lungs and felt the gentle gush of air on my forehead every time he exhaled. Want him, want, no fear, want. The sweet cramp of desire surged down between my thighs; they tightened around his leg and pulled him closer. My body, unleashed from the terror center of memories, knew exactly where it wanted his body to go.

I ached for more.

Suddenly Gus's hand closed around my throat. He threw me on the stone floor. He was quick, naked, and erect. I was naked, too, and fighting. I couldn't see his face.

He slapped me until my neck popped. His leg between my thighs became a bony knee jamming into my pelvis.

"You want me to hold her down again?"

"Nah, not this time. Gimme that ass," he ordered. He jabbed his fingers into me. "Turn over. Give it."

It's just a flashback. End it.

I opened my eyes. My heart broke my ribs. Disoriented, I shoved my tent of shawls aside and grabbed a flashlight from the tote dragging from one shoulder. My breath puffed white in frigid darkness. A coterie of herding dogs grunted unhappily as they floundered from beneath my snow-dappled woolens.

A commotion erupted, and the dog pack raised their voices.

A slender young female voice screeched back at them.

"Stop barking at me. Morons. Goat-head dick brains. Stop it."

And then a sputtering, angry sound like an old car engine trying to catch in cold weather. An angry male llama answer.

More shouts, all human, all that young female voice. Panic. Fear. Dogs barking. The thud of hooved llama feet. Grunts. I recognized llama territorial defense when I heard it. The visitor had been cornered by Michelangelo.

I staggered back to the barn. The sheep, llamas, and alpacas stirred in the shadows, agitated; the dust from wildly tossed wood shavings still filtered through the cold dim glow.

Brim towered among them, her mule muzzle curling to reveal yellow, brutal teeth.

I saw the wagging, barking dogs in a cluster around Michelangelo's shaggy tan legs. Standing, he was six-feet-six at the tip of his banana-curved llama ears. He guarded not only his small family of ten female llamas but all the other livestock and me, too. Between him and Brim, the entire livestock family of Rainbow Goddess was protected. Beyond him, plastered against the barn wall, I glimpsed spikey brown hair, a pale face glistening with llama spit, and a thick camo jacket over skinny jeans.

Megan Rowen.

I coughed up some spit, licked my lips, and managed a low whistle.

The dogs quieted. Brim snorted in disgust, but stepped aside. Megan inched toward me. She stumbled to a halt, blocked by four llamas, a dozen ewes, two alpacas, and a donkey. The overhead light revealed a lean creature with spikey brown hair, a nose ring, black denim and leather. She perched on wobbly, high heeled black boots. Her face and eyes were hypnotically pale and delicate. A deep aura, the colors of a ripe bruise, haloed her head and body.

Anger, fear, pride. A heartbeat that's lost its wings.

"I know what you're afraid of," she drawled. "I eavesdropped on your nightmare. It was hot."

Flames burst through the hay-strewn floor. Smoke and bright orange cinders floated to the ceiling, exploding. My mind filled with the acrid scent of charred wood.

Burning. Destroying.

Megan Rowen was a Fire Witch.

Megan blew out a long breath. Her shoulders sagged.

My illusionary flames evaporated. The barn returned to normal.

I nodded toward the small blank canvas Megan tried to hide behind her leg. Now I knew who'd been pilfering from my storage room.

She whipped it at me like a Frisbee. It landed on a bale of hay near my feet. "So I'm a thief. You caught me, bitch."

She needs a mother. A friend.

I remembered the softness of my mother's hands and the whisper of her voice, even though I was a baby when she died. Dad's adoration of her was a shrine in our lives; he filled the rooms in our three-story

Queen Anne parsonage with her photographs. But Auntie Teresa Parmenter, who had donated that historic Charlotte house to the church, and still controlled it and the church, always smiled at his shrines in a way that made me think of sour milk. "Your father was lucky to find such a tolerant woman," she said often. "One who likes his kind."

"Look, I'll pay for the fucking canvas," Megan said, shifting from foot to foot.

"Please, stop pretending. Who sent you here? What do you want to know?"

"I'm not gonna talk to you around all these goats. They smell like ass taint."

"These aren't goats."

"What-the-fuck-ever."

I picked up the canvas and whirled it back. "Do you want paints and brushes?"

Her eyes narrowed. "Is that a joke?"

"No. I'll give you art supplies. I'll give you art lessons. I'll teach you to spin wool, and to knit and crochet. Like everything here at the farm, you'll earn it."

Her face hardened. "I'm not dropping my panties for you or anybody else."

"No one here will ever abuse you. Ever. If you ever feel pressured or threatened, come to me, or Macy, or Alberta, and we'll take care of it. Understand? You're safe here."

"Like you really give a shit."

"I do."

"I'm not afraid of you. The witch of Rainbow Lezbo farm. That's what people call you. They say you read minds and cast spells using the old mountain hoo-doo. You turned Howard Monzell's third wife against him so she sided with his kids from his second marriage in that lawsuit against his kids in his first marriage. And then she took all her money and left. Then last fall you started trying to take Deputy Burkett away from Howard's daughter. You're trying to screw up Kern's chances of bein' elected sheriff, right?"

"Do you know what *you* are?

"What's that supposed to mean?"

She doesn't know. Doesn't understand her power.

"We'll talk about it later." I pulled my phone out. "It's almost midnight. I'll walk you back to the dorms."

"Let's talk *now*."

"All right. How about a cup of tea?"

"Whatever."

She followed me up the wooden stairs to my porch. A small light fixture illuminated the wooden door and its knob. I reached for the door key that lived in a pocket of my skirt.

A deep growl came from the shadows beyond the light. Patton leapt up on the platform. The four-footed member of the Knights. A damaged veteran, like his human compatriots. A soldier.

The scarred German shepherd pushed himself between me and Megan. He looked up at her with his fangs bared.

Her face paled. She stepped back.

The scent of smoke drifted from the storeroom.

"Run," Megan yelled.

Patton grabbed my wrist in his jaws and tugged.

Flames burst into orange flowers in the barn's loft.

10

YOU HAVE TO FOCUS. Here. In this dust and blood. Not thousands of miles away in North Carolina. Luce is safe. The fire didn't hurt her. Didn't hurt her animals. Thank God for the dog. That big shepherd—where did he come from? He heard me. He listened.

Just as the unknown soldier had listened when I told him to shoot the light out next to Kern, on the porch at the café.

THE FEBRUARY SUN rose on the barn—my home—in smoldering ruins.

All the animals were safe. After making sure that all had exited the barn, I managed to rescue my computer, my meds, and the antique spinning wheel that had belonged to one of Gus's ancestors. Delta had saved it over the years. She'd given it to me with the blessings of Gus, Tal, and Gabby.

Elam's short-legged table, however, was gone.

"Drink more," Macy ordered, squatting beside me on the frosty grass. She gently inserted another hot mug of tea into my bandaged hands. "It has chamomile in it. Very soothing." She lowered her voice. "Also two shots of bourbon."

"Just blisters and scrapes," I said, as if she'd asked.

The Jefferson County Fire Department was still spraying water on the smoking timbers. Alberta hoisted charred boards and kicked icicles that had formed on the water spigots, her grim face almost hidden under a baseball cap and the hood of a heavy jacket.

Pike, leaning on the door of his SUV, supervised as a deputy made notes.

Megan had vanished—but not without leaving clues. The farm's security cameras caught her at the front gate. A small sedan waited for her there. She was seen climbing in.

Fire witch. Fire bug. Not a spy. A paid arsonist?

The overwhelming stink of burned wool filled my mind. The entire inventory of stored roving—several seasons of hard work on the part of our woolies and ourselves—was ashes.

"Monzell did send her," I said aloud. I looked at Macy. "But we'll never prove it. I'm not sure she was the arsonist. Why would she tell me to run?"

"Sudden remorse. It takes a lot of courage to let someone die. Maybe hers failed her. She had an accomplice who picked her up."

Alberta turned among the ruins. Her hard expression reminded me she'd been a marine. "If I catch her, she's dead."

Macy clambered into the debris to shush her and give her a hug.

At the fringe of the fire, where the ashes had cooled, pretty pools of ice gleamed in the first rays of morning sun. The sheep stood at a distance, worried. Michelangelo ripped hay from bales we'd fetched from storage. He had ashes in his moptop of curls.

I'll move the herd to the old dairy barn. Get everyone set up with fresh bedding and feed and water. And then we'll all sleep. I'll sleep in the hay with them.

Brim, however, stood right behind me. Her warm breath occasionally caressed my face. At times I felt her nuzzling the heavy sock cap I wore. She even nibbled one of the shawls draped around my shoulders, as if moving it up to cover me better.

Friend. Friend?

Friend, I answered.

I can't remember how long I sat there, trying to slow the rhythm of my lungs.

Red rage unfurled slowly, vining the weak walls where fear and humiliation whispered, *Curl up, make yourself small, go to sleep. You'll feel better after a day or two in your room, sleeping and knitting.*

Those veined walls began to pulse with a new me, the Witch of the Cove—no, the Witch of the entire realm of Jefferson County, able to steal wives and daughters from powerful men, provoke rumors, fear, vicious slander, and yes, dangerous desire from an amazing man above men. Gus. Able to survive fire.

Lucy, the Unburnt. Mother of Sheep.

A new vein slithered away from the rest, growing from an alchemy of rage deeper than fear.

FOUR CARS, ONE TRUCK, and one helicopter crowded the yard and the pasture at Gear House, Tal and Doug's old Victorian, where Sam Osserman and Rose Nettie had brought Gus's mother into the world. Five days of cold rain rose off the forest floor in smoky streamers drifting toward the morning light.

The nearest of the Ten Sisters Mountains, Julia Bald and Marybeth Head, shifted from morning-glory ice-caps to umber against a sapphire sky. Horses, ponies, goats and a donkey grazed on piles of hay in the pasture. The winter world was hurtful pretty, empty of answers, a taunting mystery.

I kept to myself, hugging my arms and looking out a window of the library, where all of us had gathered to form a plan. The aroma of coffee, tea, and peach strudel formed a soothing, hypnotic cloud, just as Tal had intended: Voices came and went in my ears—Pike's and Delta's, Tal and Doug's, and attorney Quint Avery, who regularly touched a phone bud in his ear and listened to conversations elsewhere. Quint's father, George, now retired, was Jay's mentor, guardian and second in command.

Gabby was with Jay in Asheville. He continued to recover from being shot while protecting her in a Wakefield family drama up in the Little Finn Valley—a drama as complex as the one we faced at Gear House.

"Wakefields are crazy as bedbugs and mean as snakes," Delta had told me. "Greed and power. Banking and mining and fracking and real estate and murder and thieving. Jay's the only good to come out of the whole Wakefield family."

Alberta stood. "Awright, let's pull this together and keep it short." She looked down at me, sniffing, her jaw tight, her eyes wet. "You're in danger and you're putting us in danger, too. We've got a farm full of scared women and children. We've got social services snooping around, and the state is sending its goons to see if we're still qualified to call the farm a shelter. Tal and Doug want you to move in here, but we talked them out of it. They've got Eve to think of. So what we want you to do is move to Asheville. Just until things calm down. Tal and Jay will set you up in a great condo in the Wakefield building; they'll be your neighbors. With private security and no worries."

Macy, crying, stood. "Just until things calm down. We promise."

Opal settled near me. My yarn angel always appeared with the textures of freshly washed fleece. Her vapor swirled through my thoughts. *They do mean well, Miss Lucy, but you have got to stay here. In this cove. There's a battle coming, and you're gonna lead it. The old ones need you here. The giants.*

"I can't go," I said.

Pike turned from a fireplace cracking with pine logs. "If I could protect you from this nonsense, I would. But I can't promise you. I want you to be safe. I want everybody to be safe. I won't stop fighting the pure evil that's trying to take over this country."

"I know, but it's my fight, too."

Delta came over. She stroked my sweaty hair. "Monzell is out to kill you. Kern is out to . . . own you. You're a prize that has considerable value to him. None of that is your fault."

Pike spoke again, his voice deep and gruff. "I can't protect you the way I want to. I don't have the manpower, and I don't have . . . " he coughed, and Delta's eyes tightened with fear. "I'm fighting a lot of battles from a lot of different trenches, these days. There are a lot of people in these mountains who think it's time to pull in our doorsteps and arm for war. They don't have any idea who the war's against; just whatever they're being brainwashed to believe. They're scared. And for the first time in my life, I'm scared, too. Scared we're looking at a way of life—for our whole country's way—that won't be around much longer."

Delta sat down next to me, stroking a tuxedo cat who curled forward on her lap, its lime eyes watching spirits move through the room. "Jay and Gabby will treat you like a queen."

Leave the farm? Leave all my friends. My safe place. My home. The sacred pastures under a special sky, where Gus and I held our intimate conversations.

Doug, standing near Pike at the fireplace, toed a glowing log that rolled onto the hearth. "Last fall I made up stories about dangerous beasts and named them rockycockers." His deep Scottish burr was gentle. "I'm sorry to tell you that, in a way, the cockers really truly exist."

Tal knelt beside me, her hand on my shoulder. "I promise you it'll be okay. Gabby will help you practice your outings. So when Gus comes home you'll be stronger . . . "

"He's not coming home."

Everyone froze.

I took a deep breath. "Not the way you think. I can feel it. Something's going to happen to him."

Tal's face went so pale the freckles faded. "He'll die?"

"No. But something's going on. Something bad."

"Be honest with me. Are you saying Gus might die?"

I shook my head.

A part of him will die, Opal whispered.

"A part of him," I corrected. "A part of him is going to . . . die."

The chill in the room wound through the air into the old woods and rugs and the filigreed window transoms as if the house itself was contracting with alarm. Tal stood, arms spread, her freckled face pale, red hair tousled wildly around a sweater and sweaty hand marks on her jeans.

She looked wildly at Delta. "What is it that they used in the old days—they put it in the trenches under outhouses to keep the odor down?"

"Lime," Delta said.

"No, wait. Not lime. My nose is burning. When we were kids the road crews would pick up animals that had been killed by cars. I asked Daddy what happened to the bodies. He said they were taken to the landfill and then men would throw a chemical on them to make the bodies decompose."

"Lye," Delta supplied. "The same kind that makes soap and cleaners. Too much will burn your skin off."

"Lye. That's it. There is a cover up of blood and . . . anger. And somehow Gus is involved. And I'm worried about him. Lucy's right. He won't come home the same." She gagged.

Doug strode over and put an arm around her. "You and Gabs will know if anything happens to him. Sisters would know. You've told me so."

She nodded but put a hand to her throat.

I realized I was doing something with my hands, too. My hand ballet finally drew everyone's attention. Yarn reveals the heart of the spinner and the soul of the woolies it came from. That's one reason I could channel information through it.

"Lucy, hon," Delta whispered. "Lucy. What are you doing?"

I was miming the act of twirling raw wool onto a drop spindle. The tuxedo cat leapt onto the window sill next to me and looked straight at me. *We see the spirits in the worlds nearby. It's natural among our kind.*

"I see a skein of yarn, soaked in blood and manure, corrupt and filthy. Even when washed, the yarn would still be coated in oily secretions from a beast that grew coarse, sharp wool."

Quint Avery had left the room. Now he returned, looking at a message on his phone. "Megan Rowan is not a teenager, and that's not her real name. She's Ariane Taylor; twenty-six years old. She joined the army at eighteen and served two tours of the Middle East. As a sniper. Two years ago she went AWOL and disappeared."

"To become a paid killer?" Pike asked.

"Maybe. I'll find out what I can."

I and the tuxedo cat shared the view beyond the big window. He looked from it to the softly filtered frost outside, then back at me. Dust motes floated between us on the sunshine. The irises of his eyes narrowed to slits. *The courage to fight is found in the spaces between fears. It's often hidden in the knit and the purl of the pattern.*

"She wasn't there to hurt me," I said. "Whatever her pretense, she was sent to help."

Everyone stared at me. Tal blew out a long breath. "By Gus?"

"I don't think so."

Delta frowned. "She had a strange way of helping you."

"Maybe so, but we won't know why until we find her. In the meantime, Opal is telling me it's important that I stay. They expect me to stay."

"They?" Quint Avery asked. Everyone else understood.

I looked at him. "The giants in the earth."

"Oh."

Everyone began discussing the alternatives.

I got up and walked outside, holding one hand to my mouth and the other to my stomach. Fear had chewed thin spots in me over the years. I was a frayed flag, nerve endings tattered, everything struggling against the winds.

The side yard of Tal and Doug's house was undergoing a restoration to find the outline of a garden wall Sam and Rose had built in the 1930s. They'd even hired a student archaeologist from UNC. She'd located the spoked-wheel pattern they'd expected, but outside that one and off to its left, was something else. I stepped among the mud puddles and neon-sprayed wooden stakes of a large hand like the ones on the Stone Hand rock near the farm.

Had there been a hand-shaped cairn here? The student was convinced so, and that it could be found sunken and covered by the forest debris from hundreds, maybe thousands, of years. Maybe it could rise up and slap all the meanness out of the world.

Standing in the center of that ancient enigma, I fought to hear Opal among the fever thrumming my brain.

They are in the Earth, they are here, just like me, Miss Lucy. You are one of us.

A large hand gently lifted me above the tree tops. I saw the vast expanse of forest and vales. I saw the empty brick and stone buildings of Free Wheeler. I felt the ancient rhythms beneath that tragic village. Spinning wheels. Spinning yarn. The wheels of Sam and Rose's fabulous handmade bicycles. Everything, spinning. Stars and planets and the tiniest parts of the tiniest particles that link us to everything we are or ever were; our belonging to the mysteries and this tiny dot in God's own galaxies. I saw the craggy outcroppings of huge stones exposed by the centuries. The Ten Sisters smiling in the distance, and water flowing down from their heavens; deep, buried rivers, channels, caves, tunnels. I folded into a very small bird and sailed down fissures in those rocks, past carvings and symbols, the hands of gods. Into the darkness.

I came to in Tal's arms, covered in quilts and being lightly petted on the forehead and cheeks by Delta. Everyone stood around me, puffing frosty breaths in the side yard at Gear House.

"What did she say?"

"Something about staying at the farm until the blizzard."

"We don't have blizzards. This isn't Canada. In another month the jonquils pop up and the toads start croaking."

Delta's hand on my forehead. "Whatever she's saying, it's gonna happen."

11

LUCE, CAN YOU hear me? Can you feel me?

No response. I panicked, searching the caverns in my mind for the familiar empath voices and images I'd received all 36 years of my life; the sensations and knowledge that came in steadily, loud and clear.

Until now.

"Captain. Captain MacBride. We're carrying you to a chopper, Sir. Can you hear me?"

"He took the explosion on the left side. Left leg looks bad. Internal injuries, too. And his left ear's hemorrhaging."

"Captain, can you hear me? What did you say, Captain?"

"I think he said, 'Lucid,' Sir."

"Good work, Captain. Yes, you're lucid."

Not lucid. Luce.

My ears still rang from the explosion.

Luce. Bad things are coming her way. I killed a man who hid behind innocent people and got them killed. And now I can't even take care of the people I love, back home.

No pain, yet. Something that felt like seaweed and raw hamburger with sticks in it oozed through the fingers of my left hand. I lifted the mess slowly, afraid I'd recognize something of mine.

Long, dark hair.

The most powerful warlord in the province was right where I remembered him: in my grasp, which had been around his neck. I'd chased him into a mine field where he knew every safe path. I should have been blown to pieces.

My kitchen charms showed me the way. Right until I had him by the throat, staring into his shocked eyes.

Then he took one more step. The wrong one.

Everything went blank. Silent and dark in a way I'd never experienced, before.

The sound of urgent voices began to seep through again. Hands lifted me. The chop of a helicopter made the ground shiver.

"Captain, what are you saying? Clean that gore out of his hand. Get him on the stretcher. One. Two. Three. Good. Secure."

If I die I'll never get home to Luce.

Never sit beside her on our spot in the pasture at Rainbow Goddess and watch the mountains turn blue and then green in the sunshine of a spring morning again. Never brew and bottle and sell Dad's beer for him. Never make sure Mama's name was on the restaurant she deserved.

I fumbled with one hand. I found Dad's crochet hook, attached alongside a cooking charm Tal and Gabby had given me on my thirty-sixth birthday, a skillet on a thick steel necklace; and I found a shredded piece of the scarf Luce had knitted for me.

I held the lifelines as tightly as I could.

"Cap'n!" Sanchez said loudly. "We've been through too much for you to die like this. You hooked me on crocheting, and you're not leavin' me alone to go home without a letter from you tellin' *mis hermanos* I didn't turn girly. You swore, Cap'n."

Sanchez went to the ferment phase with too much sugar in her bottle. Keep a cork in it, Sanchez. I'll write that letter to your brothers.

"Cap'n!" she went on, now shouting over the roar of a helicopter that only existed in half my audible world. "No external signs of damage to your gear or clothing in the crotch area! No worries about your man-junk, Sir!"

Sangria wines aren't subtle.

Dad, I promised you I'd take care of Mama and my sisters after you were killed. I tried. But I let you down.

I've tried to make it up by joining the army. A man takes care of his people. His country. His family. His people in this village. As long as I can do that . . . Tal and Gabby have men now. They don't need me. But I can go home and take care of Luce . . .

A wave of pain rose out of the shock and took every breath out of my lungs.

What's changed. What's wrong?

A GUST OF FRIGID wind knocked me onto my right side in the pasture, setting off an even bigger wave of panic. My flock of fat ewes scattered then contracted, nosing me worriedly. My damp head shawl clung to my face, suffocating me.

I pawed long strands of hair that lifted around me.

Bugle Eye Neal, our amateur weatherman up in the Grim Bald community, said his readings were off the chart.

A Polar Vortex is about to hit. Bugle Eye pronounced it *Pole Air Vartex. Seek shelter. Now.*

I whistled.

The herd dogs urged the ewes, alpacas, and llamas toward their new home in the ancient barn that had been cleared of farm and garden equipment to give them shelter. I slept on an air mattress among them, rejecting Macy and Alberta's entreaties to take up a temporary room in the main house.

A deep, disdainful snort sounded, behind me. The crisp plop of hooves came down the barn path. I got to my feet and turned as Brim came up to me, her long ears flat-back and her muzzle curled to reveal dangerous teeth. She waggled her head at the dogs and sheep to cement her command, then halted inches from me, ears flicking forward, the snarling brown muzzle settling into soft-nibble mode.

Cold. Wind. Cold. Follow me.

I pulled a handful of corn from a pocket of my skirt. As Brim milled it to bits between her killer teeth, I leaned against her warm, winter-shaggy neck. *Send some prayers for Gus,* I whispered. *I'm worried.*

Brim and I made our way past the charred rubble of the sheep barn, with me holding onto her coarse mane for support.

I had set up my spinning wheel in the old dairy barn's long, drafty hall between the wooden berths where dozens of milk cows had munched their hay and grain. I settled on the stool and began filtering long strands of wool from a basket at my feet.

Luce.

Gus's voice came through as if he'd spoken out loud.

My bones dissolved, my legs shook, and I slid off the stool. I sat on the dirt floor gasping for air and clawing at the wool.

There are trap doors everywhere. Quick sand and invisible cliffs. Hidden meanings and riddles; windows you were never meant to open. Check under the bed, and behind the back seat of the car, and inside the closets. Never go to the store alone. Never go outside at night. Never go outside at all, if you can help it.

My heart hammered. I patted the bulge of my pill container in my skirt pocket, just for reassurance, while struggling to inhale through my nose, slowly.

It was like trying to siphon yogurt through a straw. This was bad.

Breathe in, blow out. *Though I walk through the valley of the shadow of death . . .*

Suddenly, everything turned quiet. The wool sent emotions mixed with a kind of psychic text message, sometimes clear, often muddy, like a card you find soaked in the rain by your mailbox. I listened hard, but it had stopped transmitting.

Heat, fear, the itch of my skin under layers of cotton and sweaters. *He must be hurt.*

The flock gathered around me, nuzzling me. I didn't mind their well-managed smells, and they didn't mind my well-managed agoraphobia. They knew me for the whir of my wheel, the whoosh of my carding drum, the click of my knitting needles. I was their Silent Shepherdess.

She Who Sits and Spins and Rarely Speaks.

My brain was on fire.

It was a message. Let me feel his pain. Let me. I can take it. I know pain. I can handle his pain. Just not my own.

Nothing.

I got up and staggered into a stall I used as my private cubicle. Seated on the air mattress with my laptop and phone, I tried to reach Tal, then Gabs.

No answer.

> Just checking in, Tal. Still haven't heard from Gus. Two weeks on patrol and counting. Longest patrol yet. I thought sure he'd be back at the base by today. You've heard anything?

Cookies or dill pickles. Sweet or sour. Tal and Gabby would have tuned into him through their gift, and he through his.

My heart pounded.

I jumped when my computer dinged.

> Hey, Luce! Nope, no word from Gus. But all my vibes are good. Never once have I, Gabby, or Gus been in serious danger that the other two haven't sensed it. Gabby and I have been talking about our parents. We sense-smelled them all morning. Always a good sign, when they're around us. I'll pick you up in thirty minutes for the trip to Asheville. Take your meds. We're going shopping!

I slumped.

Maybe my imagination was in overdrive. *Tal and Gabs would be calling you if they'd sensed anything. Or heard anything.* Except—what if he had been able to hide his injuries from us? Having psychic gifts was no guarantee the universe couldn't sneak past you most of the time. Gabby had almost been shot by Jay's deranged aunt. Tal had been tracked by thugs her ex-boyfriend sent.

Sweat soaked my cotton underwear and the Unbreakable Ewe tee Cathy had given me for Christmas. My feet, cased in the soft, striped socks Gus had knitted for me, felt soggy inside my hiking shoes. I could almost see steam rising from my gray wool skirt and sweater.

Breathe and imagine relief downloading into your brain. You're growing stronger. You're tougher. Breathe. Refill. Fifty percent, sixty, seventy, eighty. Almost full.

It stuck at 82 percent. Not bad, by my standards.

I'd had an ordinary panic anxiety attack, not a message from Gus.

Okay, I texted back. *Ready in 30.*

THE HARDENED HANDS of Afghani men and boys reached past the soldiers and medics to touch me, ignoring Sanchez's pleas in Pashto; they helped carry the litter, they patted my bloody face above the oxygen mask and yelled above the noise.

"They're thanking you, Sir! Thanking you for saving the village."

I couldn't save Bazir.

"We're almost there, Captain. Let's go up on that drip. Whatever's bothering him, he needs to let it go."

Maybe I'm no better than that bastard I killed today.

The keen of the woman's grief stabbed me deep inside. Revenge. She cut my voice out.

Luce, I called.

The path was empty. My voice, and hers, could no longer connect.

I had lost my charms.

I WAS TRAPPED in the produce section of Mother Nature's Super Soul Foods, Asheville's biggest organic grocery store. I kept one hand in my knitted tote bag, clutching a wooden spindle Gus had sent me from Afghanistan. I'd wrapped it in a pair of socks he'd made for me.

"Come on, Lucy. Trust us. He's fine. I know you have premonitions about him, but I think you're wrong. He's okay." Gabby prodded my shoulder with a finger. "We'd feel it if he wasn't. Gus will be home on leave in a few weeks, and you'll be living here in the city by then, and you've got to do what Macy said."

"Try not to scream?"

"De-sensitize."

"That sounds like something you do to with a scrub brush," Tal said.

Gabby gave her an evil green-eyed stare. Jay was finally back to his old arrogant self, again, after nearly dying, but Gabby was still not in a mood to coddle anyone who took her focus away from his recovery. "Push the cart," Gabby ordered.

I tightened my sweaty hand on the grocery cart's hemp-wrapped organic bamboo handlebar. Enya's famous Celtic music droned over us. Music to seduce whales and sell odd varieties of carrots.

People aren't supposed to suffer panic attacks in Asheville. It's the South's equivalent of your laidback hippy aunt, the one with the vague herbal smell and the subscription to *Yoga for Wiccans.* In Asheville, people get in touch with their inner mountain spirits. They meditate. They chant. They wear crystals. They find themselves.

I'd probably never find myself again.

Tal and Gabby had been through hells of their own, but they stood tall. Me? I stood small and white-blond, like the tassel on strange corn. I was trying to get bigger. Today, however, was not that day.

"You okay, Lucy?" Tal patted my shoulder with a strong, freckled hand. Tal was giving, huggable, fluffy. A big red-headed ewe sheep, defending the flock. "You did great in the clothing stores. When we finish here, we're going to Gab's condo and have some wine and you're going to model your new clothes for us."

"That's an order," Gabby added.

Gabby? More of a llama. Tougher wool, a biter, likely to spit . . . but very loyal and protective.

Breathe, stop sweating. No one can hurt you here among the vegetables. It's safe. It's all-natural. It's organic.

My hand shook on the cart. The entire cart shuddered.

"Calm down," Tal soothed. "You're going to crack my box of eggs. Relax your grip on the handle. You're going to pop a finger joint."

"I miscalculated. I thought I could make it all the way to the parsley."

Tal pried my hand off the handle. She rubbed it as if I needed thawing. "Remember what Macy says. Don't give up. Let the panic roll over you and just be patient. Then go on with your shopping."

Gabby bent down to peer at me. "Stop worrying about Gus coming home. You don't have to have sex with him right away. You'll tell him about your past. He'll understand."

I swore her voice could be heard all the way to the tofu chicken aisle.

I just stood there, shaking harder. "Next time we should practice going somewhere Gus might find more entertaining. He and I discuss a lot of books—what about taking him to Rabbit Glen Bookstore on book club night? That's a place we should go to next. Book Club night in Turtleville."

Both sisters gave me the side-eye.

Safe, breathe, safe. Nothing in this grocery store can upset you.

Well, except for maybe that produce clerk over there by the rutabagas. By Asheville standards he was ordinary. Tattoos, piercings, a mass of blond dreadlocks pulled back in a clump. I stared at the thumb-sized wooden plugs in his ear lobes. Didn't those things hurt? How did he protect the tender lobe-holes when he took his wooden plugs out to wash them?

Stop thinking those thoughts. Breathe. Find your comfort zone. All is well.

Gabby wrapped one strong hand around my forearm then cupped her free hand to her mouth. "We need the price of Xanax on aisle two," she intoned in a perfect imitation of the store's PA system.

Very funny. I wished I could laugh. I wished I could breathe. I wished I could leave Rainbow Goddess Farm without hyperventilating. I wished I were a MacBride pioneer woman, brave and enormous, instead of little Lucy Parmenter, a suburban refugee.

I wish I could throw myself into Gus's arms right now, wearing nothing but a smile.

Tal tugged my arm. "One foot in front of the other. Just take it slow."

Move slowly? If I move any slower I'll go backwards in time. "I need to get back to the farm before the weather turns. Carl can drop me off at the helicopter, and I'll wait for you to finish shopping." Carl, a bodyguard working for Jay, had been a Navy SEAL. He and his wife, an Asheville pediatrician, had five daughters. We talked about babies, guns, and how to drown people.

"The weather isn't going to turn," Gabby said. "We'll get a few snow flurries, that's all."

"You're blocking the aisle," a woman said loudly. "You people need to hold a counseling session somewhere else. What's wrong with . . . " She stared at Gabby, recognition creeping into her eyes. "I hope all that Wakefield money makes you happy in Hell."

Wakefield soared over the vegetable bins. Every anti-fracking, mountain-loving customer in the vicinity tuned into the signal. Jay's uncle was always in the news. Even though under indictment for a decades-old attempted murder—a case that looked increasingly less likely to ever go to trial—he continued to run the state's largest mining company. Wakefield Industries wanted to start drilling for natural gas in the state parks.

Gabby scanned the scowling faces around us. "Jay Wakefield is no longer in the mining business. He's a builder and investor. He's responsible for preserving some of the oldest buildings in Asheville. He's against fracking."

The woman rolled past, eyeing Gabby balefully. "Wakefield apologist."

"Your soul smells like rotten sauerkraut. And I don't mean that in a redundant way."

Tal's phone chimed. She plucked it out of her tote and frowned at the screen.

"Military," she said, holding up the phone for Gabby to see, her green eyes worried. She whispered, "I don't smell a thing. You?"

Gabby shook her head. "Gimme." She took the phone. "I'm older." They had a joke. Take-charge Gabby, the older one. *I'm older*, she'd say, whenever she claimed something out of Tal's hands.

"Hello? Gabby MacBride here." She cocked her head, listening to a voice that Tal and I couldn't hear. The color drained out of her beautiful face. Gabby took a deep breath. "But the explosion didn't kill him. He's going to live, correct? He's going to *live*?"

Gus.

12

"LIGHTS OUT, CAPTAIN. We have very good anesthesia here. You're going to take a nice, long nap while we work on your left leg and tidy up a few other spots."

Blinking up into the bright lights of an operating cubicle in a field hospital, I tried to see Luce. Sky-blue eyes like worlds of sadness in a delicate face framed with hair the color of white gold against North Carolina mountains. Yarn spinner. Wool charmer.

Luce. She'd been hidden down inside me, not able to come through the cloud of pain and drugs. I'd put that video on a constant loop, memorized every second of it. *I can handle this as long as she's there. Hell, yes.*

I shut my eyes and dropped down into the mental hammock where Luce always joined me. It was easy to conjure her brew-essence at will; to soothe my loneliness, my emptiness, and yes, the raw need to slide inside her and move until we both blended together. The essence of Luce . . . a taste of honey and crushed fruit, blueberry wine, too sweet to make a dark beer . . . Luce came from tender starters, that's how her brew always tasted in my mind, but there was something fragile, too . . . something easy to spoil.

At night, on patrol or in my cot at the base, I'd lay awake inside her, letting colors and textures form around the taste of her spirit, the heat and shades of light and dark, all of them gliding over my body. As if she were stroking me.

There were times, deep and powerful moments, when we'd talk all night, her nighttime in North Carolina, and she'd be outside in the moonlight with her sheep. I knew something was damaged inside her; just not what. It would be wrong to push, even playfully. But she'd say something like, "I always wear the socks you made for me, they're very comfortable and roomy," and as simple as that statement was, the essences that poured out of her would make me so hard I'd have to get up and pace my small room and try not to let the arousal creep into my voice during the rest of the conversation.

I waited. Nothing came to me. It was like being thrown into a moldy cellar after spending a lifetime living in a kitchen full of flowering hops, beer mash, open spice jars, pots of simmering sauces, and every good aroma known to every cook in every culture of the world.

I concentrated. Pinpoints of alarm crawled up my spine. *It's the pain meds. It's the fear.* Hell, no. There'd never been a moment in my life when I couldn't pull up my kitchen charms. *Luce. Wrap me in your shawls, pull me in.*

But she wasn't there, anymore.

THE BLIZZARD OF THE CENTURY, Bugle Eye called it on his Facebook page, before the internet and phones went down. CHECK ON YOUR NEIGHBORS. STOCK UP ON PROPANE AND FIRE WOOD. BRING THE PETS AND THE CHICKENS INSIDE.

Silence is a black pit filled with glowing eyes. When will their owners creep forward? When will those eyes merge with hungry mouths?

Up on Twist Thumb Ridge, where a huge barnacle of layered rock stuck out from the evergreens and rhododendrons, the cell phone tower bolted atop that ancient ledge grew an even thicker coat of ice. The tower served all of Jefferson County. Falling trees and slip-sliding vehicles took down the power lines. The county's crews kept only a few roads cleared, and those were in Turtleville.

I carried my phone with its knitted pouch tied around my neck so no reborn sound, no vibration would escape me. It lay against the skin of my breast bone with cold regard, a rectangle of ice.

In Atlanta, Chattanooga, Nashville and other big southern cities, it was as if a glacier had formed over the streets. An inch of ice. Five inches of snow. A Dixie Ice Age. Up in the highest peaks of North Carolina and Tennessee, where the level above sea water felt like Canada, we were on the look-out for wooly mammoths.

Pike worked around the clock to take care of the five thousand citizens who inhabited the hollows and backroads of Jefferson County. He took care of people. So did Delta. She rode along on the county's only bulldozer up to the north end—the high ridges surrounding the footprint of the mild Turtleville plateau—to take food to people living off the grid, or who were too old and stubborn to come into Turtleville, where the churches set up shelter at the high school and the country club supplied food and blankets. Down at the Crossroads Café, Cleo and her team shoved tables against the walls and set up pallets. Folks in need of warmth and food filled the rambling house from its front veranda to its back dining rooms.

It was all hands on deck at the farm, caring for the livestock and each other. The high country reverted to the old paths and foot travel at times like this. Neighbors rode horses or hiked along razorback ridges to check on each other in isolated cabins and rickety house trailers. Deer haunches were pulled from meat coolers. Jars of homemade soup bubbled on camping stoves. Thermal underwear was already part of the standard wardrobe; also quilted camo overalls, waterproof boots, ski masks, and cords of firewood, propane tanks, generators, four-wheel drive and lanterns. Iron skillets and lidded pots older than the great-grandmothers who used them were set into fireplaces, heaped with coals, turning out cornbread and biscuits.

Everyone with a bulldozer, a backhoe or a garden tractor scraped trails along the side roads. Alberta used the farm's ham radio network to coordinate the work. We were far better off than the counties around us—Jefferson County had a helicopter, thanks to Cathy and Tom Mitternich. People gossiped about Cathy's wealth; did her movie star money beat Howard's chicken fortune? *Variety* reported that her *Dazzle the Dragon Rider* paycheck was well into seven figures now—just for voicing the animated character in the highly successful franchise.

Delta shrugged and smiled when outsiders dug around for clues. After all, Cathy and Howard were both cousins of hers. But when people pressed her, Delta answered with the glint of sugared victory in her eyes. "Howard says he pays enough in taxes. Howard buys favors, Howard buys wives, Howard buys influence. But Howard won't give a penny to help local causes. Does it bother him to hear folks wonderin' if me and mine have got more from givin' than he's got from gettin'? You bet your donkey it does. When Cathy bought that whirlybird for the sheriff's department? Boy howdy. You coulda heard a pinfeather drop in Howard's camp. His *cockadoodle-do had been cockadoodle out-done.*"

I WAS TRAPPED at the farm; I was trapped in my own fears.

"HE WOKE UP at the base hospital and asked about you right away," Tal told me via the ham radio. She, Gabby, and Jay were about to board Jay's private helicopter for a flight from Asheville to the ice-free coast, where they'd take a chartered jet at the Coastal Carolina Regional Airport in New Bern. "Gabby and I are a little worried about his vibes. He's disconnected from us, just as he is from you. But that's probably temporary. Normal for a man who just killed a warlord, saved a village and almost lost a leg. I wish you could come with us." Tal paused. "No, you're not a moldy olive. That's not what Gabby thinks."

"She knows I have panic attacks when I travel."

"You don't have any choice. We can't retrieve you fast enough. The storm's too big."

"He'll think I don't care."

"No, he won't. He's got broken ribs, he lost his spleen, and his left leg's a mess. He's on heavy medication. He won't even realize you're not there. And with any luck, we'll get him home soon. Jay knows a couple of generals."

"But what if he asks . . . "

"We'll tell him the truth. You're stuck in the mountains. You wanted to come, but you couldn't get out."

"Time's up," Gabby called. I heard her voice in the background. "Helicopter's waiting."

I bit back a groan.

Tal wrapped me in a psychic hug. "You listen to me. I'm the biscuit witch, and I *know* my food molds. Molds are the reason we have delicious mushrooms. Blue cheese, sake, and oh, penicillin, by the way. Yeast. Without molds there'd be no antibiotics, no bread, and no beer—which would make Gus *very* unhappy. I don't know why terrible things happen to sweet people like you. But the darkness gave you a charmer's gift, and maybe more than that. Maybe your moldy spots are growing a future we can't live without."

I thanked her and said goodbye, then sat in Alberta's office staring at the mic on the ham radio as if it might explode.

I can't be there for Gus when he needs me most.

"WELCOME TO GERMANY, Captain MacBride."

They sent me to Landstuhl. That's how bad this is.

Lights revolved, and people moved my body without me engaged in the process; conversations happened around me, but they were all ordinary. All among the living and the present. No psychic flavors, no intuitions, no kaleidoscope of sensations. Luce was hidden by walls and curtains; thousands of miles away, over the curve of the planet. Where were Mama and Dad, filling my senses with comforting whispers?

Tal and Gabby and Jay came and went. I heard their voices, saw them through bleary eyes, but never *felt* their emotions.

A cool washcloth dabbed my forehead. "Up and at 'em, soldier.

Wake up. Your sisters have assigned me to greet you, man to man." Jay's deep, boardroom drawl seeped through the ringing in my ears. "It's to inform you, man to man, that you still have a penis and testicles."

He's wiping my face with a washcloth, like I'm helpless. They're taking charge of me.

When we were kids growing up in the over-the-river backwoods of West Asheville, Jay, the richest orphan in western North Carolina, had himself dropped off at our house by George Avery, his lawyer and guardian. Without invitation or warning, Jay intended to make good on his father's pledge to redeem what the Wakefields had done to our grandparents.

Instead he ended up in a slug-out with me on the front lawn, while Tal made excited chirpy noises from her hiding place in a forsythia hedge and Gabby tried to smack him with a serving spoon. He'd taken one of her meat-stuffed pickles out of a smoker, tasted it, then tossed it in the hedge. That meant war.

I was back in that yard, wrestling him.

"Outta my face. Kick your ass. Where's the pickle?" My throat felt like a sandpaper tunnel. "Where's the goddamn pickle?" In my bleary, humiliated thoughts, it all came down to that.

"Your pickle's fine. I swear to you. The doctors explained to us that the first thing most soldiers want to know when they wake up is, 'Do I still have my junk?' Yours is right where it's supposed to be. I'm not really interested in playing 'Male Nurse Fantasy,' but if you insist, I'll snap a picture for you with my phone. I'd prefer that you just trust me."

My eyes felt gummy. I was weighted or weightless—hard to tell which. I heard the beeps of machines, the shush of an air compressor adjusting the mattress under me, and the voices filtered through speakers, somewhere. *Hospital.* Vague memories of being transported began to surface.

Where's Luce? I need Luce.

"Luce?"

Jay kept dabbing my face. "Snowstorm in the mountains. We couldn't get her out in time, or she'd be here. She desperately wanted to come."

It took all my effort to unglue my eyes. In the middle of the ordeal the washcloth came down on them, and I didn't protest. I blinked and saw dim outlines, and for a panicked moment thought I'd lost part of my eyesight. Then my vision cleared and I made out the hospital room, drapes drawn, light low, an edge of sunshine outlining a window. What were all those odd things in the foreground?

Those were me—left leg propped on cushions with steel pins and a frame attached to it. IVs went into my arms and side; a catheter tube snaked under the sheet down lower. Wires straggled across my bare chest, nursing at nipple-sized electrode pads stuck to the shaved spots in my chest hair. I felt . . . puffy, like a blow-up doll.

A hand appeared in front of my eyes, middle finger up. "How many do you see?" Jay asked. His voice was loud, the way people talk to an old person whose hearing aid battery's gone dead.

I turned my head toward him and raised my right arm to flip him off back, taking a tangle of IV's with it. The arm couldn't be mine. It was bloated.

Jay clamped a hand on my wrist. "Don't move around. They'll come in and rearrange your catheter. Neither of us want to be part of that."

I studied him, squinting. He was only six weeks into recovery from a near-fatal bullet wound to the chest. A little pale, a little thinner than his usual brawny self. A visitor's pass dangled over a gray sweater with a coffee stain on it. And his eyes were tired. Or maybe full of worry. For me.

I lowered my arm. On the edge of my brain, pain receptors said I'd regret the arm wrestling. My whole body was stuffed in a glove of drugs and bindings and surrounded by a halo of dark fear unlike anything I'd ever felt before. The fear of being flat on my back, broken, and unable to take care of myself or anyone else. But also, that emptiness. A world without the taste and flavor of Luce.

"Tell me," I whispered. "No bullshit."

Jay tossed the washcloth and pulled up a chair. "You have a punctured lung, broken ribs, a concussion, a really unhappy spleen—which has been donated to science, thank you—a lot of interesting shrapnel wounds that will give you fascinating scars to show the grandkids, and, last but not least, a seriously torn up lower left leg. The surgeons debated amputating it above the knee, but you're in the clear, for now. They've left some of the incisions open. Looking for infection."

They're cleaning debris out of me. They're hunting for more tiny pieces of dirt and shrapnel, and the exploded body of the man I killed. Pieces of Sarbanri. The bastard's vaporized body is inside my leg.

"Get. Him. *Out.*"

"Who, buddy?" Jay's voice was gentle. He didn't understand.

I tried to explain but the words made no sense.

"You'll get knee replacement surgery, and then the army is sending you home." He paused. "They don't want publicity. Wouldn't look good to court-martial a soldier who disobeyed orders to kill a sadistic warlord the U.S. put on its payroll. So . . . you're getting an honorable discharge. You're done. You're out."

"*Good.*" My voice was gravel on a washboard. It hurt to move my lips. "Call. Luce. Now."

"The storm's shut down everything at home. Tell me what you want her to know. Besides the fact that you're in one piece and you're coming home."

My eyelids sagged. "Tell her to watch her back. Have to move on this situation, pronto."

"What situation?"

"Him."

"Who?"

"All of him. Them."

I felt his hand on my shoulder. "She's safe. I swear to you."

A nurse marched in. "Awake and talking?"

"Yes, thank you. And he's doing pretty well, also."

She laughed, then began checking my tubes and fiddling with IV bags. Jay leaned down and spoke close to my ear. "You're a bonafide hero, in our book. And you're going home. Lucy's waiting to meet you."

Her blueberry and honey will come through now and conquer the blood and the fear.

But only her screams filled my darkness.

"Gus? *Gus.*" Jay shook me a little and touched the oxygen cannula taped under my nose. "He's breathing hard."

"I'll bump up his flow."

I could live with the physical damages from war. No problem. But if I'd lost my way of understanding people—life—through the taste and texture of the grapes and hops and grains and grasses that distilled into their thoughts . . .

I'd be disabled.

"MORE SNOW COMING. Shit." Alberta grunted as she chugged by on a tractor, heading toward the communal dorms. Ice dotted her ear-flapped gray-green hat. I had knitted it for her. She was short, thick, pug-nosed and burly. Threats and humiliations bounced off her aura like firecrackers thrown at a tank. "This is when I worry the most about

Tayton Hornsby. His wife gets mean when she's hemmed in. Lemme know if you get a wooly-sense on him."

I nodded. Tayton and the missus lived in a doublewide two miles from Rainbow Goddess. He did plowing and maintenance work for us. Tayton was physically huge but mentally small. His wife bullied him. I stroked my wool scarf. "Things have been better since I told him the rabbits don't hate him. If she eats them, they won't blame him."

Alberta grunted again and drove up the snowy slope, swaying like a large Hobbit. Her ear flaps bounced. A wool and rayon blend. Mixed signals, to me.

I went back to the barns to wrap more insulation around the hose bibs. I barely knew when I was touching them. Even the bitter cold couldn't penetrate my wool mittens. *Gus will be all right, the injuries aren't life threatening. His leg will heal. He'll come back inside me, inside my mind.*

Swaddled in coats, shawls, a sock cap, gloves, arm warmers, sweat pants under my skirt, and knee-high rubber boots, I fed livestock and helped break ice on the water troughs, toted firewood to the big hearths in the community house, and entertained bored kids by making sure war didn't break out over the selection of movies and games.

Two large propane-powered generators ran enough electrical service to keep the lights on at the main house, the dorm areas, and community center and, more important, the blowers that circulated heat from the gas furnaces. But not at my stall in the barn. "Come bunk on our couch," Macy ordered.

"I might sleep too sound and miss a call." I pulled out my cell phone, convinced it had buzzed. Snowflakes feathered the screen. Still dead.

By nightfall I couldn't sit still, couldn't even calm myself with yarn. Swaddled in layers of coats and shawls and a blanket, I plowed through the snow to the special spot in the pasture, dragging supplies behind me on a blanket. I sat down with the blanket and my skirt cushioned under me, and closed my eyes. Several dogs burrowed under the blanket and curled around my hips. Our combined breath puffed from the fabric tent in soft silver curls. Smoke signals.

I built a fire, set a camp grill over it, then placed a large stock pot atop the grill. I scooped snow into it first, then added vegetables and beef I'd already cooked on a gas camp stove in the barn. As if arranging china on a banquet table, I placed deep metal bowls in the snow alongside a bucket of silverware. I unwrapped loaves of bread and laid out blocks of butter.

Shadows formed in the snowy mist. A dozen of them, one using a cane, several crouching like assassins, and one on four paws. All of them carrying long rifles.

The lost and forgotten, veterans, most with PTSD and some wanted for minor crimes. Hiding in the vast woods and caves beyond my pasture. Protecting the farm from a distance, protecting me. The Knights had come to sit with me.

I couldn't bring Gus home; yet, I could bring the warrior spirit he embraced.

When they were all seated around the fire, holding steaming bowls of stew, Gutsy ordered, "Speak, Yarny. Whazzup with your captain?"

"He may walk with a limp. But he should be able to come home to a normal life."

When several of the Knights snorted I added, "I understand that 'normal' won't be the same for him. He's already not the same person. His . . . emotions. His reactions. That's why I want to ask you all some questions. He didn't suffer a head injury. And as far as we know, his psychological evaluations are on track with this type of experience and recovery."

Trey cleared his throat. "It may seem that way, at first."

"I'm hoping you all can tell me what might be going through his head."

"Everything," Sink said. Sink was lean, with jet-black hair braided in a long que down the front of a thick brown jacket smeared with dark stains that might be dried blood. Deer blood, I hoped. "Every fucking thing is going through his head, and he wishes it would stop."

"Or nothing," Cowboy added. "Like it's a big, empty room with no windows."

Gutsy swallowed a mouthful of stew, nodding as she did. "I had the *nothing*. Felt like my mind was blank as shit. Didn't start to see any light until I was racing the state patrol in Alabama." She paused, smiling. "They didn't catch me."

"I broke a Dumpster once."

We all looked at The Berg. Short for Iceberg. Six-five, at least, with a prosthetic left arm and a right arm as thick as a small tree. A vertical scar slashed one side of his dark-skinned face, making a deep dimple beside a mouth that rarely smiled.

"Ran over it with a jacked-up monster truck. Tires taller than me."

Sink craned his head. "Where the hell did you get a truck like that?"

"Stole it. I needed my psych meds adjusted."

"Speakin' of crazy," Cowboy said. He set his stew aside and fumbled in a backpack, producing a bulky plastic bag. The tousled hair and dazed eyes of several Barbie dolls peered out the top. Patton raised his muzzle from his bowl, sniffing at them. "Corporal Patton was having a weird day. He doesn't usually take kids' stuff. These came from the Shelton farm. Can you find a way to drop 'em off at the mailbox?"

I stashed the bag by my feet. Patton's heists mainly focused on towels and yard tools.

Cowboy's smile hardened. "Swear to me you'll return those dolls to the children. I don't steal from children. I don't harm children. Not anymore."

I felt the blood leaving my face. Bandit, slurping stew with his head down so far that the brim of his camo hat hid his face, looked up quickly. "He means in combat. Artillery."

My breath caught. "I would never harm a child. Or steal from one. You have my word."

Berg clamped a hand on his shoulder. "Deep breath. She's not the enemy, man."

"Steady," Trey ordered. "Settle down."

Cowboy shut his eyes, then opened them. "I apologize."

"No need. I understand."

"So, Yarny," Gutsy barked. "About your captain. We don't need to know anything else about him to tell you what's wrong with him. It's brain damage."

"But I told you . . . "

"His brains are rattled," Doc said. "That's not a clinical term, of course." Doc was the oldest of the Knights; fiftyish. He had been a surgeon in a field hospital. Other than that I only knew what I deduced. The broken veins on his nose combined with the image of a yarn that had been torn apart and mended at a weak spot. I sensed the challenge of addictions around him.

"It's called a Traumatic Brain Injury. TBI. Hell, kids playing high school sports get a TBI sooner or later. It's very common. In the best case scenario the person feels a little down, can't sleep, gets edgy. It goes away in a few days, a couple of weeks. The not-so-mild cases can make the person lose words and memories. There's a whole range of symptoms."

"Some people get mad as a fucking rattlesnake." That comment came from Dragon, who wagged her spoon at me and hissed.

This must be why Gus lost his psychic ability. "In the worst cases, does the person eventually heal?"

"Yes, but it could take months."

Berg said, "Your captain probably feels like a zombie right now." Berg lifted his artificial arm. "Even though he didn't lose his leg, it's a foreign object. It doesn't work the way it should. He can't control it right now; he can't depend on it. He's crippled."

Sink leaned toward me, so close to the camp fire that snow melted on his jacket. "He can't see himself anymore," Sink said softly, his accent rolling the *more* into a dark skein of meaning. "He's blind inside."

"Can a TBI affect a soldier's basic senses? Vision, hearing, sense of smell—"

"I heard Christmas music for a month," Berg said. "And it was July. In the psych ward, they called me 'The Summer Santa.'"

Gutsy smiled. "I liked seeing halos and sparkles, but when I stepped off curbs and my eyes said I was free-falling from ten-thousand feet, well . . . let's just say it takes a lot to scare a New York driver, but there's a few whose assholes still clinch up every time they think of me flailing like a duck right in front of their bumpers."

At the corner of her right eye, the slightest twitch appeared. She looked away.

Bar Code was watching me with his head tilted. A long black braid hung down one shoulder, dividing the camo pattern on his jacket into twisted faces. I blinked to erase the image. He said slowly, "I come from a family of chefs. They own the finest restaurant in Miami. I was to retire from the Army after twenty years, and become one of them." He lifted a hand toward his braid then pulled the swath of hair aside, revealing a bald area above one ear and a divot deep enough to hide a marble. "But my ability to taste food, it is gone." He lowered the braid. "I never want my family to know."

Pain and protest roared inside me. Suddenly I wanted to leap at them, hug and hold them, tell them we would not surrender to the valley of the shadow of death, and we would fear no evil.

I will help Gus heal somehow . . . but what if I can't, what if the valley of shadows is too deep? And what if my own valley is too deep?

13

"I WANT TO HEAR Lucy's voice. Now. Or I'll use the copter to come there and track her down."

"She's safe and sound," Alberta told him. "Stop stalking her."

Alberta and Macy sat stone-faced in front of the ham radio. Kerosene lanterns flickered in the warm confines of the office. The scent of hearth-baked cornbread filled the farm house. The sound of crackling firewood mingled with the low voices of women and children who were watching a movie on a generator-supplied TV in the living room. They were wrapped in deep, cozy afghans I'd made.

I stood rigidly, staring at the radio unit as if Kern could reach through it and grab me by one arm.

"Don't lie about my motivations," Kern snapped. "I'm in charge of your part of the county. When I ask for a roll call, everyone answers. It's a security measure. Don't make me come up there. I'll do background checks on every new resident, and you know what that means. ICE will get involved."

Alberta clicked the mic. "You're not worried one goddamn bit about Lucy's safety. You're trying to find out if she went to Germany to see the captain."

Macy held up a sheet of paper for me to read.

NARCISSIST, she'd written on it. SOCIOPATH.

"Let me talk to her," he shouted. "Or I'll be the worst enemy you and your cunt girlfriend ever made."

That word raised the challenge to a whole new level. Macy grabbed Alberta's wrist before Alberta, furious, flipped the mic switch again. "No threats," Macy ordered. "No pissing contest, please."

Alberta nearly growled.

I reached between them and pushed the switch. "I'm here. What do you want?"

"Why do you play these games?"

Macy scrawled on another sheet. GASLIGHTING.

One of her favorite warnings about toxic relationships. *Gaslighting.*

A bully's attempts to convince his victim that everything is her fault or merely her imagination. The term came from a 1940s Ingrid Bergman film set in turn-of-the-century London. Ingrid's new husband wants her inheritance. He uses many tactics to convince her she's losing her mind, including tricks with the gas lights in their home.

"The games are all yours," I said. My voice sounded far stronger than I felt.

"He calls you *Luce*, doesn't he?"

"Stop spying on me."

"He's a traitor, *Luce*. He disobeyed orders and killed a U.S. asset. He should be going to prison, not coming home with an honorable discharge. Wakefield pulled strings for him. I told you the MacBrides are nothing without Wakefield money. *Now* do you believe me?"

"You wanted to know that I'm here. Well, now you know. Don't ever call me *Luce*, again." I released the switch. Breathing hard, I wobbled to a chair and sat down.

"I'll get you some wine," Macy said. "We have to have a toast." She sprinted from the room.

Alberta swiveled in her chair, slapping her hands on her denimed knees. "Parmenter, you make me proud."

I discreetly rested a hand on the slim outline hidden under my skirt. The only time my hands didn't shake was on wool or guns. Guns were the opposite of wool. They had no soul. They didn't talk to me the way wool did. No love, no memories, no regrets. I considered them a blessedly neutral therapist.

I traced the outline.

Only Gus can call me Luce.

I HAVE STEEL PINS inside my leg. And a new knee. I'm made of manmade parts, now.

Tal and Gabby held my hands, discussed me, made plans for my future, and told me they loved me.

Where is Luce?

Why isn't she here?

My sisters had always come across as one taste, to me. A sweet and sour beer, wrestling for which flavor would come out on top; they weren't good at sharing . . . sharing what?

Me.

"You're in the recovery room, Gussy. Your knee replacement went off without a problem. We're here. We love you. Gabby and I are right beside you. Look at his skin. It's got the texture of an over-baked wheat loaf. Sun damage. He hasn't been moisturizing or using enough sunscreen. When we get him to my house we'll tell him that skin treatments at Bah Spa are part of his physical therapy. We'll figure out how to convince him. Even Doug goes to Bah Spa. I hope he likes Doug."

A snort. I knew that snort. Gabby. "Tell him Lucy wants to give him a lanolin-and-lavender grease rub. He'll go for that. He does look crusty and pale. Let's be honest. He's going to have to recalibrate his pressure cooker, if you know what I mean. Deal with being an invalid. Come to terms with the distinct possibility he may eventually lose this leg if it doesn't heal well. Even if it does, he'll walk with a limp."

"Why are you being such a downer?"

"Because something else is wrong with him. That's why we can't communicate the way we used to. And . . . we're not his baby sisters anymore. We're grown women, Tal. We've waited all these years for him to come home and lead the way. We were conditioned to believe we needed our big brother, our man of the family, to build a family business. But we don't. He'll have to accept that he's not the leader of this family anymore."

"Look, all that's important is that he comes home, and gets well, and the three of us—along with Jay and Doug—come up with a plan for the future of Free Wheeler. All of us have a piece of our heart in it."

"We don't even know if he'll stay in North Carolina. Especially if things don't work out with Lucy."

"They will."

"*Tal.* Even if there hadn't been a blizzard, she wouldn't have been able to . . . "

For the next minute they spoke too softly for me to hear. I caught a word here and there. *Damaged.* And *broken.*

Skunk Fruit Ale. *That's their brew name. My sisters. Sweet with an underbelly of stink.*

Going home to Luce. Damaged. Broken. Both of us.

No more fighting for lost causes.

I have to tell her not to go there.

Not to leave the farm.

Why? Not go where?

I don't know how much time passed, but eventually I realized I was back in my private room. "Hullo, Captain America," said a smoky

British voice. That voice had kept me company in a lot of bars and beds. "I hear that I'm the 'other woman' now. That's fine. I didn't reach my exalted state of fame and misery by running away from competition."

Hands slipped over my face, stroking my jaw. "I hear she's a wounded little dove. Exactly your type. She and I obviously have a lot in common." I knew the smell of that lonely kitchen. Roast beef left out to dry. Congealed butter on the verge of going sour, hiding her grief and memories, pressing the pain points like an infection we shared.

Hana.

14

Yarnspinner—

WE'VE GOT SATELLITE gear that can patch you through to Captain MacBride. G will bring it to you—recon with you at the usual spot if you send OK. BTW, we checked stats at Landstuhl. Captain is out of surgery and Good. N. Owl.

My breath streamed into the cold sunshine. My brain flooded with relief.

"Hey. Parmenter!"

Alberta's voice.

I looked up.

"Doc Firth radioed for help. Come talk to him."

So far, Doug had rescued ten motorists, a hiker, five dogs, ten cats, several lambs, two donkeys, and four hamsters.

"I need knitted blankets, ya kin? And any kinda sweaters you can make for pigs and hens. It's cold enough on the farms to freeze the willy off a polar bear."

Since his deep Scottish burr carried throughout the main house, and a dozen women were in the kitchen at that time, laughter erupted.

We'll knit for ya Doc, but can you show us your willy?

Soon I and the others filled the shed where I stored all the finished yarns. Hands flew with needles and crochet hooks. I guided and instructed and watched with satisfaction as stacks of small blankets and critter sweaters grew tall.

A farm cat leapt onto a table and nuzzled me. I jumped at the brush of his snowy fur on my hand.

It burns.

I stepped outside where the rest couldn't see me examining my completely unharmed skin. The sensation ebbed then returned even hotter. I thrust my hand into a snow bank.

The wool sense came first. Then the faintest, distant smell. I examined my hand for burns while I searched the horizon, where snow-laden clouds still pancaked the Ten Sisters.

A blue-gray smudge pushed into the lowest clouds between the smallest mountain top, Little Clara. There were five townships in Jefferson County. Voting districts, post office routes—the names were just oddities on a map to outsiders. Corn Haint. Big Walk. Turtleville, Crossroad's Cove.

And Devil's Knob.

That township, named for the giant rock that jutted high above the western side of Hog Back Mountain, was the most remote part of the county, home to only a dozen fulltime residents, and served by only one old, crumbling, macadam road that dead-ended at the entrance to a wistful fairytale. The Everlast Inn.

I had seen photos and Technicolor postcards in albums Delta kept at the café. As much as Delta disliked Howard—probably the only cousin of hers she had ever rejected—she spoke warmly of his mother and the Bavarian-style hotel Marvis DeClare Monzell had built in the shadow of Devil's Knob during the 1950s. Marvis dreamed of an Alpine resort that would bring fame to the high peaks.

Everyone else nicknamed it *The Chicken Haus.* It failed within a dozen years, and when she died soon after, Howard turned it into his private retreat, where he threw parties for his business cronies.

"Marvis had the Whimsy," Delta told me. "Whether it came from drinking too much or cussin' God for having given her Howard as her only child, it was a special light. Howard dimmed it."

Nausea rose in my throat.

Fire. At the same time, a skein twisted hard inside my chest. *Pike.*

"GET OUTTA MY sight, goddamn you. You've been helping Monzell hide these women up here. Holding them prisoner. Like slaves. Running a goddamn whore house."

"Pike, calm down. They *work* for Howard."

"Dancing naked and giving blow jobs to his business buddies?"

"They're housekeepers and cooks and bartenders."

"On the side, you mean. Don't bullshit me, boy. Not a one of them has a green card. This godforsaken place is so isolated they couldn't run away. All the outside doors were locked. Two women burned to death because they couldn't even get out into the goddamn yard when the fire started. You piece of shit. I've given you every chance to be a good man, to become a good law officer. Cleo begged me to put up with your shit just a little longer. Now, I'm done. I'm gonna throw the book at Howard and you, too. You're no nephew of mine. Not anymore."

"Here's the thing, *Uncle* Pike. I don't give a fuck whether you consider me family or not. I'm going to run this county, and this state, and even the whole country, one day. There's nothing you can do to stop me or Howard."

"Sheriff! We got a third death. EMTs can't get her heart going again. She's burned real bad. The medivac copter's still twenty minutes out. She's lost."

"Collateral damage," Kern said. "Just another immigrant taking American jobs. Nobody cares."

"Sheriff, don't! Don't shoot him!"

DELTA

Pike was twenty-five years old and six-five and built like a big stone chimney. A house could fall down around him and he'd still stand in the lost wreck of the homestead, doing guard duty. Justice showed in his eyes. He went off to Vietnam a raw-boned yahoo and came home knowing how to kill. How to be a tough-but-fair country sheriff like his daddy and granddaddy before him. Wouldn't talk about the war. He bought a big motorcycle and smoked weed and drank and raised Hell. All the girls wanted to belong to him. But not me.

I wanted him to belong to me. I used my kitchen charms to win him. He believed the law is sacred. He took care of people. He took care of me. I took care of him. Oh, my Lard, we were a hot ticket. Love is made on hope and sorrow and the desperate business of living life instead of life living you.

PIKE HAD HAD a heart attack.

The Chicken Haus was no more. Three women were dead.

Had the mysterious Alaina, aka Megan, set the old hotel on fire? Was she a *freelance* arsonist?

"I can't get a reading on that," I confessed to Macy and Alberta. "But I can tell you those women were forced to do a lot more than clean rooms and make beds."

I sat on the edge of a hard, vintage secretary's chair in front of the farm's ham radio, waiting for more news on the fire and Pike's condition. He'd been helicoptered to the nearest hospital, which meant across the state line in Tennessee.

"Maybe they set fire to the place so they could escape," Macy said. "Opal tells me they were locked in."

Alberta grunted. "Either way, they're fuckin' doomed unless we can find them. They know too much. Monzell will never let them talk to the authorities."

"And it's not like immigration will be on their side," Macy said. "They'll end up in a camp."

Alberta grimaced. "We have to figure out where Kern has stashed them." She tapped me on the forehead. "You got a GPS in there?"

"I'm trying my best to find them." I wound a scarf in my hands.

We all flinched when Kern's voice came over the receiver. He gave his call sign and the usual intro jargon. Then he added, "Sheriff Kern Burkett calling for Lucy Parmenter. Official business. Confidential."

Sheriff? Macy mouthed at us.

Alberta picked up the mic. "Sonuva . . . "

I clamped a hand over hers. "I'll talk to him. He's tangled and on the defensive."

"Tangled?"

"When strands of wool tangle, if you're not careful about the way you handle them, they'll mat and turn into felt. Tough and unworkable."

Macy gently pried the mic out of Alberta's fist. "We need to keep him fluffy." She handed the mic to me.

I shut my eyes, pushed a button, and replied with the farm's call sign, then, "This is Lucy."

"I said 'Confidential.' Are you alone?"

Alberta and I traded a look. Macy held up a sheet of paper. PLAY HIS GAME.

"Yes. I'm in charge of monitoring the radio for updates on Pike."

"I gave him CPR. Saved his life."

I spread my hands on Alberta's desk. I watched my fingers quiver. *Careful.* "That's what we've heard. You did a good job."

"Yes, I did my best. I called to tell you that I'm in charge, now."

"As Acting Sheriff. Of course."

"No. The county commission has named me sheriff. Pike is done."

Alberta, Macy, and I traded a horrified look.

"But . . . is that legal? There's an election coming . . . "

"Let the traitorous lawyers fight over the details. I'm the sheriff now. Constitutionally, sheriffs are the only legitimate law officers in this country. We're the only ones who are chosen by the people, for the people. The Constitution demands that we rule above police chiefs, federal agents, judges. We're even higher that the Supreme Court. America is finally getting back to its true greatness. What happened today was meant to be. My destiny. *Our* destiny. The best and the brightest. The strongest and the smartest. Survival of the fittest."

My stomach twisted. Kern went on, "You know that I did right by Pike. He was my opposition in the election, and some people will always distrust me. But you . . . you see the real me. You see into people's minds and spirits."

Humor him and his twisted interpretation of authority. "There's no doubt in my mind you did what you . . . what you had to do."

"I need you more than ever."

Chills went up my spine. "Could I help you with those poor women who worked at the hotel? Are they Hispanic? I speak fluent Spanish. I went on missionary trips to Central and South America with my dad."

"Don't worry about them. They're well-fed and well-paid little *mamacitas*. Here on work visas. My father-in-law is taking care of them personally. Last I saw, they were in a convoy of trucks behind a bulldozer, making their way to the Daw Ridge plant. Howard was in the convoy with them, like a father figure. They'll bunk at the plant for a couple of days, and when the snow and ice clear they'll get re-homed."

Re-homed. Like unwanted pets.

Clouds began to part. I wound my scarf around the hand that held the mic. "Any clue what caused the fire?"

"We'll do an investigation, but my money is on a *mamacita* who stole a bottle of tequila from the bar, got drunk, and dropped a lit cigarette."

"They must have been freezing up there, with the power off. Maybe they were trying to build a fire. To stay warm."

"Are you questioning my judgment?"

I sucked in a breath. "No . . . I . . . look, I need to confess. I was worried about you when I heard there'd been a fire."

"My God, sweetie. Music to my ears. Here's what I'm going to do. Appoint you as the department's spokesperson. I'll even deputize you. You can use your voodoo to help people accept the new rules. Help them understand that freedom can't exist without order and discipline and sacrifice. Agreed?"

I stared at the mic, unable to force my thumb onto the speaker button. The scarf twisted around my arm, twirling like a snake up and then around my shoulders, the tasseled ends dancing. Alberta slashed a *Cut* signal across her throat. Both she and Macy leapt for the controls.

I held onto the microphone with white-knuckled fists. "I'd be honored."

"Are you sure no one else can overhear us?"

"Yes."

"Amber doesn't have to know about you and me. We'll make it

work." He paused. "Eighty eight."

Love you, in ham radio lingo.

"Say it back," he ordered.

I released the mic. It clattered to the desk. Alberta ripped the mic cord from its plug. We sat in silence. A kerosene lamp hissed on a shelf, flickering shadows of flames on the walls. I watched my scarf return to an ordinary reality. The tassels curled into patterns on the desk.

It's your time, Miss Lucy. You can see what to do.

Opal put her small arms around me. Suddenly I realized how young she'd been. No more than a child.

Why did you die young?

Because no one like you was there to stand up for me.

"They're at the café," I said. "And I'm the only one who can get them out."

"THERMAL BLANKET," Alberta said, stuffing the folded silver fabric into a bulging bag strapped the back of the saddle. It was already filled with scarves, mittens and sock caps. She followed the blanket with various pouches. "Flare gun. Matches. First Aid kit."

"Granola bars," Macy added, handing her another packet.

"GPS tracker." Alberta strapped a band around my wrist. She held up the hunting equivalent of a bad-ass switchblade. The scabbard was leather, etched with a skull and crossbones. "Utility knife. Wear it around your neck at all times."

I dutifully put the scabbard's braided leather strap over my head, and patted it gently among the canyons of my jacket and shawls.

Brim snorted. She was not happy that I'd coaxed her from the warm barn.

Friends don't make friends go out in the cold.

She stood in the knee-deep snow with her long, gray-brown ears pinned back and her upper lip wrinkled in a sneer. Her lower lip, an agile creature that operated separately from the rest of her head, protruded in a pout. Occasionally it tried to suck in one of her hackamore reins, like an old woman rolling a wad of chew tobacco.

The hackamore had long metal shanks attached to a braided nose piece. Pull on the reins and the nose piece tightened. Stop, turn left, turn right. For a pleasant equine and a skilled rider, the hackamore was plenty.

In Brim's case, I just prayed she'd halt before we hit a tree. Dad put me on ponies at church carnivals. I always fell off. People snicker when the minister's daughter falls off a Shetland pony. It's seen as righteous penance.

Brim's angry ears flattened even more. Her big, brown eyes shifted my way with betrayal. *Friends don't use friends as pack animals.*

Cold air pummeled my face with intense sensations, alive with meaning. I saw every tiny hair on the dark skin around the smooth round jewel of her beautiful oculus. The dark well of the pupil had a fire deep inside it; not a hellish one that deserved her name but a heart of bleak, dull sorrows.

I pulled my top shawl over my head and swept it around her head in a hugging motion. We stood there, tented inside the wool-scented warmth, our heads bent together. For a moment she drew her head up, blowing hard out of her nostrils. I waited. Slowly, she relaxed. I leaned my face against the hard, bony plane of her temple.

Thank you, my friend. I am afraid of this journey. I need your help.

She snuffled my shoulder, then blew out a long breath.

I will carry you.

"Last but not least." Alberta stuck an extra clip of bullets into the bag. "You *do* have your Lady Parts gun on you, right?"

I patted my lower stomach. Heavy artillery guarding the mound of Venus.

Macy stepped to one side, blonde hair feathering the fleece-lined hood of her coat, mittened hands clutched in front of her, breath puffing white. "It's not supposed to snow again today. You should have no problem getting to the café in two hours, tops." She grabbed my gloved hand. "Be careful."

"I will. But we have to get those women out of there. I just have to figure out *how*."

Brim shifted ominously. I patted her neck. *If there were any other way, my friend, I would not ask you to do this.*

No answer. She was sulking.

Macy tucked a small canister of pepper spray into a deep pocket of my skirt. "In case you need to season a salad," she said wanly. Macy watched me sadly, as if I were an Inuit about to cast off on a lonely ice floe. Judging by my knitted gray leggings, my all-weather knee-high boots, my long woolen skirt, and multiple shirts and shawls, I might open up to reveal smaller Russian dolls inside.

Alberta put a thickly jacketed arm around Macy. "She's tougher than she looks, honey. I did a good job. Hell, I'm hoping to upgrade her from her little lady pistol to a .38."

"I'll be fine," I said. "Brim and I are a team."

"She looks very unhappy," Macy said.

Alberta scowled at me. "What if this mean dyke of a mule throws you off and heads back here? Do you really *know* how to control this mule, Parmenter?"

I slowly eased a boot into the broad wooden stirrup on Brim's saddle, then swung up. I gathered the reins. "I know how to hold on," I said.

SNOW DRIFTED among the steep hollows and curving ridges around Free Wheeler.

Each of Brim's plowing footsteps sent echoes into the earth and through my bones. The air came alive; blue-gray in the frosted sunlight, with mysterious whorls of dark, earthy currents rising from the snow and swirling around the empty buildings.

I grabbed the edge of a shawl. The wool, ancient in its magic, grounded me.

This is real, Miss Lucy, Opal whispered. *This right here is a kingdom over a kingdom under a mountain and beside a river of death. You're meant to save it.*

I swayed dizzily atop Brim's back. A saddle has an erotic quality, spreading and intimate. I moved on four legs now, not two. I was much taller, and I walked the earth as a new animal. I put a shaking hand on Brim's shaggy shoulder. *Thank you, again.*

I carry you.

As Brim plodded down the lane between the haunted, empty brick shops with their boarded windows and chained doors I kept glancing to my right, at the woods and hollows and caves where the Knights hid.

Brim stumbled. "Easy, easy," I coaxed. She recovered, carefully putting one hoof ahead of the other, sinking through the soft white layers to the old cobbled main street. *Clop.* A solid foundation, there.

I glimpsed movement to my right. I pulled on the reins. Brim swiveled her head toward the motion, too.

Suddenly a tall figure separated himself from the background, and then another, shorter one. Gutsy, my feminine guide to all things warrior. Berg, a six-five mountain with a prosthetic right arm inside his coat.

Both Berg and Gutsy were covered in bulky white jumpsuits with white hoods and ski masks. Even their rifles were wrapped in white cloth. Gutsy signaled to me with a forefinger. Then she pointed to the top of the village general store.

The hair stood up on the back of my neck. I turned Brim and stared, my heart racing, into the snowy forest. Brim raised her head and sniffed the wind, then snorted.

Megan, aka Alaina.

She raised from a squat on the roof, camouflaged in white—like Gutsy and Berg. A rifle was slung over her shoulder. She held up a hand. More of a salute than a wave.

Flames rose up around her. Snow and ice dripped from the eaves, shimmering into deep, glowing puddles.

She's one of them. Not an enemy.

I WAS BAGGAGE, being prepped for transport. Oxygen tank nestled between my thighs, IV pouches piled on top of me like ready-to-microwave dinners. Flying stateside courtesy of Uncle Sam on a military medical plane, then transferring to Jay's chartered jet.

One last leg in my military career, then cut free.

Luce. Talk to me. If anybody can get through, you can.

I felt Tal's hand on my arm. Every physical sensation was strange. The part of me that knew what it might mean was vacant. "Gus," she whispered. "We're still trying to get in touch with Lucy, I promise you."

"We're not going to tell Lucy about Hana." Gabby's voice.

I kept my eyes half-shut. Even the single light over my bed hurt. "Nothing to tell. Was over a long time ago. And Luce knows."

I heard more whispers. Jay's low voice, joining the chorus. Then he leaned over me. I caught a whiff of bourbon and cigars. "I can pay Hana off if she's just here for money."

"She's here because she's in trouble again. She's scared."

"Hana always has problems. We understand why, but you need to concentrate on healing, not trying to babysit her."

"I made a promise to Hepswith. What happened to him . . . what she saw . . . "

"All right, she can stay," Gabby interjected. "But let us keep her at a distance. You don't have your kitchen charms at the moment, big brother. You're a bat flying with no radar."

"Then I'll have to slam into a few walls."

"Trust *our* radar."

I began to drift into another sleep-drugged cycle. "Just . . . let her . . . hang around."

"Okay, but on our terms, not hers."

Gabs moved to a corner along with Tal. Very low voices. Not low enough.

"He's asleep. Good. We can't let that soul-sucking demon near him."

"Gus is not going to be unfaithful to Lucy. You know that."

"Not intentionally. But you and I both know how Hana plays her games."

"He'll stay with Doug and me. She won't have access. We have a big bedroom at the back of the house. It's where Doug stores veterinary supplies. We'll renovate it and add handicapped access to the bathroom."

"He'll need a wheelchair. Let's get him a super-charged motorized one. He liked motorcycles when we were growing up in California."

"Jay will set up a checking account for him. He'll have plenty of money to play with."

"Yes! Gus always talks about starting a brewery. Let's encourage him to start planning. Something to keep him busy during rehab."

"Tom Mitternich will work with him on the architectural design. At Free Wheeler. It's time we made a decision about its future."

"Put a beer brewery in that abandoned ghost town?"

"If the investment fails, so what? Let's just get Gus motivated. And, hopefully, Lucy will . . ."

"That situation is outside our control. We should tell him about her history. Her . . . liabilities. For her sake, not just his."

"No." Tal's firm voice. "That's between her and Gus. We promised her."

"Look, Baby Sister, preserving food means stopping its original life. You save it, but it's not the living thing it once was. You heat it, you add salt and vinegar, you put it in a jar and seal out the air. It's beautiful, it's useful, it's special. But it's not alive, anymore. That's what I get from Lucy. She's never going to break out of her jar and be fully alive, again. I don't want Gus stuck protecting yet another hopeless soul."

"Like us?" Tal's voice. Angry. "Like he joined the Army rather than compromise our relationship with the Rodriquez family?"

"He seduced our sister. He broke the family bond."

"Our adopted sister. And Amelia Rodriguez was five years older than him. And he was only eighteen. And she was the aggressor."

"He abandoned us."

"He made a mistake. He took responsibility for it. They kicked him out."

"*I* took care of you after he left. Never forget that."

"Oh, as in always looking for a substitute for Jay while pretending you were a big independent California woman and I was just your little stupid cookie-baking sister? Why do you think I left for New York?"

"You didn't have to leave. You deserted me."

"'You deserted me."

"This is all old history. You've got Doug now. You and Eve caught the golden ring on the carousel. So did I, with Jay. Now let's see if we can help Gus catch that ring, too."

"I agree. But don't ever talk trash about Lucy to me. Never again. She protected Eve from my ex's goons. Don't ever . . . "

"You're smelling like burned bread. Calm down."

"And you stink like rotten peppers. I love you, but rotten!"

"Your brother's still awake," Jay said grimly. "He's blinked about fifty times in the past minute. You might want to apologize to him."

He had my back.

My sisters converged on me, each grasping a hand. They didn't say a word out loud. In the past, everything between us would have been said inside our circle, stronger than any spoken language.

"I can't hear you that way anymore," I said hoarsely. "Just leave me alone."

They left the room. No one was happy. Especially not me.

THE BROAD AND majestic Cove sprawled beyond the fringe of skeletal oaks, with the wonder of the Ten Sisters behind it. Snow lay high against the porches of Delta and Pike's big farm house. The snow was stunning in its illusion; its white was made up of endless shades of color. Above the mists of the gray-white sky the Ten Sisters etched themselves in delicate forevers.

Everything worried me. The exquisitely mysterious shades of blue. They worried Brim, too. She laid her ears back and tossed her head. We were *sympatico.*

The café loomed ahead, down the alley of a snowy lane hooded by oaks sheathed in ice. The sounds of guitars and fiddles rose from the rambling former farm house.

"Miss Lucy!" Larry yelled as I rode up a back trail behind the Crossroads Café. He waved from the end of the snowy lane, his full-length apron flopping around a tall body that remained lanky even padded by a blue quilted jacket. His title was assistant kitchen manager; his main job duties were bussing tables and washing dishes. He loped up to us. His fuzzy blue hat had huge ear flaps; they flew back like the ears of a happy Beagle when he ran. "Look at you, out here alone! Hey, Brimmy!"

Brim didn't try to bite him. A mark in his honor.

"I came to offer scarves and caps." I patted the big bundle tied behind me.

"I think I found some rockycocker tracks over by Stirwater Creek! I took pictures and measurements! The snow covered them before I could make plaster casts! But I'll be ready next time!"

"Have you seen anything else strange around here?"

"Just Miz Cleo." His expression fell as he strode along beside us.

"She's stranger than usual?"

He nodded. "I guess 'cause Sheriff Pike got sick. She's yelling at everybody. I don't like it when Miz Delta is away and Miz Cleo's in charge."

"How many people are staying here during the storm?"

He pulled his phone from a pocket and waggled it at me. "Thirty-seven. I keep count and record their data."

"You make an excellent observer."

"Scientist," he corrected solemnly.

"Scientist. I misspoke. I apologize."

He sighed. "I admit I don't have the whole number. I didn't get to count the ones in the Yellow Jellyfish Room."

My ears perked. What Larry called the Yellow Jellyfish Room was otherwise named the Turse Nettie Dining Room. One of Delta's great aunts from the Nettie branch. Turse had been a masterful flower gardener, Delta said. The wallpaper was a florid swirl of blooms and vines. It did appear to be swimming out to sea.

"Who's in the Jellyfish Room?"

"Some girls that aren't from around here. I got just one peep at them when they came through the back hall before Miz Cleo grabbed me by my ear. It hurt." He raised a flap to show me the red mark.

"Can you guess how many there were?"

"I never guess, Miss Lucy. That would be unscientific."

"How about giving me your best estimate? Just a hypothetical count."

"More than ten. Fewer than thirteen."

"And you haven't seen them outside that room, since?"

"No. Only Miz Cleo gets to go in the Jellyfish Room."

We reached the back of the café—its kitchen entrance, storage sheds, ice machine, and outdoor freezer. Icicles hung from the whitewashed eaves and the railings around the kitchen porch. Larry bolted ahead. "I better get back to work. I only have one good ear left."

As he disappeared through a double door wide enough for deliveries, I climbed down from Brim and removed her hackamore. I fed her a granola bar. *Wait here.*

She crunched the treat and air-kicked an invisible annoyance.

I followed a shoveled trail to the front veranda. People were camping there. There was music and bonfires and laughter, and the snow had been shoveled from the graveled parking lot. Tents sprouted throughout.

Cleo strode onto the veranda, her short arms planted akimbo on her hips. Snow dappled her graying hair. Food stains smeared her full chef's apron. As she eased down the salted steps she watched me warily from under the brim of a baseball cap with MOTHER OF A VETERAN embroidered on it. Dark bags cusped her eyes. "Did Delta send you to spy on me?"

"I came to bring some scarves and . . . "

"She blames Kern for what happened to Pike. It's not fair."

"I haven't talked to her. I only know that . . . "

"She says Howard kept women up there for sex and Kern helped hide them. That's not true. There were women, yes, but they were maids and cooks."

"I have scarves—"

"Kern's taking care of them. They'll be on their way back to Mexico as soon as the snow breaks."

"Do you know where they are? I speak Spanish—"

"You speak *heathen.* I see what you're up to. Nosing around. Why else would you be here? Out and about by yourself. Miss Scaredy Cat working up the gumption to cause trouble."

"Please let me talk to them. We can move them to Rainbow Goddess. Help them. That's all I care about at the moment."

Cleo grabbed my arm so hard it hurt through all the coverings. "You want to cast untruths about Kern. You've hurt his marriage, you've chased him but pretended to be innocent, and now you'll say something ugly was going on up yonder and he's involved. I won't let you spread lies about him."

Your other son—the one who lost a leg in Iraq—is harboring a group of damaged veterans in the woods at Free Wheeler. You haven't been able to find Trey for two years. But you're worried about Kern?

"Let go of me."

She shook me, but it wasn't violent; it was desperate. "Pike is fighting for his life, and Delta depends on me to run things here. You've got to help me. Work with me."

"Let me see those women."

She shoved me away. "Go back to your goddess farm. Go. *Git.*"

Suddenly, I understood. "I feel the waves of guilt pouring off you. Kern's not a foster child you adopted. *You gave birth to him.*"

Her face froze in a chilly mask. "If I go inside and come back and you're still here," she said in a low voice, "I'll shoot you."

IF A MULE CAN tiptoe, Brim did her best. We had a brief chance to accomplish our mission. I based my hopes on Cleo's arrogance; it never occurred to her that I was capable of this subterfuge. She simply assumed I'd turned tail and left the property.

Brim followed me along a shoveled path behind the café. When we reached a window in the Turse Nettie dining room, I stood beneath it, my head on a level with the bottom sill. My heart pounded.

Gus, I could use some advice. I want you to be proud of me. Failure is not an option.

I climbed into the saddle and steered Brim so close to the window my knee brushed the screen. Beyond the lacy curtains, a dozen young women huddled around a table, hands clasped, heads together. I glimpsed faces swollen from crying and desperate with fear.

Here goes.

I pulled out my bad-ass knife, flicked it open, and punctured the screen with it. The mesh cut easier than expected. I notched a hole large enough to stick my hand through. Balling a fist, I put it inside and knocked softly on the glass.

The group swiveled toward me, mouths open, hands rising to throats. Scared. "*Una amiga,*" I said slowly, mouthing the words so they might lip read. "I am a friend. *Ven conmigo por favor.* Come with me, please."

No one moved. Suspicion fringed them. I put a hand to my heart, then gestured for them to come. Still, no one moved . . . except one. She was small and delicate; swamped inside baggy pants and an oversized coat. Thick black hair ringed her face in a heavy braid. She went from frowning at me in puzzlement to a wide-eyed gasp.

She turned to the others. I couldn't hear what she said, but she was clearly excited. She pointed to her hair, then at me.

The rest shifted nervously but regarded me with less fear.

My ally rushed to the window. She unlatched it and struggled to raise the heavy frame. The others joined her warily, their sharp eyes on me the whole time.

As the window rose in their merged hands, the first woman placed her palms on the icy screen. "You're the moon witch!" she whispered in lightly accented English. She pointed to my pale hair and rapidly explained to the others in Spanish. That I was the mind reader from the women's refuge.

"I'm here to help," I told them. Trying not to mimic Arnold Schwarzenegger, I intoned, "Come with me if you want to live."

"What do we do?"

"Pry this screen off. Climb out. As quietly as possible."

Within seconds the screen toppled aside. I climbed off Brim. "Here. Reach over and hold onto the saddle horn to help you get down."

As Brim gave me the evil eye, each woman levered herself through the open window. I unloaded my Santa bag of scarves and hats. Though all the women had coats and gloves, they eagerly donned the new items. "We have a long walk," I told them in Spanish. "Stay in a single line behind her." I pointed to Brim. "She'll make a path through the snow."

Mounted on Brim again, I led the way. I took a path that skirted the property through deep woods hooded in evergreens. Better hidden, but would add nearly an hour to the long trek in freezing temperatures.

I headed for Free Wheeler.

BY THE TIME WE reached the old town, daylight had begun to fade and the temps had dropped. I now walked in front of Brim, staggering in the snow as she followed me. Three of the smallest women sat astride her, much to Brim's sneering disgust. The one I acknowledged as their leader, Maria, had a white-knuckled grip on the saddle horn.

"We're going to stop here," I announced, pointing to the bakery. It'll be warm and safe. You'll wait inside while I ride the rest of the way and bring back help."

"What is this place?" Maria asked, sharing the furtive looks of dismay. Alarm and distrust circled them in steely threads.

I gave them the abbreviated history.

"But who owns it? What if they find out we're here?"

I thought for a moment. They wanted profound reassurance.

"My boyfriend and his family own this property. I have their permission to come here anytime I want. They're good people. They'd want you to feel safe here."

My boyfriend.

The threads evaporated. Shoulders relaxed.

We slogged to the bakery. I found a key Tal had left, tucked above the back door. The women streamed inside gratefully. The interior had to be a good twenty degrees warmer than outdoors.

Brim gave one of her snorts. *Stranger Danger.*

Megan/Alaina stepped out of the forest and plowed through the knee-high snow. Her rifle still hung from one shoulder. The other dipped beneath the weight of a large back pack.

As she reached me she shrugged the pack off and pulled it behind her. "Food. Water. Heat packs for their hands and feet."

"How did you know?"

"I was sent here to find them and get them out. Happily, you did the job for me. At least phase one. I'll take it from here."

"So, you work with the Knights?"

"The what?"

"My friends in the woods."

"That's their code name around here? Cute."

"Who sent you?"

"That intel is above my pay grade, Yammy. That's what they call you?"

"Yarny."

She thrust out a hand. "Good to meet you, Yarny. Sorry for being a dick at the farm. I was using it as a cover to gather information. I got word that your sheep barn was an arson target. That's why I was jerking you around that night. Trying not to blow my cover, but making sure you were safe."

"Who targeted me?"

"People who want you dead or scared off."

"Monzell?"

"Probably one of his associates. Although he probably approved the plan."

"Associates? *What*?"

"He's been laundering dirty money for years. The casino in Mississippi that went bankrupt? He was a silent partner in that. He owns a lot of politicians and a lot of judges. How do you think Jay Wakefield's psycho uncle got off on that murder charge?"

"Laundering . . . for *who*?"

"This is no time for a chat, Yarny. Let's just leave it at this: There's a 'They' out there, and they want to get rid of trouble makers. That includes anyone who's a rallying point for the resistance."

"I'm not a rallying point. I'm not a leader. I have panic attacks and fall apart."

"Really?" She nodded at the bakery. "Those women trust you with their lives. Nice job, Yarny." She hoisted the backpack. "Tell them your goodbyes, introduce me, and go back to the farm. You know nothing, saw nothing, did nothing to help them escape. Got it?"

"I want some guarantee that you're going to protect them."

"I'll do more than protect them. After they're de-briefed, I'll get them out of the country and make sure they're in happy new digs, with good circumstances."

"Why should I trust you?"

She tilted her head toward a small radio mic attached to her snowsuit. "Yammy needs reassurance."

"Yarny."

She shrugged. "Here." She pulled a receiver from one ear.

I scrubbed it on my shawl then slowly tucked it into my own ear. Trey's voice came through. "She's the real deal. Part of our organization. It's okay. Do what she says." He paused. "You did a helluva job today. Out."

I handed the earpiece back to Alaina. *The Knights have an organization?*

"All right, but . . . " I halted. Dark, bleak fear flooded me. Brim raised her head, her long ears pricked in alarm, her eyes on the cloudy sky. "A helicopter's coming."

Alaina looked up, frowning. "I don't hear anything."

"I feel it. Big shadows, the sensation of a cleaver chopping wool roving into useless bits."

"Oh, come on. I know you're psychic, but really? Calm . . ."

The sound of the engine and blades became a dull throb to the west.

Kern.

"It's the sheriff. He'll search every building. You have to get these women into the woods. I'll go meet him. Try to convince him it's just me here."

Alaina dodged past me into the bakery, speaking fluent Spanish as she ordered the women to come with her.

"Go with her. Go!" I called to them.

They rushed out, watching the sky fearfully. Alaina waved them toward the woods. At the edge of the trees I glimpsed several of the Knights, rifles in hand.

"Tell them to let me handle this!" I yelled. "No shooting!"

Maria was the last to leave. She hugged me. "You are a blessing," she said. "You were put in this world for a great purpose, and you saved our lives. We will never forget you."

BRIM AND I STOOD in the churned snow of the old main street, watching the small helicopter hover then settle in front of us. Icy wind blasted my face and made Brim bow her head against it. *Miss Lucy, he's coming for you. Get ready.*

It was not the county's copter.

It was Howard Monzell's.

Brim exhaled in long sighs of frosty air. The shadows of failing daylight sunk us both into blue-black suspicions. As the copter settled into the snow, its blades slowing, I slid my hand inside the band of my skirt. Grasped the pistol, slipped it free of the soft holster without revealing it, and hid it behind the long drape of a shawl.

Flicked the safety off.

Practice makes perfect.

The end was near. It walked toward me in the snowy half-light.

Broad and tall and corpulent; knee-high mountaineering boots, with cream-colored camo pants tucked into them. A heavy jacket, high-tech, quilted, with fur-lined lapels. Above that, a thick, middle-aged face with hard cheekbones and sharp eyes beneath bushy, graying brows. When he stopped no more than five feet from me, he pulled his coat back. My eyes went to the large pistol holstered on his belt.

Brim showed her teeth. I grasped the reins tightly below her muzzle.

Monzell looked down at me with utter disdain. "Where are my women?"

"I have no idea."

With a speed that stunned me, he pulled the heavy pistol from his belt, pointed it at Brim's forehead, and fired.

The blast deafened me. She collapsed and dragged me down with her, falling with her neck and head across my legs. I couldn't hear; couldn't access any thoughts or other sensations; like watching a movie in a dark room with the sound off. I stared at the amazingly small trickle of blood between Brim's eyes. *Friend.*

Brim, don't go. I stroked her jaw frantically.

Her dark eyes quickly lost their sight.

Monzell stood over us, heaving for breath. He pointed the gun at my head. "I could kill you just like this mule, and nobody'd care. But I'll give you one more chance. "Where are my goddamn women?"

Hot spew. Take it, bitch. Lick it.

I pointed my blood-smeared hand toward the woods. When he looked in that direction, I raised the gun.

He never realized I had one, in the shadows.

Never expected that Lucy Parmenter could take control of her fate, and shoot him.

I pulled the trigger until the chamber emptied.

DARK WATERS ROSE up, hidden like forgotten creeks beneath highways and skyscrapers, but never lost. Living in concrete tombs under my sane layer of mindfulness. Always moving towards the sea, no matter what. Even though I was under some kind of curse that blocked most of them, a trickle came through. What was left of my damaged abilities connected with Luce.

Something is wrong with Luce. Something is happening. I'm flying in the dark. No radar. But I can sense that much.

I sat up on the gurney during transport to the plane that would take me back to the States. I began methodically ripping IVs and electrodes from my body. Medical staff swarmed me. My fist connected with someone's face. The noises and shouted orders became a tornado.

"We're going to sedate him," someone said. "He'll hurt himself."

"Hell, he'll hurt one of *us*."

I LAY BY BRIM'S body, my face against her cooling neck. Monzell was spread-eagled on his back, his eyes sightless and blood pooling under his body. Snow fell along with the darkness.

You'll go to prison for this. You'll be locked away for years. You'll be helpless. You'll be raped again.

Never. I'll die, first.

A hand on my shoulder. Gutsy's voice. Then Berg's and Cowboy's and Sink's. Bandit, silent, picked up the phone I'd dropped then carried mysterious equipment to the copter.

"My phone."

"He's gonna disable the GPS," Gutsy explained. "And then he's gonna set up a fake one. By morning it'll look like you're halfway to Canada."

I watched numbly as they dragged Monzell's body back to the copter and loaded it in the passenger seat. Cowboy and Bandit climbed in. I felt mildly astonished when Cowboy piloted the copter out of sight. Out of sight, out of mind?

"Yarny, come back to the *now*."

Fingers snapped in front of my eyes. I squinted at Gutsy, who squatted beside me. She gave me a shake. "It'll take hours for them to find that fucker's body at the crash site."

"How will Cowboy and . . . "

"Bandit's got all sorts of gadgets. Remote control."

"I shot Monzell. Can't hide that."

"Nope, but we can hide *you*."

"I'd do it again."

"Good. If you said any different I'd give you a smack on the head. Come on."

She dragged me to my feet, although I tried to keep one hand on Brim. Berg and Sink were busy emptying my bag.

"Don't leave anything," Gutsy told them.

Looking at Brim as the snow slowly covered her, I sobbed. "I can't just leave her like this. All alone."

"We'll get her body loaded on a big truck tonight and take it someplace . . . private."

"Where?" Berg dug my gun out of the snow and tucked it inside his jacket. I thrust out a hand. "I want it."

Gutsy shook me again. "The gun has to disappear. The mule has to disappear. And *you* have to disappear, too."

The Ten Sisters made a gray-on-gray wall in the distance, behind the snowy wilderness. The last glimmer of light showed dark eyes of the forest, waiting for me.

Go with them, Miss Lucy, Opal whispered. *You're a different kind of outcast, now.*

15

HIGH ABOVE EUROPE, I had been strapped in like cargo on a shelf. The medical transport plane was full of other wounded soldiers. We traveled via special gurneys and isolation pods. The med staff worked quietly. The lighting was low. The patients who weren't badly injured sat up in their beds, listening to music or audiobooks. Others lay like mummies. Mummies with parts missing, attached to machines.

I was flat on my back with oxygen strapped to my nose; my arms were connected to IVs, and I wore a heart monitor. I drifted on clouds, targeting the words spoken about me; words within my missile range. They sprouted curlicues of bright color and shot off fireworks.

Look at me as a kid, serving up fried okra, field peas, and meat loaf at Ma's diner on Lexington Avenue, back when most of the steep old side streets were ghost towns with boarded-over storefronts from the early 1900s.

And then in California, getting the shit kicked out of me by a gang behind the restaurant owned by our foster parents, the Rodriquez's. Then kicking back, by the time I was sixteen or so, walking out of the restaurant with an apron low around my food-stained jeans, flicking a cigarette into the ally.

Kicking ass for *mi familia.*

Back to reality. Or at least, the present. Butterfly knee. That was an odd one. My knee was a butterfly? Look, it's flitting up yonder to perch on a section of ribbing. It's sparkling.

Bones, tell me what that means.

Dammit, Jim, I'm a doctor, not a butterfly-ologist.

"No, Sir, your knee's not a sparkling butterfly," a nurse said. He adjusted my drip. "Get some rest, Captain. I'm giving you a little extra help."

The words grew legs and slick, furry hides. They spider-walked across my bandaged rib cage then crawled up the injured leg, which was elevated on cushions. When they reached the knee—a misshapen form hidden beneath a small sheet—they squatted, rubbing against the sheet and grunting.

Sweat slid down my forehead. *I still have microscopic pieces of that bastard's body inside me.*

I retreated deeper inside my own world, hoping for a magical phone call from Luce; her imaginary body next to mine again, her hands touching me, her mouth on me. I saw a panorama of soft gray mountains. Barns and buildings and the big house she'd shown me in photographs; the sheep and dogs, cats, chickens, rabbits, dairy cows, and horses, big trees and fields . . . then snow falling and mist rolling in along a background of hills and wooded hollows.

Luce walked out of the winter mist with her woolies close behind. Sheep, llamas, and alpacas, following their shepherdess. And there was Brim, the cranky she-mule. Luce's head was uncovered. Her pale hair flowed around her shoulders and down her arms. A soft shawl draped between her arms and her body, which made a slender outline that moved like water.

She gazed straight at me, her eyes somber and worried, sad and hopeful, looking at me, God, looking only at me, while her lips flexed in a smile that scared me. Hurt. Uncertain. What was she worried about? *No more yarn metaphors, baby; I want you to strip and wiggle. Gimme the real thing.*

No. It wouldn't be like that.

Luce, relax. We're a team.

A butcher odor suddenly rose.

I gagged and took a deep breath. The oxygen cannula in my nose made a hissing sound. Sharp fingers pinched my neck. *Liver.* The stink of the worst food in the world. *I don't like what this means.*

"Gus," she said, stopping so close I could see flecks of snow landing on her hair. "I can't let you be responsible for me . . . " a large llama poked his periscoped head in front of her and stared at me.

Luce, who was no more that five-foot-six to my six-five, reached up and gave his head a pat. His dark eyes narrowing into suspicious slits, his lips moving in cud-chewing annoyance, he stepped away at her command. She looked directly at me again. "I love you." The honey and tea of the Carolina flatlands sang in her voice. God, I felt it down between my legs.

The llama poked his head in front of the camera again, chewing, staring at me. *You're all busted up and angry and you don't want to fight anymore. So how are you going to save her from the trouble?*

What trouble?

The blood smell filled my mind. Blood on the mountains. *The trouble here. Danger here.*

A homing beacon pulsed blood-red in my brain. I had a new purpose, a new mission in life. *War is only ethical if it's personal. Peace is temporary. Love is forever. Prove you earned it. Kill. This time, kill the ones who threaten your own family.*

That's it. The danger is at home. For Luce. Why can't she hear me?

I've got to get her out of there.

16

"BEWARE THE JABBERTALK, my child! The jaws that flap, the words that quack!

Beware the Hearsay bird, and shun The Farteous BanAllfacts!

On bended knee, Mr. Lewis Carroll, I hope you're square with this admiring fun. DF

WELCOME TO THE Online Community Bulletin Board for the Crossroads Cove,

Ten Sisters Mountains, and Wild Woman Ridge Districts of
Jefferson County, North Carolina
Dr. Doug Firth, DVM, moderator

SHERIFF WHITTLESPOON came through quadruple bypass surgery with no more than a wee hitch or two. He was transferred to the hospital in Asheville. Delta says he may not come home until after he starts cardiac rehab. Delta dosed his doctors with some of her mystical biscuits and convinced them to keep him there.

Because this is a community news site and I try to keep my ill feelings out of the reporting, I'm passing along this information with not a hint of my mood. Not much, anyhow. Howard Monzell's memorial service was held at his private farm here in Jefferson County.

Lucy Parmenter is being sought as a suspect in his shooting.

That makes no sense to me or anyone else who knows Lucy. Just as it makes no sense that Monzell was shot multiple times but managed to get back in his bird then fly it into a mountainside.

All we know for sure is that Lucy disappeared along with her mule AND the women Howard stashed up at that old hotel. Let's call that what it was—a private party house staffed with women forced to have sex against their will.

Monzell's heirs can sue me for libel if they've a mind to. But they have to prove what I said—and what a lot of people are saying—isn't true. I'm looking at you, Kern Burkett and Amber Monzell Burkett.

Kern Burkett is now Sheriff of Jefferson County. I'm imagining he'll move as fast as he can to undermine God and country for the sake of Monzell business interests. Mayhaps we'll see Jefferson County get a SWAT team and one of those military-style armored vehicles that rams into buildings for fun. And police in military gear will come knocking on our doors without warrants?

'Tis an irony that Lucy Parmenter has become a symbol of proud rebellion amongst us—she, who has been talked down about and regarded by some as a peculiar creature with a little of the Spooky Fright about her—yet now she's accused of shooting Monzell, and for good reason, I predict.

The gun that was found with his body had been fired. There was blood in the snow at Free Wheeler. Not just Monzell's. Equine blood.

In my opinion, Lucy was trying to defend herself and her pet and maybe those abused women, too. Some are saying she's a hero. Others say she's a murderer.

I say let's find the truth. Trust no view of normal that's not sound. Look for the facts, not the fancy.

And take no guff from the Monzell empire's propaganda.

I SLEPT FOR MORE than forty hours, Gutsy said later.

It wasn't really sleep. I went away. Hard to say where.

I shot Howard Monzell. I killed him.

I enjoyed it.

Self-satisfaction, as Macy called it in our therapy sessions. An important healing and self-love measure. Not that she meant shooting people.

I was no stranger to putting my hand between my thighs. But self-satisfaction was more than reclaiming control of the body, the urge, the orgasm; it was about reclaiming the soul. About the strength to overcome violation; to dismiss violations of the body as nothing more than scratches on the hard surface of the soul's fortress.

And yet . . . the old voices seeped poison into me.

Someone might think I was asking for it.

Hadn't you been leading them on, Ms. Parmenter? Flirting with them at your apartment complex? Bringing them cookies in the evenings after you came home from your teaching job? Engaging them in conversation?

Sir, that's . . . that's how I how I was raised to treat my fellow human beings. That's called outreach. Ministering. They had drug problems.

Move to strike that comment, your honor. Prejudicial against my clients.

Ms. Parmenter, just tell us your own motives.

Yes, Ms. Parmenter, tell us if you were trying to get sex and drugs from my clients, two employees of the apartment complex who felt pressured by a pretty blonde school teacher looking for thrills.

Block out that memory. Block it.

A dark stink rose up in my mind, a blood smell, and a distant sound that didn't quite register until it grew louder. I was distracted, whispering, "I want to be normal, I just want to be normal."

What's wrong? What's changed?

He's injured, he's on medication, don't overreact.

No, he's listening to the same sound. He's smelling that same butcher odor.

A coyote shrieking somewhere high on a ridge? A female fox uttering her unearthly scream for a mate? Not in the middle of winter. And not something I'd hear inside a cave.

I am in a cave. Swear to Dear Methodist Jesus. A cave.

A woman, screaming.

It's me. It's my scream. In my mind.

Run, Luce. Run.

I stumbled back inside myself.

Lost in the blood. *I love you Gus. Stay safe. Don't look for me. I can't come back. I won't come back.*

Dad died because my pain broke his heart. Brim died for me. I avenged her as best I could. And those Mexican women. And everyone in every culture and country and eon and century who's been killed or enslaved or subjugated.

Live your life. Love your life. I intend to survive without asking anyone's permission. Never again. I'm in pieces, but I'm not a victim anymore.

The End

Coming in Fall 2017

The Moonshine King

The next installment in Lucy and Gus's story.

About Deborah Smith

Deborah Smith is the author of more than thirty-five novels in romance and women's fiction, including the *New York Times* bestseller, *A Place to Call Home*, and the *Wall Street Journal* bestseller, *The Crossroads Café*. She is also a founding partner of BelleBooks/Bell Bridge Books, a Memphis-based publishing company known for quality fiction and non-fiction by new and established authors. *The Pickle Queen* is the second of *The Crossroads Café* Novellas, spin-offs set in the Appalachian world of *The Crossroads Café*.

Coming soon: Gus and Lucy's story, *The Kitchen Charmer*.

Visit Deb at www.bellbridgebooks.com. Also on Facebook at Deborah Smith Author.

CPSIA information can be obtained
at www.ICGtesting.com
Printed in the USA
LVHW111113190720
661081LV00006B/1679

9 781611 948356